LESSONS IN EVIL

A Bridget Bishop Thriller: Book One

Melinda Woodhall

Melinda Woodhall
Visit my website at www.melindawoodhall.com
Printed in the United States of America
First Printing: February 2022
Creative Magnolia

CHAPTER ONE

The needle on the gas gauge hovered on empty as Libby Palmer steered her mother's old Buick down the Wisteria Falls exit ramp. The heavy traffic on the interstate had added an extra hour to her drive back from D.C., and Libby had just decided she was going to run out of gas when the Gas & Go sign came into view.

Eyeing the gas station with relief, Libby turned into the parking lot, brought the car to a jerking halt beside an available pump, and shut off the engine with a resigned sigh.

Her trip into D.C. certainly hadn't turned out the way she'd hoped when she'd left home that morning. Despite her new clothes and valiant efforts to impress the hiring manager at the Smithsonian, she was still woefully unemployed.

So much for showing Mom once and for all that majoring in art history wasn't a colossal mistake.

A fat drop of rain plunked onto the windshield and slid down the glass as Libby opened the door and stepped out into the dusky twilight, credit card in hand.

A hand-written note had been taped over the card reader.

Machine broken. Pay inside.

Looking up at the darkening sky in irritation, Libby pulled

the hood of her jacket over her dark curls and hurried toward the store. She hesitated as she saw the missing person flyer taped to the glass door.

It was the third time that day she'd seen one of the flyers with a picture of the pretty blonde girl who'd gone missing from her apartment near Dupont Circle the week before.

Brooke Nelson hadn't been seen since; foul play was suspected. The FBI had been asking anyone with information to call a dedicated tip line, and a slew of the flyers had been posted around Washington D.C. and the surrounding area.

"You going in or not?"

A man in a black jacket and faded jeans held the door open, waiting for Libby to pass through.

"Uh...yeah, sorry about that," she said, ducking her head as she stepped into the brightly lit building.

Wrinkling her nose against the pungent scent of stale coffee which hung in the air, Libby made her way to the counter and presented her credit card to the clerk.

"Twenty dollars on pump one," she said, hoping her card wasn't maxed out. "And can I get the key to the restroom?"

The clerk looked her up and down, taking in her disheveled curls and rain-spattered jacket as he handed her a receipt and a silver key on a red plastic keyring.

His eyes held a suspicious gleam.

"Restrooms are outside to the left." He held up her credit card. "You'll get this back when you return the key."

Libby nodded and stepped back, bumping into the solid figure of a man in line behind her.

"Sorry," she murmured, avoiding eye contact as she

turned and headed outside.

Keeping her head down against the spitting rain, she hurried around the little building to the restroom, stuck the metal key in the lock, and found the tiny, tiled room surprisingly clean.

She stopped in front of the chipped mirror over the sink, wiping at the mascara smudged under her disappointed brown eyes.

"You didn't want to work at that stupid museum anyway, did you?" she asked her reflection. "I mean, who'd want to live in boring old Washington D.C. when they could live in exciting Wisteria Falls?"

Rain was falling in a steady downpour by the time Libby had returned the key to the clerk, retrieved her credit card, and pumped twenty dollars' worth of gas into the Buick's big tank.

Dropping back into the driver's seat, she started the engine and pulled back onto the highway, lowering the volume on the radio as she picked up speed, uninterested in the local weather and traffic report.

As she drove over Landsend Bridge, she glanced down toward the Shenandoah River but could see nothing of the dark water churning below the metal and concrete structure.

Always fearful the ancient truss bridge might suddenly give way beneath her, Libby drove cautiously, holding her breath until the Buick's wheels were back on solid ground before pressing her foot toward the floor, eager to get home.

She didn't see the girl standing on the side of the road until she rounded the sharp curve just past Beaufort Hollow.

Stomping on the brakes as the Buick's headlights lit up a pale face framed by sodden blonde hair, Libby brought the car to a sudden stop in the middle of the empty road.

Worried another car may round the curve behind her and plow into her rear bumper, she steered the Buick onto the shoulder and shut off the engine.

With a quick glance in the rearview mirror, she climbed out into the rain and ran toward the girl, who stood beside a black sedan. The car's trunk was wide open, and the emergency lights were blinking.

"Are you okay?" Libby called as she approached the car.

The girl's face was hidden in shadow, no longer illuminated by the Buick's headlights, but the jarring *blink, blink, blink* of the sedan's emergency lights revealed the outline of her bowed head and thin shoulders.

"Did your car break down?"

Libby's question was met with silence. She wondered if the girl had been in an accident. Perhaps a tire had blown.

Maybe she hit her head on the dashboard. Or maybe she...

The thought was interrupted by the girl's raspy whisper, but Libby couldn't make out what she was saying.

Stepping close enough to put her hand on the girl's thin shoulder, she inhaled sharply.

"You're trembling," Libby said, impulsively pulling off her jacket and draping it over the girl's shoulders. "You must be hurt. Come with me to my car and..."

"*Help...me.*"

As the girl lifted her head, the emergency blinkers lit up a heart-shaped face, which looked strangely familiar.

Libby stared into the girl's tormented blue eyes, her pulse quickening as she pictured the missing person flyer on the door at Gas & Go.

"You're that girl, aren't you? You're Brooke Nelson."

"I'm...sorry," the girl croaked and swayed on her feet as if she no longer had the strength to stand. "I'm so sorry."

The crack of a branch behind Libby sent her spinning around just as a dark figure loomed up in front of her.

A scream froze in her throat as she stared up, gaping in terror. The man's face was half-hidden by the hood of his jacket, but she recognized his cold stare.

Adrenaline shot through her as she saw the knife in his hand. Lunging toward the road in a desperate bid to get back to the safety of the old Buick, she slipped and fell to her knees.

An iron fist reached out and grabbed a handful of her hair.

Snapping her head back, the man pulled her to her feet and wrapped his free arm around her neck.

He tightened his hold until Libby could no longer breathe.

"Brooke and I were...waiting for you," he hissed, his breath coming in excited gasps. "The time...of reckoning is...here."

Waves of dizziness washed over Libby as she scratched and pried at the unyielding arm around her throat, and hot tears blurred the flashing lights around her.

"Stay still...or I'll break your neck."

His breath was hot in her ear as he dragged her toward the open trunk of the sedan, then forced her inside.

She opened her mouth to scream as she looked back and

met Brook Nelson's anguished eyes but could only manage a raspy cry before the trunk slammed shut, throwing her into darkness.

* * *

Water trickled somewhere nearby as Libby struggled to open her eyes. Her throat burned, and it was hard to swallow as she blinked around the dimly lit room.

Where am I? What is this place?

Rough walls and a cracked wooden floor held a small metal-framed bed and a straight-backed chair. Rickety stairs led up to a small landing and a narrow door.

"You awake?"

She jumped at the man's voice.

"I thought maybe I'd squeezed too hard."

A dark figure stepped into view. The man who'd forced her into the trunk of his car stared down at her.

"It'd be a shame to go through all that trouble to snatch you only to kill you off so soon."

Studying her face, he reached out a hand to tuck a still soggy curl behind her ear.

Libby cringed in terror but found she couldn't pull away. Her hands were bound to the chair with bright blue duct tape, as were her ankles.

"Where am I?" she croaked, wincing at the pain in her throat. "Why are you doing this?"

He appeared not to have heard her questions as he moved toward the stairs. Propping a booted foot on the bottom step, he stopped and cocked his head as if listening.

"I know what to do," he finally said, giving a resolute nod. "I've read the handbook. I won't take any chances."

Libby looked around the room, confused.

Who's he talking to?

She suddenly remembered Brook Nelson's terrified eyes. The poor girl must have been abducted, too. Was she being held in the same place?

"Where's Brooke?" Libby wheezed out, ignoring the stabbing pain in her throat. "What have you done to her?"

Turning to face her, the man frowned.

"You're not gonna try anything stupid, are you?" he asked, shifting his weight on the creaking wooden floor. "My mentor warned me you'd cause trouble. He told me not to be fooled."

"Who warned you?" she asked, looking up the stairs toward the door. "Is someone else here?"

The man cocked his head.

"I guess you could say that. Now stop asking so many questions. I've got important work to do."

"Please," Libby called out as he turned away. "Tell me what you did to Brooke. Tell me where she is."

Looking over his shoulder, the man shrugged.

"She's served her purpose," he said softly. "As will you."

CHAPTER TWO

Bridget Bishop stared at the crime scene photos in the case file with a puzzled frown. Her report on Felix Arnett was due in the Wisteria Fall's prosecutor's office by the end of the month, but she was finding it hard to wrap up her evaluation with a nice, neat conclusion when she still had so many unanswered questions.

Flipping through the contents of the file, she stopped to study a wallet-sized mugshot, noting Felix's ashen complexion and dilated pupils.

"What really happened that day, Felix?" she murmured, before closing the folder on the desk. "What is it you can't bear to remember?"

Hank stirred at her feet and lifted his head, staring up at her with curious brown eyes.

"Ignore me," she told the Irish setter, scratching the soft reddish fur between his ears. "I'm talking to myself, *again.*"

Bridget turned her gaze toward the window, the rosy-pink flowers on the redbud tree outside reminding her that spring had officially arrived in the Shenandoah Valley.

Almost two months had passed since the Wisteria Falls PD had found Felix Arnett standing over his wife's dead body.

According to the police reports on Bridget's desk, Felix had appeared to be in shock, a gun still hanging limply in his hand.

"I shot her."

His eyes had been wide and unblinking as he faced the responding officers.

"I killed Whitney. She's...dead."

The officers claimed they had yelled for Felix to put down his weapon, but he'd continued walking zombie-like toward them, slowly raising the gun as he'd moved closer.

The shot to the chest had knocked him back onto the concrete porch steps, causing a significant head injury as well as massive bleeding from the gunshot wound.

Somehow, he'd survived.

Once he'd regained consciousness in the hospital three days later, Felix had been read his rights and placed under arrest on suspicion of first-degree murder.

Insisting he was unable to remember anything that had happened leading up to his wife's death, Felix had refused counsel from a court-appointed lawyer.

The presiding judge had eventually ordered a forensic psychological evaluation, and Bridget had been called in to determine if he was mentally fit to assist in his own defense.

Her task, as a private psychological consultant, was to produce a written report for Liz Reardon, the Commonwealth's Attorney in Wisteria Falls.

That report would be used by the prosecutor to determine which charges, if any, were to be brought against the young widower. And if Felix went to trial, Bridget would no doubt be called to testify as to her findings.

The problem was, she wasn't sure her findings made sense.

Although Bridget believed Felix Arnett to be mentally sound, she had serious doubts the traumatized young man was capable of inflicting the injuries found on Whitney Arnett or of shooting his young wife in the head.

By all accounts, he and his wife had enjoyed a happy marriage, with no history of violence, and Whitney's death had devastated Felix, who was overwhelmed by guilt and grief.

Although Bridget had been hired simply to determine if Felix was fit to stand trial, she'd become preoccupied with a more pressing question. One that had been keeping her up at night.

Did Felix Arnett really shoot his wife in cold blood?

The question had eaten away at her, and the urge to investigate the circumstances of the shooting had eventually proven too strong, prompting her to examine the crime scene reports and conduct interviews of all the responding officers.

It was the kind of work she'd handled in her past profiling role within the FBI's Behavioral Analysis Unit. The kind of work she'd excelled at before she'd decided to quit almost two years earlier.

Now staring out the window and absently twisting a wayward strand of chestnut brown hair around her finger, Bridget watched as a sleek Lincoln Navigator turned into the psychology practice's parking lot.

The dark gray SUV rolled to a stop outside her window and

a tall man in a dark suit and even darker sunglasses stepped out and looked toward the door.

What in the world is Terrance Gage doing in Wisteria Falls?

Bridget's stomach tightened as the man ran a hand over the smooth, bronze skin on his head and adjusted his tie.

Her old boss at the Bureau would only make the hour and a half drive over from Quantico to see her if something had gone seriously wrong.

She stood slowly, her mind turning to the last time she'd seen Gage in person outside the federal courthouse in downtown Washington, D.C.

Holding on to the edge of her desk, Bridget grounded herself to the room, and to the present moment, reminding herself that the man she and Gage had hunted down together, the man who had been convicted inside that courtroom, was no longer a threat.

The monster who had wrought so much suffering and pain was no longer able to hurt her or anyone else.

So why are you trembling like a leaf, Bridget? And why are you hiding out here in Wisteria Falls, anyway?

Ignoring the soft voice and its unwelcome questions, Bridget leaned over and peeked out the window just as Gage started toward the front door.

She ducked out of sight as Hank watched with interest, his head turning to follow her as she again leaned over and surveyed Gage.

Noting the hard set to his jaw, she saw no sign of the smile the BAU agent had worn after the jury's guilty verdict that day on the courthouse steps.

He'd been thrilled to successfully close the high-profile case, but Bridget hadn't managed to match his smile with one of her own.

The Backroads Butcher case had still been too fresh. The horror of what she'd been through hadn't yet faded. She hadn't been sure that it ever would.

And she hadn't known then that she would be sending Gage an email announcing her resignation less than a week later

Feeling she'd had no choice after she'd gotten news of her father's stroke, Bridget had emailed her resignation to Gage from Bob Bishop's hospital bedside.

She'd pressed *Send* with a mixture of relief and regret, convinced she could leave the BAU behind, along with the indelible images of death and torture she'd witnessed during the search for the Backroads Butcher.

By the time Bob Bishop was out of danger and able to function independently again, Bridget had decided not to return to her role as a behavioral analyst in Quantico.

Wanting to live closer to her father, she'd joined the Wisteria Falls Forensic Psychology group, and after a year of private practice as a consultant, she was finally starting to sleep through the night again.

So, why is Terrance Gage walking back into my life now, as if he has every right to be here?

A hesitant knock sounded on the office door.

Hank stood and trotted over, sensing a chance to get out and stretch his legs as the door swung open.

Aubrey March stood in the hall with wide eyes. The group's

receptionist was tall and willowy. She towered over Bridget by a good six inches.

"Special Agent Terrance Gage is here to see you," Aubrey said, her voice breathy with excitement. "He's with the *FBI*."

"Yes, I know who he is," Bridget replied, stalling for time, looking back at the window, thinking of escape.

A shadow fell over Bridget as Gage's face appeared in the doorway behind Aubrey. He'd removed his sunglasses to reveal tired eyes framed by a faint web of lines and furrows.

"Bridget, I need to speak to you. It's urgent."

He brushed past Aubrey to step into the room.

"We've got a...*situation*."

His eyes took in Aubrey's eager expression, then flicked back to Bridget impatiently.

Taking the hint, Aubrey looked down at Hank.

"How about I take this big guy out for a walk?" she asked, giving the Irish setter a smile. "It's a perfect day out there."

Bridget waited for Aubrey and Hank to disappear down the hall before she pushed the door closed behind Gage, then turned to stare at him with wary eyes.

"Two young women have gone missing in the last ten days," he said, not bothering to ask how life had treated her during the last two years.

"I've seen the posters for Brooke Nelson," Bridget admitted, the image of the pretty blonde woman flashing through her mind. "There's been another one?"

Gage nodded.

"Libby Palmer went missing three days ago," he confirmed.

Reaching into his suit pocket, he pulled out a photo of a young woman with dark curls in a graduation cap and gown.

"Her abandoned car was found not far from here near the Shenandoah River."

A momentary tightening of Gage's jaw drew Bridget's eyes away from the photo. She studied her old boss, taking in his stiff shoulders and fisted hands, registering his agitation.

Gage wasn't the type to put his emotions on display, but Bridget sensed his heightened anxiety and felt her own rising up to match it.

"A body was discovered out by Moonstone Cavern last night," he said bluntly. "The local police chief realized who it was and called the Bureau."

When Bridget didn't respond, Gage continued.

"Brooke Nelson's family has already been notified. The news will be hitting the press soon if it hasn't already."

Inhaling slowly, Bridget concentrated on the top button of Gage's crisp white shirt, not wanting to imagine Brooke Nelson's dead body. Not allowing herself to wonder where Libby Palmer was or to imagine the horrors the young woman might be suffering.

She'd earned her doctorate by exploring the darkest corners of a madman's mind and had spent two years in the BAU chasing monsters out of her worst nightmares. She was done with all that now. Wasn't she?

"I'm sorry to hear about Brooke," she said in a strained voice. "And about Libby. But why tell me? I can't imagine you'd need to hire in an outside consultant with all the analysts you've got at the-"

"Brooke Nelson's arms and legs were bound together with blue duct tape," Gage interrupted. "And the ring finger on her left hand was missing. Sound familiar?"

The knot of dread in Bridget's stomach tightened as he continued.

"The perp's MO matches that of the Shenandoah Valley Strangler," he said. "Unless Ernest Crast has somehow come back from the dead..."

Bridget pictured the expression on Ernest Crast's face as he'd described what he'd done to his victims. How he'd used the blue duct tape to restrain them. How he'd left them discarded like broken dolls for the police to find.

She shook her head to dislodge the disturbing images.

"So, you're thinking a...a *copycat* killed Brooke Nelson and abducted Libby Palmer in an attempt to imitate Crast?"

"That would make the most sense, but there's one problem with that theory," Gage said, running a nervous hand over his smooth, shiny head. "The tape used to bind Brooke Nelson came off the exact same spool of tape Crast used to bind up *his* last victim. His fingerprints were even on it."

Leaning back against the heavy oak desk, Gage crossed his arms over his broad chest.

"It sounds crazy...we're talking about crimes committed almost twenty years ago."

"There's got to be a mistake," she said. "A mix-up."

Gage shrugged.

"The lab at Quantico is analyzing all evidence," he assured her. "But, in the meantime, I want you on board this investigation from the beginning."

Bridget shook her head in disbelief.

"It's not possible," she murmured. "Ernest Crast is dead."

"Yes, I know," Gage replied, his voice softening. "And I know you were there to witness his execution."

Turning haunted blue eyes toward the window, Bridget inhaled again, trying to maintain her composure, not wanting Gage to see the effect his words had on her.

Oblivious to the vivid spring morning beyond the glass, she tried to block out the memories that had plagued her for the last seven years, but an image of Ernest Crast's broad, pit-marked face flashed through her mind, and a rough voice sounded in her head.

You wanna watch a man die? I think you might enjoy it.

Recoiling at the remembered growl of Crast's voice, Bridget shook her head in mute denial.

Yes, she'd seen the confessed serial killer die with her own eyes. But only because he'd requested her presence in the witness room. Only because she'd known it hadn't been right and had felt obligated to make her objections known.

She hadn't wanted to be there. She hadn't enjoyed it.

Are you sure? You practically jumped at the chance.

"He killed seven innocent women," she protested aloud, spinning to face Gage with a frown, as if he was the one who'd spoken, instead of the phantom voice in her head. "But he was psychotic. He was having delusions. I told them he wasn't mentally fit, but...no one would listen."

"I know that, too," Gage said.

He hesitated, studying her as if weighing his options.

"Look, Bridget, you knew Crast better than anyone else in the BAU," he finally said. "It's public knowledge you conducted research on Crast and attended his execution before you joined the Bureau."

Moving closer, he lowered his voice, adopting a softer tone.

"If our killer is trying to imitate Crast, or maybe even has some closer connection to him, you're our best bet for being able to figure out who he is, and what he might do next."

"I told you I'm not coming back to the BAU," Bridget said, trying to sound firm. "So, what do you want from me?"

"Take a drive with me."

Gage's voice was calm, almost soothing.

"There's something I want you to see. Something that may change your mind."

CHAPTER THREE

Opal Fitzgerald leaned over the autopsy table and pulled down the white sheet covering Brooke Nelson's body. The seasoned forensic pathologist had worked for Virginia's northern district medical examiner's office for over a decade, but the sight of the young woman's stiff, discolored face, and the circle of bruises around her thin neck, still elicited a grimace of anger.

"What a pitiful shame," she muttered, pulling on a second pair of gloves, and checking the tray of tools her forensic assistant had prepared.

The door behind her opened and a voice called out.

"Opal? The folks from the FBI are here."

"Have them suit up. I'll be right out."

Looking down at the small face and closed eyes, Opal pulled the sheet back over the dead girl's head in a protective gesture.

Brooke Nelson was in her care, at least for the time being, and she wasn't about to leave her alone and exposed.

The dead might not know what was going on around them, but Opal preferred to act like they did, just in case.

She moved to the door and pushed it open.

"Well, if it isn't Special Agent Day and her trusty sidekick, Agent Halo," Opal called out as she pulled down her mask to greet the two people in the adjacent room, who were both pulling protective coveralls over their business attire.

"I figured you'd be the one to catch this case, Opal," Charlie Day said, tucking a shoulder-length strand of blonde hair under a disposable blue cap. "Seems like you always get stuck with homicides when the Bureau is involved."

"I'm the only one around here that knows how to handle feds," Opal shot back. "Y'all would have the other examiners running in circles if I wasn't here to rein you in."

Her eyes flicked to the man next to Charlie.

"Isn't that right, Agent Halo?"

"It's *Hale*," the agent said, pulling protective booties over his shiny black dress shoes. "Special Agent Tristan *Hale*."

Opal raised her eyebrows as if unconvinced.

"Well, your partner here told me they called you Halo when you worked undercover," she said. "So, I just thought..."

"She's not my partner," Hale corrected her, glancing at Charlie. "Special agents aren't assigned official partners."

Nodding as if she understood, Opal watched as Hale adjusted the cap over his dark head of hair.

"I get it. You two just like to work together," she said, nodding her approval. "You do make a good couple."

She didn't wait for either agent to reply as she turned and pushed open the autopsy suite door.

"I was just getting ready to begin," Opal said, crossing to the metal table. "And let me start off by saying you two better catch the bastard who caused this child to end up on my table."

A sharp knock stopped Opal from removing the sheet draped over Brooke Nelson's body.

She turned as an unexpected figure appeared at the door.

"Sorry we're late," Terrance Gage said, meeting Opal's eyes before nodding to Charlie and Hale. "I had to pick up Dr. Bishop over in Wisteria Falls. It took longer than expected."

"Bridget's here?"

Opal's face crinkled into a surprised smile as Gage stepped aside to reveal a familiar face.

"Dr. Bishop now, is it?" she said, shaking her head. "First, it's Agent Bishop, and now Dr. Bishop. I can't get used to it."

Bridget returned the smile.

"How are you, Dr. Fitzgerald? It's good to see you."

She lifted a hand to cover her nose as her watery eyes flicked to the sheet covering the body on the table.

Opal realized the sickly-sweet smell of death that permeated the room must be getting to the psychologist. She'd grown so used to it herself that she often forgot the effect it had on those not exposed to dead bodies on a daily basis.

"You two need to get suited up if you plan to witness the autopsy," Opal said, then added in Bridget's direction, "and there's some vapor rub on the shelf if you need it."

As Bridget and Gage disappeared back through the door, Opal put away the camera she'd used earlier to take the initial photographs of the body, then reached for her voice recorder.

"Cecil told me she'd been abducted," Opal said as she

pulled back the sheet, exposing Brooke Nelson's face and shoulders.

"That's right," Hale confirmed, his face tightening as his eyes fell on the dead girl. "We managed to track down security camera footage of her abduction in the District near Dupont Circle. The assailant forced her into her car. Twenty minutes later he drove past a toll camera on I-66 westbound."

A flash of outrage rolled through Opal.

"He's got some nerve snatching her up in the middle of a busy city," she muttered under her breath, then looked up at Charlie. "You guys know who the perp is, yet?"

"No clue," Charlie admitted, looking toward the door where Bridget and Gage had appeared wearing coveralls and masks. "Which is why we called in the BAU to assist."

Turning her full attention back to the body before her, Opal clicked on the recorder and began to speak in a crisp voice, revealing none of the anger brewing in her chest.

"I've got a well-nourished white female measuring sixty-four inches and weighing one hundred seventeen pounds," she said. "External appearance consistent with the victim's age, which is known to be twenty-three years. Lividity fixed in the distal portions of the limbs. Eyes are closed."

As Opal continued to dictate notes, she felt all eyes glued to the dead girl on the table.

"A series of contusions and abrasions are visible around the neck, the pattern being indicative of manual strangulation."

Using a gloved finger, Opal lifted first one eyelid and then the other. She wasn't surprised to see the tiny red spots that often appeared when blood vessels had ruptured.

"Petechia is present in both eyes."

After examining the mouth, ears, and nostrils, Opal hesitated, then gently pulled down the stiff, white sheet to reveal the body's torso and arms.

Bright blue masking tape had been wound around the young woman's wrists, binding her arms together in front of her. Pulling the sheet off altogether, Opal revealed the same blue tape wrapped around the ankles.

"Blue masking tape, approximately two inches in width, has been wound around both arms and ankles," Opal dictated.

She looked back at the faces transfixed behind her, pausing momentarily, before continuing in a subdued voice.

"The left ring finger is missing," she said. "Based on the wound, it appears to have been excised postmortem."

Deciding to take a break before she moved on to the internal exam, Opal stopped the recorder and repositioned the sheet.

"I imagine you aren't interested in sticking around for the cutting and sawing," she said, waving them toward the outer room. "And I'll need room to work with my assistant."

She pulled down her mask as they gathered around her.

"I think we all have a pretty good idea as to the cause and manner of death at this point."

"Homicide by manual strangulation," Gage said with no hint of a question in his voice. "The same as all of Ernest Crast's victims. And a section of the blue duct tape was collected at the scene. It's already been processed at the lab in Quantico. It's a match."

Opal frowned.

"A match with what?"

"A match with the tape pulled off Crast's last victim," Gage said. "I thought you knew. Didn't Agent Day tell you?"

Shaking her head, Opal raised both eyebrows.

"Whoever killed Brooke Nelson used the same tape Ernest Crast used to bind his victims," Charlie said as she pulled off her mask and protective cap.

"Ernest Crast? As in the Shenandoah Valley Strangler?" Opal asked. "As in, the man who was executed years ago?"

Charlie nodded, her gray eyes somber.

"The forensic results suggest the tape on Brooke came off the same roll Crast used," she confirmed. "His prints were even on it. We'll want the tape from the body sent to the FBI lab for further testing."

"Hopefully the lab geeks will get lucky and find DNA. Maybe we can even get a hit in CODIS," Hale added.

Still trying to process the fact that executed serial killer Ernest Crast was somehow involved with the death of the woman on her table, Opal was momentarily speechless.

Gage spoke again before she could regain her composure.

"What we need to know is how long you think she's been dead. How long this guy kept her before he killed her. That'll tell us how closely he's following Crast's MO."

He gestured toward Bridget, who stood behind Opal. The psychologist's mask and cap had been discarded to reveal a pale, drawn face and unreadable blue eyes.

"Bridget studied Ernest Crast and interviewed him about his crimes. She knows how he operated," Gage explained. "If our unsub is trying to reenact Crast's murders, she may be able to figure out where he is, and what he's likely to do next."

Opal turned to Bridget, remembering the news coverage of the Shenandoah Valley Strangler's execution, and how the press had hounded young Bridget as she'd made her way into the Greensville Correctional Center to act as a witness.

"I wasn't working here when Crast's victims were autopsied. That was before my time," Opal said softly. "But Cecil was driving patrol back then and he was called to a few of the scenes. Once in a while he still has a nightmare."

Opal had met her husband on the job, just before he'd been appointed Wisteria Fall's chief of police, and they often shared war stories about their jobs over dinner. But he still didn't like to talk about the series of killings that had terrorized the community before Ernest Crast had been caught.

"Have you estimated time of death, yet?" Bridget asked.

"When I got to the scene, she'd been dead about forty-eight hours," Opal said. "Maybe a little longer."

Bridget looked stricken.

"So, Libby Palmer disappeared while Brooke Nelson was still alive," she murmured. "That's the way Crast liked to do it. He'd abduct a new victim before disposing of the previous victim. He didn't want to be alone."

The quiet words sent a chill up Opal's spine.

"That's why he was so mad at Althea Helmont," Bridget

said in a distracted voice. "She'd disrupted his routine."

"Who's Althea Helmont?" Opal asked.

Bridget seemed surprised she didn't know.

"She's the one who escaped," Bridget said. "The only one of Crast's victims who ever got away."

* * *

Opal typed Althea Helmont's name into her search engine and waited as the page of results loaded.

Lifting a hand to smooth back the graying curls framing her round face, she clicked on the top link and found herself staring at an image on the Wisteria Falls Tribune website.

She recognized Harry Kemp's stocky figure. The detective led a thin woman with frizzy brown hair out of the courthouse.

She dropped her eyes to the caption below the image.

Althea Helmont Gives Damning Testimony in Crast Trial.

Scanning through the article, Opal felt a stir of admiration for the young mother who had managed to escape the psychopathic killer of seven other women.

"Opal? Do you have a minute?"

Bridget Bishop stood hesitantly in the office doorway.

"Sure, I do," Opal said.

Closing the browser, she waved Bridget toward the chair across from her desk.

"I was meaning to ask how your father's been doing anyway," Opal said. "Cecil updates me now and then, but I'd rather get my information from a more reliable source."

A smile softened Bridget's face as she sank into the chair.

"Dad's doing well. In fact, he's been making noise about going back to work. I had to remind him he's retired now."

A hint of strain in Bridget's voice told Opal that Bob Bishop's stroke had taken its toll on his daughter.

"Well, your father was a detective for over twenty years," Opal chided. "It must be strange for him to be a civilian again."

"Yes, I guess it is," Bridget agreed. "He's always talking about the big cases he closed. He can remember all the details from decades ago. Sometimes I wish he couldn't."

Bridget cleared her throat and sat forward.

"But that's not what I wanted to talk about," she admitted. "I wanted to ask you something else. You see, I'm working in private practice now. I'm consulting on a case for Liz Reardon in the Wisteria Falls prosecutor's office."

The change of subject took Opal by surprise.

"Liz brought me in to conduct a psychological evaluation of Felix Arnett," Bridget explained. "I know you collected Whitney Arnett's body from the scene and performed the autopsy, and I was wondering..."

Her voice faltered.

"Wondering what?" Opal asked, cocking her head.

"Well, I was wondering what you think really happened that night," Bridget admitted. "Based on what you saw."

Faint furrows appeared on Opal's forehead as she recalled the grisly scene at the Arnett house the night Whitney died.

The poor woman had been shot in the head. Blood spatter had coated the porch and the front door, and Opal had seen clear signs of a struggle. There had definitely been some sort of altercation as Whitney had attempted to leave.

"I think Felix Arnett shot his wife in the head when she tried to leave him," she said bluntly. "I think they had an argument and it got out of control. I think he should never have been allowed out on bail."

"But Felix had no prior history of violence, so..."

Raising a hand to stop Bridget, Opal leaned back in her chair.

"Yes, I know. Cecil told me he was stunned when he'd heard what had happened," Opal admitted. "Felix worked the dispatch desk for the WFPD, so Cecil knew the boy quite well. Said he was quiet...never caused any trouble."

"And what does Cecil think?" Bridget asked. "Does he believe Felix Arnett murdered his wife?"

Opal shrugged.

"You'd have to ask him, I guess. But it doesn't really matter what he *thinks* happened," Opal said. "As Cecil always reminds me, it only matters what the evidence *proves*."

CHAPTER FOUR

Terrance Gage followed Charlie and Hale out to a dusty black Expedition. The agents had been called back to the Washington field office to set up a new task force, which Gage figured was about time. Bringing local and federal resources together might give them a chance to find Brooke Nelson's killer before it was too late to save Libby Palmer.

"You planning to take the lead on this one?" Gage asked as Charlie pulled open the door.

"Absolutely," she said without hesitation. "Our perp snatched the first victim in D.C. and dumped her in Wisteria Falls. No telling where we might find Libby Palmer, if we find her at all."

"And if this guy really is anything like Crast, the locals are going to need our help to find him," Hale added.

Gage wasn't so sure Chief Fitzgerald would agree with the agents' logic.

"If I remember correctly, it was the Wisteria Falls PD who discovered Ernest Crast was the Shenandoah Valley Strangler."

"That's right," a voice said from behind Gage. "My father

28

was one of the detectives working the case. He and his partner Harry Kemp helped bring Crast in."

Spinning around to face Bridget, Gage detected a hint of pride in her voice.

"Your father put Crast behind bars?" he asked in surprise. "Is that why you wanted to interview Crast in the first place?"

She nodded.

"I was a teenager when the Shenandoah Valley Strangler started showing up on the nightly news," Bridget said. "I was scared, like every other girl I knew, but I wanted to know more. I wanted to know why the Strangler killed innocent women. And why he chose *those* women."

She looked at Charlie and Hale, who had both paused beside the SUV to listen with interest.

"I figured something inside him must be different than other people. Then, when my father found Crast, I tried to learn everything I could about him."

Bridget lifted a distracted hand and tucked a strand of dark hair behind her ear.

"When I started working toward my doctorate in psychology, I decided to focus my dissertation on the effects of childhood trauma on people who later become serial killers."

"What kind of trauma?' Hale asked. "Like PTSD?"

Bridget shrugged.

"Any kind of mental or physical trauma, such as brain injuries or some kind of abuse."

"I'm surprised Ernest Crast agreed to cooperate," Charlie

said. "First your father catches him, and then you convince him to let you study his brain? No wonder the Bureau wanted you in on the Backroads Butcher case."

A frown flickered across Bridget's face, but she didn't respond as Charlie and Hale climbed into the SUV.

"I'll let you know once the task force has been assembled," Charlie said to Gage through the open window. "In the meantime, you need to convince Bridget to help us find this guy. She may be our best bet."

Gage watched the Expedition pull onto the highway before turning to catch Bridget checking her watch.

"I'll give you a ride back to your office if you're ready."

As they settled into his Navigator, Gage mentally rehearsed the arguments he planned to use to convince her to return to the BAU.

His phone buzzed in his pocket before he'd had the chance to start the engine. Glancing down, Gage saw a familiar name pop up on the display.

Vivian Burke.

He quickly swiped away the text message that had come through, hoping Bridget hadn't seen the sender's name.

"Based on Opal's findings, we know Brooke Nelson was kept alive for about a week before she was killed," Bridget said, forestalling the discussion of her return to the Bureau. "Crast liked to keep his victims for at least a week or even longer, so that fits with the new strangler's M.O."

She looked out the window as Gage steered the Navigator across the lot toward the road and waited for a break in traffic.

"Of course, we'll have to wait for the full autopsy report," she continued. "But if this guy really is following in Crast's footsteps, there won't be any biological fluids or DNA on the body. Nothing that will help us identify him in CODIS."

Gage lifted his eyebrows hopefully.

"You said *us*. Does that mean you're coming back to the-?"

"No!" she interrupted before he could get the words out. "It means I'm willing to consult on the case as long as I feel I can be helpful. But I don't want the press to get wind of it."

Her shoulders tensed and a guarded look fell over her face as she turned to study his profile.

"The media has been pretty much leaving me alone lately, and that's the way I'd prefer it to stay."

Gage kept his eyes on the road, not sure how to respond. He didn't want to upset Bridget. Didn't want her to withdraw her offer to assist. He needed her to create a profile of the man who was copying Ernest Crast's deadly crimes.

Her help in the investigation might be the difference between life and death for Libby Palmer. If Bridget thought the media might target her, it could scare her off for good.

After all, the image of the attractive young psychologist arriving at the serial killer's execution had been splashed across every newspaper and television screen in the country.

The stories had only grown in fervor when it had been revealed Crast had stipulated his brain could only be autopsied and studied after execution if Bridget was present during the procedure and if she led any associated research project.

"I guess having a serial killer invite you to his execution

and leave you his brain for research is a sure-fire way to get your picture in the paper," Gage said in an attempt to lighten the mood. "I'm not sure you told me how that all came about."

Bridget sank back into the passenger's seat with a sigh.

"I sent Crast a letter while he was on death row. Told him I was Bob Bishop's daughter, and that I was working on my dissertation about the effects of childhood trauma on serial killers."

"And he responded?" Gage asked. "Just like that?"

Turning to face him, she nodded.

"Yes, it was that simple," she admitted. "He added me to his approved visitor's list, and I drove over to the state prison in Waverly."

She grimaced at the memory.

"Of course, my dad begged me not to go. He said Crast wasn't some lost soul I could save. As if I was going there to try to redeem the man."

Gage raised an eyebrow.

"That hadn't crossed your mind?" he asked. "The thought that you could find out what was broken inside him and fix it?"

Bridget gave a firm shake of her head.

"No, I went there to *study* him," she insisted. "I knew full well he was beyond *saving*, in any sense of the word."

"Okay, so you went to see him. You weren't scared?"

She hesitated.

"I almost chickened out," she admitted. "It was frightening to come face to face with a man who'd killed seven women."

"It would have been eight if Althea Helmont hadn't escaped," Gage reminded her. "What happened when you went in? What was he like?"

"He was big. Aggressive. Talkative," Bridget said. "He told me about his childhood. Said his father was abusive. Claimed he'd had various head injuries. He ticked all the boxes. He was exactly the kind of subject I'd been looking for."

Her voice was thoughtful.

"Looking back, it's possible he knew just what to say."

"You think he was manipulating you?"

She shrugged.

"Probably. At least in the beginning. After all, he was a serial killer who preyed on women. He would lie and say what he needed to say to get what he wanted from them."

"And in the end?"

Considering the question, Bridget again looked toward the window and the scenery rolling past.

They were nearing the outskirts of Wisteria Falls, and the maple, pine, and poplar trees were giving way to street signs, shops, and office buildings.

"In the end he was psychotic and suffering delusions," she said. "He'd lost touch with reality."

Surprised at her candor, Gage prodded.

"Why'd he ask you to witness the execution? You were the only one he requested to be in the witness room, right?"

"That's right," she agreed. "By that time, he was...*attached* to me. I guess that's the way I came to think of it. Attachment might be the closest thing he ever felt to a true emotion."

Her voice sounded almost tender.

"Crast believed I was the only one who understood him. The only one he could trust. At least, that's what he told me when he asked me to witness his execution."

Gage waited, sensing she wanted to say more.

"When I found out he'd stipulated that his brain could only be used for research if I was in charge of the study, I started to think he might have been telling the truth, about one thing at least. Maybe he did really trust me."

"And what did your research show?" Gage asked, growing more curious about the man who'd inspired Bridget's career. "Did you find signs of trauma in Crast's brain?"

Bridget nodded.

"We did, actually. Based on my previous interviews with people who'd known Crast growing up, I'd confirmed he'd sustained various head injuries over the years. Then when Tony and I went in to dissect his brain, we found-"

"Tony? You mean Dr. Yen at Quantico's RSU?"

Picturing the clean-cut young research scientist who had often stopped by to see Bridget during her days as a behavioral analyst, Gage had a hard time imagining Tony Yen slicing through Ernest Crast's brain.

"Yes, Tony and I partnered on the research project," she said. "That's how I got recruited to join the Bureau in the first place. But that's a whole different story."

She shook her head as if to clear it.

"Tony and I found damage to Crast's frontal cortex. It corroborated the findings in my dissertation," she said. "You add that to the reports of abuse and neglect he'd suffered as a child, and it isn't hard to figure out how he became a killer."

"What we need to figure out is how he's linked to the man who killed Brooke Nelson," Gage said. "That's where I need your help. Will you come over to Quantico tomorrow and help the team come up with a profile of our new strangler?"

The question hung in the air for a long beat before Bridget slowly inclined her head.

"I'll help you work up a profile," she agreed. "But no press. And I'm just a consultant. This is a one-off."

Gage nodded. He didn't need the hassle that would come along with the media, either.

The press will go nuts if they get wind Bridget is profiling a new serial murderer who is copycatting the Shenandoah Valley Strangler.

Seeing the sign for Wisteria Falls Forensic Psychology up ahead, Gage looked over at Bridget.

"I'm glad to have you back on board," he said, then quickly added, "even if it's not a permanent thing."

Bridget reached for the handle as the SUV rolled to a stop, then she hesitated and turned back to Gage.

"Remind Charlie and Hale to track down Althea Helmont. I have a feeling she could be in danger."

* * *

Bridget's solemn pronouncement played over in Gage's mind as he watched her disappear into the building.

Would the copycat strangler really go after Crast's only

surviving victim? The question prompted Gage to tap out a quick text message to Charlie before he steered the SUV back onto the highway.

Bridget advises you find Althea Helmont. Could be in danger.

Dropping his phone on the seat next to him, he turned the vehicle toward Quantico and settled in for the ride.

The drive home to Stafford County would take over an hour, but he was in no hurry. Sarge would be the only one waiting for him. That is if he wasn't already out on the prowl.

Gage smiled at the thought of the big tomcat as his phone buzzed beside him.

He looked down, expecting Charlie to be calling back about his text, but instead saw Anne's number on the display.

"What's up, little sister?" he asked. "Everything okay?"

"Yeah, I'm good. I was just calling to make sure you made that appointment for Sarge," Anne said.

Her disapproving tone made it clear she was doubtful.

"I meant to do that today, but we have a big case starting up," Gage said with a wince, wondering how his sister always managed to make him feel like a deadbeat.

"You want a litter of tiger kittens running around your neighborhood?" she asked. "Cause that's what's going to happen if you don't get that cat fixed."

Before he could think up a witty reply, Gage heard the beep of another incoming call. His stomach dropped when he looked down at the phone and saw Vivian's number on the display.

"Look, I have another call coming in. I have to-"

"Don't you hang up on me, Big Brother," Anne said in the

no-nonsense tone that reminded him of their mother. "We haven't discussed what time you're coming over tomorrow."

Gage sighed as another beep sounded.

"Tomorrow?" he asked.

"I knew you'd forget," Anne declared, sounding vaguely triumphant. "You're supposed to be coming for dinner. I told Chris you'd try to get out of it."

Heart sinking at the thought of spending his Saturday night with Anne and whichever friend she was trying to set him up with this time, Gage tried to think up an excuse.

"I'm not trying to get out of anything," he protested. "It's just this new case. You've heard about the woman who went missing by Dupont Circle. Well, her-"

"Save it," Anne said, her tone turning sullen. "You promised you'd be here, and I've already made all the arrangements. There's someone I want you to meet, so be here at eight. And bring some wine."

The line went dead before he could protest.

Gripping both hands around the steering wheel as he saw his exit approaching, Gage glanced at the phone again.

His shoulders relaxed as he saw Vivian hadn't left a voicemail. Perhaps she wasn't available tonight. After all, it was a Friday.

She'll want to spend the evening with her husband, won't she?

Scolding himself for getting involved in the first place, Gage spent the rest of the drive debating whether he should try to call her back. Maybe it was best to just end things now.

He still hadn't made up his mind by the time he pulled into the garage of the spacious, two-story house he'd purchased a decade before, back when he'd imagined marriage and children in his future. Back when he'd considered himself to be in the prime of life.

But lately, Gage had started to think of himself as being slightly past his sell-by date, and the big house with plenty of room to expand only emphasized his still-single status.

The house was dark when he pushed through the garage door into the kitchen. Dropping his laptop bag on the table, he reached for the light switch, then froze as he heard a faint rustling.

Squinting across the shadowy room, he held his breath and inched his hand toward the gun in his holster as the kitchen door swung slowly open.

At the sound of soft paws scampering toward him, Gage exhaled loudly, feeling Sarge brush past his leg on the way to his food bowl.

"You gotta stop sneaking up on me like that, little dude," he said, flipping on the light switch. "You're gonna give me a heart attack. Then who will feed you?"

He scooped the cat up and held him against his chest, ruffling the soft, tiger-striped fur as he crossed to the counter.

Wondering how he'd ended up spending Friday night alone, with only a cat for company, he opened his refrigerator and pulled out a bottle of beer.

After taking a few long gulps of the ice-cold liquid, he stopped to listen to the soft rumble of Sarge's purring before setting the bottle on the counter and reaching for his phone.

CHAPTER FIVE

Bridget was rubbing her tired eyes and stifling a yawn when Aubrey March opened the door to allow Hank to trot into the room. The Irish setter's mahogany coat gleamed in the glow from the desk lamp, causing Bridget to look toward the window in surprise. The daylight outside had somehow faded into full darkness without her noticing.

"Good, you're back," Aubrey said, her face pink and flushed. "Hank was getting antsy, so I took him over to Highland Park. He sure does have a lot of energy."

"Thanks, Aubrey, you're a lifesaver."

Bridget ruffled Hank's fur as the dog settled in at her feet.

Smoothing back her hair, which she always wore in a high, sleek ponytail, Aubrey hovered beside Bridget's desk, her eyes taking in the file of crime scene photos before darting away.

"Dr. Zepler was asking what the FBI wanted," she said, glancing toward the door. "I told him I didn't know, but he's still in his office, so..."

"So, he's going to want an update before I leave?" Bridget finished for her. "I appreciate the heads up, but I'm sure you have something better to do on a Friday night than hang around here and dog sit."

Aubrey's face fell as she realized Bridget wasn't going to tell her why the FBI had come calling. Turning to leave, she stopped at the door and looked back.

"Oh, and Dr. Thackery called looking for you," she said, biting her lip. "Something about a missed appointment."

Bridget's stomach dropped as the receptionist disappeared down the hall. Reaching for her phone, she grimaced at the messages on the display.

She'd missed a dozen calls and voicemails after activating the *Do Not Disturb* option on her cell phone.

But she'd had no choice, had she? It was the only way she could concentrate. The only way she might have a chance to finish her report on Felix Arnett.

"I'm sorry, Faye," she said into the receiver after the therapist's voicemail had picked up. "I had a busy day and I got side-tracked and...I'm sorry I missed our session. I'll call back tomorrow and reschedule."

She waited until the beep sounded in her ear before dropping the phone on her desk with a sigh.

Of course, Faye has already gone home for the day. It isn't like she'd be waiting around for me to call with some lame excuse. She'll probably think I'm just trying to get out of it...and maybe I am.

Tucking the thought away for later consideration, she looked down at Hank with a weary smile.

"I bet you're hungry, boy. Let's go home and get you something to eat."

The statement reminded Bridget she should be hungry, too. After all, she'd missed lunch and it was inching past her normal dinnertime. But then, she hadn't felt much like eating after witnessing Brooke Nelson's autopsy.

As she stood and reached for her laptop bag, a knock on the doorframe stopped her.

"Aubrey told me the FBI was here earlier."

Dr. Gary Zepler's sizable figure filled the doorway, an expectant expression on his round, bearded face. Thinning white hair and metal-framed glasses lent the older man the appearance of a department store Santa on his day off.

"There's a case...a homicide," Bridget said. "And an abduction. It's been in the news..."

She hesitated, unsure how much to share with her boss.

"The Bureau is setting up a task force with the local PD," she explained. "Agent Gage wants me to work up a profile of the unsub. He thinks I may be able to predict what the guy is likely to do next."

Zepler frowned.

"Why you?" he asked. "The FBI must have plenty of behavioral analysts chomping at the bit to get involved in a high-profile case. Why drive out here to seek *you* out?"

Bridget stiffened at Zepler's insinuation. Clearly, he considered her skills as an analyst to be nothing special.

Opening her mouth to issue a sharp reply, Bridget heard a familiar voice in her head. It was a voice that spoke to her often; a voice that sounded remarkably like her mother's voice, or at least what she remembered of it.

Check your ego, Bridget. That's not what he meant, and you know it. He's just worried he'll lose you to the Bureau.

She exhaled and let her shoulders relax. The little voice

41

was probably right. Over the years she'd learned it usually was.

"The case requires an analyst with certain experience that isn't easy to find," she said evasively. "And they understand I would only be working on this case as a consultant."

The assurance didn't soften Zepler's frown. The respected psychologist had spent considerable effort persuading Bridget to join his lucrative private practice. He wouldn't be eager to see her return to the BAU.

"I'll be working plenty of billable hours," she added. "And I'm still working on the Felix Arnett case."

"And you have the bandwidth to do both?" he asked gruffly, his resolve weakening at the mention of billable hours as she knew it would. "You won't be taking on too much?"

Bridget shook her head, despite her misgivings, knowing that she couldn't back out now. Not after seeing Brooke Nelson's body on the autopsy table.

That's what Gage counted on. He manipulated me to get what he wanted, just like Crast would have done.

"I'll be fine," she told Zepler, slinging her laptop bag over her shoulder. "I've got everything under control."

* * *

A headache began to throb behind Bridget's eyes as she turned her old Ford Explorer onto Fern Creek Road and followed the winding street to a modest red brick house with white shutters and a wraparound porch.

Pulling onto the driveway, Bridget lifted a hand and waved as she noticed Jacey Wallace standing on the sidewalk.

She parked the SUV in the garage, then led Hank out toward the road to check her mailbox.

"You're getting home late," Jacey called as her miniature teacup Yorkie pulled on the leash in her hand. "Working on a big case?"

Bridget shrugged as she pulled a stack of envelopes out of the mailbox and began to rifle through them.

"Just bills and ads as usual," she murmured, ignoring Jacey's prying question as she turned back toward the house.

"You heard they found that missing girl's body over by Moonstone Cavern, didn't you?" Jacey asked, her eyes wide and her face pale under the streetlights. "And another girl's been taken. Makes you wonder who could be next."

Calling to Hank as he trotted over to sniff at the Yorkie, Bridget shook her head.

"I'm sure whoever is responsible will be caught soon," she said, moving up the driveway, eager to get inside.

"Aren't you scared to live alone?" Jacey called after her. "Ever since Parker left, I can hardly sleep. I keep hearing all sorts of noises. Checking the windows and doors every five minutes. Luckily, I've got Pixie to scare off anyone who tries to break in."

Bridget smiled and dropped her eyes to the tiny Yorkie, but when she looked up at Jacey, she saw that her neighbor hadn't been joking.

"Yes, you're lucky. Hank isn't much of a guard dog."

Bridget gestured to the setter's frantically wagging tail.

"He's way too friendly to scare anyone off."

"I guess you've got a gun, haven't you? I mean...since you were with the FBI," Jacey prodded, nervously twisting at the long, dark braid that had fallen over her shoulder. "And I bet you know how to use it, too, don't you? Maybe you could teach me how to-"

"I'd try not to worry too much about intruders, if I were you," Bridget said quickly, urging Hank toward the house.

But Jacey was tugging Pixie up the driveway after her.

"You could teach me how to use a gun, couldn't you, Bridget?" Jacey asked again. "I mean, just for peace of mind."

Hearing the anxiety in her neighbor's voice, Bridget found herself nodding reluctantly.

"I guess I could take you over to the range on Rockbridge Road next weekend," she said, already regretting the offer as Jacey's face lit up with pleasure.

"That's great," Jacey gushed. "Parker never would trust me with a gun. Said I was too clumsy. Thought I'd end up shooting myself. I guess there are some benefits to getting a divorce."

Bridget unlocked her door and herded Hank inside, relieved to see that Pixie was once again pulling Jacey toward the sidewalk as she called out her goodbyes.

Following Hank into the kitchen, she prepared his dinner first, then studied the contents of the refrigerator without much enthusiasm, finally settling on a toasted cheese sandwich and a glass of merlot.

Setting her plate on the kitchen table, Bridget took a bite of the sandwich, washed it down with a gulp of the rich, red wine, and opened her laptop bag.

If she was going to work up a profile of Brooke Nelson's killer, she might as well get started. She'd have to be willing to work nights and weekends if she wanted to keep her promise to Dr. Zepler.

By the time the sandwich was gone, and her glass of wine was empty, Bridget had reviewed the key details of the Shenandoah Valley Strangler case and Ernest Crast's crimes and had arranged eight photos on the table.

The photos showed the seven women Crast had killed, along with Althea Helmont, the one who'd gotten away. The women had all been young and attractive. Just like Brooke Nelson had been. Just like Libby Palmer.

Head pounding, Bridget carried her empty plate to the sink and poured herself a second glass of wine.

Staring out toward the darkness beyond the window, Bridget's mind turned to Libby Palmer and her abductor.

If the copycat is following in Crast's footsteps, he'll try to keep Libby for at least a week, maybe longer. He'll hide her away until he's finished with her. So, where would he take her? Where would he feel safe?

The image of a darkened room materialized in her imagination, then flitted away as her phone buzzed on the table and her father's number appeared on the display.

Perhaps he'd heard the news about the blue duct tape found on Brooke Nelson. He might even know Bridget had been seen with the FBI, and that she'd gone to view the autopsy.

Although Bob Bishop was officially retired, his ex-partner

Harry Kemp was still on the force, and she suspected he provided her father with the latest WFPD news and gossip.

"Hi, Dad, how's it going?"

Bridget took another sip from her glass, then impulsively poured the rest of the wine into the sink. She turned on the faucet, washing the blood-red liquid down the drain.

Getting drunk wouldn't erase the images from her aching head, and it wouldn't help her find their copycat.

"Everything's good, honey," her father said. "Just wanted to check in. I haven't heard from you for a few days and-"

"Let me talk to her, Bob. I want to ask her something."

A high-pitched voice in the background drowned out her father's words, and then Bridget's stepmother Paloma was on the phone.

"Bridget, how are you, dear?"

The nasal voice reverberated like nails on a chalkboard in Bridget's ear.

"You never called to tell us how your date with Angelo went," Paloma complained. "Did you kids have fun?"

Bridget grimaced at the thought of Paloma's nephew.

Angelo Molina worked for the floundering Wisteria Falls Tribune, doing everything from writing articles, commissioning photos, and even delivering papers when needed.

His determination to keep the paper going at all costs was commendable, but his keen interest in Bridget was suspect.

Like every other member of the press Bridget had encountered, Angelo was determined to get her to recount her experience watching Ernest Crast's execution, or to provide lurid details of the Backroads Butcher's crimes.

The date Paloma had arranged, after much resistance from Bridget, had been an excruciating bout of twenty questions, in which Bridget had resisted answering any of the questions.

"It was fine," she lied, not wanting to cause further stress for her father. "But I'm really busy right now, so can I..."

"And Angelo's so handsome, isn't he?" Paloma said as if Bridget hadn't spoken. "And so smart. He takes after my poor brother, bless his soul. I think it's in the genes."

Holding the phone away from her ear, Bridget let Paloma ramble on until she heard Bob Bishop's deep voice come back on the line.

"Sorry about that honey. I'm sure you're busy, but I've heard some rumors, and I wanted to make sure you're okay."

"Harry Kemp never was able to keep a secret," Bridget said dryly, wondering what her father's ex-partner had revealed. "But there's no reason for you to worry. I'll fill you in on Sunday when I come over. Now, I gotta go."

Once she'd ended the call, Bridget considered how much she should share with her father about the new case.

He and Harry Kemp had been the lead detectives searching for the Shenandoah Valley Strangler. They'd played a huge role in bringing Crast in after the serial killer had terrorized the community.

Her father might even be able to help with her profile of Crast's copycat if she let him, although she still wasn't convinced he had fully recovered from his stroke.

The last thing Dad needs is to be stressed out worrying about me.

Turning back to the photos and documents spread out on

the table, Bridget let her eyes drop to the graduation photo Libby Palmer's worried mother had provided to the police.

A pretty girl with pensive brown eyes and a headful of dark curls stared up at her.

"Who took you, Libby?" Bridget whispered into the quiet kitchen. "And where are you, now?"

CHAPTER SIX

The disciple stood in a harsh circle of light cast by a single bulb hanging from the ceiling. The rest of the musty room was blanketed in the predawn darkness, its rough wooden walls and floors doing little to keep out the nighttime chill that often lingered in the Shenandoah Valley well into spring.

Keeping his dark, feverish eyes fixed on the wooden table before him, he studied the collection of relics he'd inherited.

Finally, it's my turn to add to the offerings.

A jolt of pride raced through his body as he removed a small cloth bundle from the pocket of his jacket.

Unwrapping the bundle, he admired the three small keepsakes he'd spent the day preparing. The finger bones were clean and smooth, having been boiled, scraped, and cleaned, just as the handbook had instructed.

The bones rattled softly in his hand as he lifted them out of the cloth and arranged them on the table next to the others.

He smiled at the sight of his handiwork next to that of his mentor, letting his eyes wander over the objects on the makeshift altar with greedy pleasure.

Picking up the tattered handbook, he opened it to the front page and began to read aloud the words his mentor had written by hand in red ink.

"Ecclesiastes 7:28 (Mama's Favorite)
-And I find something more bitter than death:
the woman whose heart is snares and nets, and
whose hands are fetters. He who pleases God
escapes her, but the sinner is taken by her."

The disciple nodded his head in agreement.

The women would try to snare him, just as they'd done to his mentor. They'd want to trap him and trick him. But his mentor had shown him the way.

And now that his mentor was gone, now that he'd been betrayed and sent to his death, it was up to the disciple to carry on his legacy. The second coming was at hand, and it was time to make the sinners pay.

Tucking the handbook under his arm, he turned toward the door in the far wall, lighting his way across the worn wooden floor with the soft glow from his cell phone's display.

As he neared the scarred, splintered wood of the old door, the disciple held his breath and listened patiently, determined to remain vigilant, just as the words in the handbook urged.

Stay watchful, listen well. Trusting the succubus will lead to hell.

Although he heard nothing within to arouse his suspicion, he kept his ear pressed against the door for several more minutes, wanting to be sure the girl downstairs hadn't managed to break free.

If she managed to escape as Althea Helmont had escaped, his mission to fulfill his mentor's legacy would end in failure.

Putting a hand on the butt of his gun to assure himself it was in its usual place, he took the old metal key off the hook on the wall, inserted it into the lock, and pushed the door open.

The light from his phone lit up the dozen rickety steps leading down to the windowless room on the lower level, then shone across the dark space to reveal a motionless figure.

Libby Palmer hadn't moved since he'd left her on the bed. Her arms and legs were still tightly bound with the bright blue duct tape and the cloth gag he'd used to keep her quiet was still firmly in place.

A vague worry filled his chest as he stared down at her.

Shouldn't she be awake by now? Or had she suffocated? Maybe he'd misjudged the blow he'd delivered to her head.

Taking the steps two at a time, he strode across the small room and crouched beside Libby's limp figure. Positioning two fingers on the side of her neck, he sat back on his heels as he felt the slow *thump, thump, thump* of her pulse.

Good work, kid.

A gravelly voice sounded in the darkness. He jumped up and spun around, his eyes searching the room.

You're doing fine. All you gotta do is stick to the plan. Just follow what's written in the handbook and you'll never get caught.

He pulled the handbook from under his arm and gripped it in both hands, holding it up toward the low ceiling as if offering up a sacrifice.

"I remember everything you told me," he said aloud. "And I've read every word in the handbook."

Sensing movement, he looked down to see Libby awake and cowering on the bed. She stared up at him with wide, scared eyes.

"You're awake," he said. "I thought maybe I'd killed you."

When she didn't answer, he bent over to untie the gag.

"I guess you're getting pretty thirsty about now."

She hesitated, then nodded slowly, not attempting to speak.

Realizing he hadn't brought any water or food with him, he frowned and cocked his head, then checked his watch as his stomach growled in protest.

"Not sure any stores around here are open yet."

He scratched at his chin.

"But I could use something to eat. Maybe I'll head up to the Moonstone Diner."

He stood and stretched his back, enjoying the sense of power that flooded through him as he stared down at her, then bent to push the gag back in place.

"Don't you worry, now. I'll be back soon."

The words hung in the air as he bounded up the stairs to the small landing. Pushing through the door, he closed and locked it behind him, throwing the room into darkness again as he strode out to his car.

Careful to keep the sedan under the speed limit, he arrived at the diner just as the sun was rising over the hills to the east.

Seeing that the lights were on, but that the *Closed* sign still hung in the window, he continued on to the shop next door.

The store was open and brightly lit, with fresh coffee brewing on the back counter next to a stack of newspapers.

"You can get a large coffee and a Tribune for two bucks," a gruff voice said as he hovered beside the counter.

Not sure if the voice was coming from inside or outside his head, he turned to see an elderly man stocking the candy shelves at the front of the store.

"Sounds like a deal."

Picking up a paper off the top of the stack, the disciple read the headline across the top with a sense of triumph.

One Woman Dead, One Missing as Police Search for Shenandoah Valley's Second Strangler!

"Terrible, isn't it?" the clerk said, shaking his head. "I can still remember when nobody knew who the Shenandoah Valley Strangler was. Everybody around here was scared to death."

Crossing to the register, he held up two fingers.

"That'll be two bucks. Cash only."

The disciple dug in his pocket and pulled out his wallet, careful to keep the butt of his gun concealed under his jacket as he pulled out two one-dollar bills.

"Once the cops figured out Ernest Crast had killed those poor women, everybody went back to leaving their doors unlocked, again."

The disciple handed the bills to the clerk and made for the exit, his heart pounding as he scanned the article.

"Hold on, Mister!" the clerk called as he reached the door.

Adrenaline shot through the disciple's body as he turned toward the older man, who was pointing to the back counter.

"You forgot your coffee."

He stared at the clerk for a long beat, then smiled.

"You can have it," he said, holding up the paper. "This is all I need."

Sucking in a breath of cool morning air, the disciple folded the paper under his arm and hurried down the sidewalk, arriving at the Moonstone Diner just in time to see a server turning the sign in the door to *Open*.

CHAPTER SEVEN

C harlie Day rolled to a stop by the curb outside the bulky concrete apartment building and put the big Expedition into park. Pushing her oversized sunglasses on top of her head, she pulled out her phone, tapped in a text message, and stared impatiently toward the front entrance.

Wishing she had taken the time to prepare her usual double-shot of espresso before she'd left home, Charlie checked her reflection in the rearview mirror.

Her calm, gray eyes betrayed nothing of her frantic, late-night efforts to coordinate resources from various federal, state, and local departments.

After multiple phone calls, email chains, and online meetings, her fledgling task force was finally in place.

Moving forward, she would officially be acting as lead investigator, with Hale as her backup.

But her relief at getting the task force rolling had been short-lived as she realized it would be up to her to find Brooke Nelson's killer, and to bring Libby Palmer home before it was too late. The weight of it all had kept her tossing and turning most of the night.

When she'd gotten the call that morning from the witness security program informing her that Althea Helmont was back in D.C., Charlie had immediately decided they needed to find the woman and offer her protection. They couldn't take the chance that Crast's copycat might get to her first.

Flinching at a sharp rap on the passenger's side window, Charlie turned to see Tristan Hale smiling in at her, his face freshly shaven, his dark hair still damp from the shower.

"It's illegal to be in a good mood this early in the morning," she said as he climbed into the SUV and buckled his seatbelt. "Or if it isn't, it should be."

"*You're* the one who called *me*," he reminded her. "I'm just trying to make the best of a bad situation."

She shot Hale a look that would wither most men, but it only served to widen his grin. Her irritation grew as she detected the faint scent of his cologne, although she wasn't sure why.

"Okay, so where are we headed?" he asked as she pulled away from the curb and merged into traffic.

Charlie's phone buzzed on the dashboard before she could respond, and her eyes flicked to the display.

"Uh-oh, it's Calloway," Hale said, raising his eyebrows in mock dismay. "What have you done to earn a call from the SAC on a Saturday morning?"

An uneasy pang joined the empty ache in her stomach as Charlie stared at the name and number of the Special Agent in Charge. She doubted he was calling with good news.

Most likely Calloway's about to throw a wrench in my plans.

Glancing at Hale with a sigh, she reluctantly pressed the

hands-free button on the steering wheel.

"Roger, how are you?"

"I'd be a hell of a lot better without all these damn leaks to the press," Calloway said by way of a greeting. "I just got my ass chewed out by the Deputy Director over this morning's article in the Post. Apparently, we've got a new serial killer in Virginia, even though we only have one body to speak of. Hardly newsworthy if you ask me."

Charlie opened her mouth to ask just how many bodies Calloway considered worthy of a spot on the front page, then closed it again. The man wasn't worth it.

"I haven't seen the Post this morning," she said instead. "But I'll be sure to get a copy, and-"

"All the other newspapers have the same story, not just the Post," Calloway complained. "Now I want you to make sure everyone working on this Second Strangler task force keeps their mouths shut."

Frowning over at Hale in confusion, she mouthed the words, "*Second Strangler?*"

Hale just shrugged.

"And that goes for the locals, too," Calloway blustered on. "I don't want the police over in Wisteria Falls or any other pissant little town to talk to the press. This needs to be contained until we know what we're dealing with."

Before she could ask Calloway just how exactly he expected her to control what the local police told reporters, she realized he'd disconnected the call.

Turning wide, outraged eyes to Hale, she saw that he was no longer smiling.

"Forget all that," he said, giving a firm shake of his head. "Don't let him get to you. Now, where are we going?'

"We're going to one of those pissant little towns Calloway was talking about," Charlie said dryly. "We're going to find Bridget Bishop. And if she agrees, we're going to take her with us to talk to Althea Helmont."

Hale studied Charlie's profile as she merged the big Ford onto I-66 heading west.

"Okay, I get it," Hale said, though his tone said otherwise. "She's a psychologist. She knows how to talk to victims of trauma. But didn't she quit the Bureau a while back?"

"She's not just any psychologist," Charlie protested. "Bridget has a way of getting through to people. Both victims and criminals. I've worked with her on a few cases, including the Backroads Butcher case, so I know what she's capable of."

Not wanting to get into a discussion of the horrific crimes involved, Charlie swallowed hard and cleared her throat.

"Let's just say, Bridget Bishop is one of the few people I'd trust with someone like Althea Helmont. Someone who suffered at the hands of Ernest Crast and barely escaped with her life. The woman is bound to be emotionally fragile."

"You never know," Hale said, turning to look out the window as they left the congestion and traffic of D.C. behind. "Sometimes an experience like that can toughen you up and make you even stronger. I've seen it happen."

Charlie was tempted to ask exactly what he'd seen, but something in his voice stopped her.

Hale had worked undercover for years before he'd been

compromised and reassigned to the Washington field office.

From the little he'd told her, his experiences infiltrating a human trafficking syndicate had put him in close contact with some very dangerous people.

People who made a living off victimizing vulnerable women and children. People who dealt out pain and suffering with callous indifference.

She imagined Hale had witnessed the worst of human nature on a regular basis, just as she had over her years working abductions and homicides as part of the Violent Crimes Unit. She knew better than most that the constant exposure to violence and death could be soul-destroying.

But she also knew that on occasion he'd likely had the chance to witness virtue prevail over evil, despite the odds.

Perhaps that rare glimpse of justice, and the rush of satisfaction that went with it, had kept him in the game and at the Bureau. If so, then they had something in common.

Seeing the sign for Wisteria Falls ahead, Charlie took the exit, merging onto Landsend Road. She glanced at her gas gauge as she passed a Gas & Go station, deciding she had enough in the tank to get them back to D.C. without stopping.

As they crossed an old truss bridge that appeared to have seen better days, Hale leaned forward to get a better view of the turbulent Shenandoah River below.

"This is close to where Libby Palmer's car was found, isn't it?" he asked. "Maybe she wasn't abducted after all. Maybe she got out to look at the river and fell in. Or jumped."

"We've gone through this already," she reminded him. "There were signs of a struggle on the ground beside Libby's car, and tire marks from a second vehicle at the scene matched the tire marks near Brooke's body. It was an abduction."

Charlie slowed down as they reached Fern Creek Road.

Following the winding street to a neat red brick house she remembered from previous visits, Charlie brought the Expedition to a stop along the curb.

"Did you let Bridget know we were coming?" Hale asked as they climbed out and surveyed the empty porch. "It's still pretty early to-"

His words were cut short by a high-pitched cry.

"Pixie! Come back here, girl!"

A small woman in a tracksuit and tennis shoes appeared on the porch next door. She charged down the walkway toward them, her long black braid flying out behind her.

Charlie pulled Hale back onto the grass to make way for the frantic woman, but he shook off her hand and laughed as he pointed to a tiny dog racing down the sidewalk toward them.

Bending over, he scooped the Yorkie up with one big hand and cradled it against his chest.

"Oh, thank goodness," the woman said, puffing to a stop in front of them. "I thought I was gonna have to run a mile to get this little girl back."

Hale handed over the runaway dog as the woman gazed up at him with undisguised admiration.

"You're not from around here, are you?" she asked, running an appreciative eye over Hale's suit as if appraising the lean, muscular body underneath it.

"Uh, no, I'm just visiting," Hale said, suppressing a smile as Charlie prodded him up the path toward Bridget's door.

Ignoring the longing stare of Pixie's owner, she knocked on the door harder than she'd intended.

Eager feet approached the door, and a furry head peered out of the glass insert. Charlie could see the dog's tail wagging enthusiastically behind him.

"Well, at least someone's glad to see us," Hale said as a figure appeared in the hallway behind the eager dog.

"Charlie? What are you doing here?"

Bridget Bishop stood in the doorway wearing a pink cotton robe and holding the collar of her excited Irish setter, who appeared to think he was going for an impromptu walk.

"Inside, Hank," Bridget ordered, then stepped onto the porch as the disappointed dog retreated into the hall.

She waved to her neighbor, who still stood on the sidewalk holding the little Yorkie, before turning to Charlie with a questioning stare.

"Has something happened?"

Charlie hesitated, suddenly wishing she had called before they'd made the hour drive.

"Althea Helmont is back in D.C.," Charlie said, deciding it would be best to get straight to the point. "Our contact at the Witness Security Program confirmed it this morning. I thought you'd want to go with us to talk to her."

But Bridget wasn't listening. Her eyes were fixed on the doormat and the Wisteria Falls Tribune next to it.

"So that's what Calloway was talking about," Charlie said, bending over to pick up the paper. "Now I know why he called the guy the *Second Strangler*. The press have given our unsub his very own nickname."

Taking the Tribune from Charlie's hand, Bridget turned and walked slowly back inside, reading the article as she went, leaving the door open for Charlie and Hale to follow her in.

"I can't believe Angelo wrote this," Bridget said, pointing at the byline. "I mean, how did he get all this information?"

"You know the journalist who wrote this?" Charlie asked in surprise. "Have you discussed the case with him?"

Bridget's forehead creased into an indignant frown.

"Of course, not," she insisted. "I would never do that, even if I liked the guy, which I don't."

A flush of color filled Bridget's cheeks.

"I didn't mean that like it sounded. I don't *dislike* the guy, it's just that he's my stepmother's nephew and she tried to hook us up and he's always..."

Her words trailed off as she met Charlie's eyes.

"We need to find Althea Helmont before she sees the news and panics," Charlie said. "We can worry about the press later. For now, we need to get to D.C."

CHAPTER EIGHT

Bridget rapped on Jacey Wallace's front door and waited as Hank shifted impatiently at her feet, deciding she'd have to leave the Irish setter with her father if her neighbor wasn't available to dog sit. After all, Hank was a sociable dog. He didn't like being left on his own for long.

"Any chance you could keep Hank today?" Bridget asked when Jacey opened the door. "No problem if you've got plans."

"No, Pixie and I are free as birds all weekend," Jacey said, her eyes drifting past Bridget to where Charlie and Hale stood beside the Expedition.

Leaving Hank settled in beside Pixie on Jacey's porch, Bridget crossed to Charlie's SUV and climbed into the backseat.

"You can ride shotgun if you want," Hale offered, but Bridget only shook her head.

She hadn't gotten enough sleep, and what little sleep she'd managed had been filled with disturbing dreams in which Ernest Crast played a starring role.

As they rolled down Fern Creek Road, Bridget's mind drifted back to the first time she'd seen Crast in person. By that time, he'd been on death row at the state prison in Waverly for almost eight years.

Bridget stood on shaky legs behind the stone-faced guard as he unlocked the door to the visiting room and pulled it open.

Resisting the urge to turn and run, she followed brusquely given instructions to step inside and take a seat at the small metal table in the middle of the room.

"They'll bring Crast in shortly," the guard said. "He'll be cuffed at wrists and ankles, and I'll be right outside, but keep your distance."

Bridget nodded, her throat too tight and dry to speak.

Heavy footsteps sounded behind her, and then Ernest Crast appeared, his wide shoulders filling the doorway, his tall figure dominating the tiny room.

Feeling suddenly claustrophobic, Bridget struggled to catch a full breath as she recognized the serial killer from the pictures and videos she'd seen on the news, and from the case files her father had kept in boxes in his home office.

The convicted killer's reddish hair had begun to thin above his broad, craggy face since he'd been on death row, but it looked as if he'd managed to maintain his intimidating physique.

As Crast dropped into the chair on the other side of the table, a ripple of fear rolled through Bridget. Her eyes fell to the cuffs on his thick wrists, and then to his big hands, which were clasped in his lap.

She couldn't stop the shudder that rolled through her as she realized those same hands had been used to strangle seven women.

"So, you're Bob Bishop's daughter," Crast said in a

conversational tone. "Now, why would a nice girl like you want to study my brain?"

"It's for my psychology dissertation," Bridget said in a numb voice. "I'm researching the effects of childhood trauma and brain injuries on men who...well, who do what you've done."

Crast cocked his head and frowned.

"Hmm...and what exactly do you think I've done?"

Swallowing hard, Bridget met his narrowed gaze.

"You abducted at least eight women and killed seven of them," *she said, suddenly angry. "And I want to know why you did it."*

A gleam entered Crast's small, close-set eyes as they took in her flushed face, then dropped to her clenched fists.

"Now that sounds more like the truth," he said, producing a wide grin. "As Mama always told me, anger or alcohol will always bring out the truth in a man, for good or evil."

"Bridget?"

Charlie's voice called to her from the front seat, bringing Bridget's mind back to the present moment.

"I was just asking if you could think of anyone who might have access to Crast's supplies or his souvenirs."

"Souvenirs?"

She looked up to meet Charlie's eyes in the rearview mirror.

"You know, any items he took from his victims."

Bridget thought back to the files she'd combed through the night before, then shook her head.

"From what I remember, he didn't take any souvenirs," she said, then hesitated. "Although, the fingers removed

65

from his victims have never been found."

As her words hung in the air, Bridget glanced out the window, noticing that they were passing the distinctive white building which housed the Wisteria Falls Tribune.

Angelo Molina stood outside, talking on his phone, and smoking a cigarette, although he'd made a point of telling Bridget that he didn't smoke and abhorred the nasty habit.

I had a feeling he was a liar. Now I've seen it with my own eyes.

Ducking down in her seat, Bridget tried to hide. She couldn't let Angelo see her riding around with two FBI agents. No need to give the journalist material for his sensationalized stories.

You should never have gone out with him, no matter how much Paloma nagged you. You've got to learn how to say no, Bridget.

The little voice was right. It didn't matter that Angelo was handsome and single. His show of interest in her was likely just a ploy to get her talking anyway.

Thinking of the probing questions Angelo had bombarded her with over their dinner of pasta and wine, she wouldn't doubt he was hoping to include her in some sort of feature article or exposé. Maybe even a book.

Dozens of journalists, reporters, and writers had contacted Bridget over the years hoping to interview her for projects on Ernest Crast, the Backroads Butcher, or one of the other serial killers she'd studied or profiled, but she'd always refused.

I'm not about to take part in promoting a serial killer's legacy.

Bridget sat up again just in time to see the Moonstone Diner as the SUV flashed past it.

Gasping in dismay, Bridget looked back.

"What's wrong?" Hale asked without turning around.

"I promised to meet a friend for lunch," Bridget said. "Now I'll have to cancel, and she's going through a rough time."

She didn't add that Daphne Finch often seemed to be going through a rough time, usually of her own making.

Pulling out her phone, Bridget tapped in a text, then sighed.

For the first time in years, Bridget and her best friend were living in the same city. A return to the BAU would mean moving further away from Daphne and closer to Quantico.

Just one more reason that I'm not going back.

* * *

Bridget stared out at the D.C. traffic as Charlie drove slowly past the Healthy Lotus Yoga studio, then circled the block and parked the Ford across the street under a *No Parking* sign.

Noting the small *Closed* sign on the door, Bridget settled back in her seat.

"You sure this is her place?" Hale asked.

"That's what Witness Protection told me," Charlie confirmed. "She moved back to the District two years ago."

She craned her neck to look back at Bridget.

"Apparently they've kept tabs on Althea ever since she was in the program, back before Crast was executed," Charlie said. "The guy I spoke with wouldn't say much, but he indicated Althea and her kids were still considered to be at risk."

"Her kids?" Hale asked.

Bridget sat forward in her seat.

"That's right, she had twin toddlers at the time of her abduction," Bridget confirmed. "A girl and a boy."

"Well, they're not toddlers anymore," Charlie said. "They're both students at Georgetown, which must be why Althea moved back to D.C. to open up her studio."

The theory sounded about right to Bridget.

"I read all the notes from Althea's interviews after she escaped," Bridget said. "She said the only thing that kept her alive was the thought of her kids. Said she couldn't leave them on their own, so she had to find a way to escape. And she did."

She was about to tell them how Althea had outwitted Crast and managed to get away when she saw a tall, thin figure striding down the sidewalk.

"That's her," Charlie said, sitting up straight. "We'll wait until she gets inside before we approach."

"Hold on a minute," Hale cautioned. "If we think our unsub might be coming for Althea, shouldn't we survey the area and make sure it's clear before we make a move?"

Bridget shook her head and opened her door.

"Our guy's a coward," she said in a hard voice. "He attacks lone, unarmed women and binds their arms and legs so they can't fight back. He's not the type to go after three agents with weapons."

Charlie and Hale both looked back at her in surprise.

"The only reason Althea Helmont survived Crast was because he misjudged her. She was stronger than she looked."

CHAPTER NINE

Althea Helmont walked toward the studio with steady, even strides. She clocked the black SUV parked under the *No Parking* sign when she was only ten yards away from the entrance, noting that the Expedition's left, rear door was slightly open.

Keeping her face impassive and her shoulders relaxed, she dropped her head, pretending to search her bag, and surreptitiously raised her eyes to survey the vehicle.

Noting the dark tint to the windows, her eyes flicked down to the standard Washington D.C. license plate. There was nothing suspicious about the vehicle, other than the illegal parking and the open rear door, but Althea had been feeling as if someone had been watching her for the last few weeks.

Perhaps she was about to find out who it was.

Continuing on to the front door, she stopped to pick up the paper resting beside it, then slipped inside.

As she dropped the paper on the reception counter, the headline on the front page caught Althea's eye.

FBI Task Force Hunts Shenandoah Valley's Second Strangler After Body of DC Woman Found Near Moonstone Cavern.

Grabbing up the paper, she scanned the story as her heart

began a frantic drumbeat in her chest.

Once she'd reached the end of the article, Althea studied the photo next to it. The young blonde woman in the picture beamed out at her with a wide smile.

Althea had seen the photo on missing posters throughout the city during the last week or two. She'd tried not to let the posters get to her. Tried not to think of the posters she'd seen plastered around the city after her abduction and escape.

The posters in which her own face had stared back at her.

Almost eighteen years had passed since she'd escaped from Crast, and her abductor had been dead and buried for close to half that time. But he had taken her peace of mind with him to his grave.

She was still unable to venture outside without looking over her shoulder or listening for footsteps behind her. Still paranoid that Crast had somehow managed to fake his death and would eventually show up seeking revenge.

Opening her bag, Althea unzipped the side pocket and pulled out her Glock. Feeling better with the heavy gun in her hand, she stood next to the window and peered out at the black SUV.

But the rear door was closed now, and she could see no movement without or within.

Had she been imagining things again? Was this just her PTSD coming back for another round?

A firm rap on the door sent her pulse jumping but she remained motionless as a woman's voice called out.

"Althea Helmont? I'm Special Agent Charlie Day with the FBI. I need to speak to you. It's urgent."

Risking a peek through the window, she saw an attractive blonde woman in a fitted blazer and slim black trousers.

The woman held up an identification badge when she saw Althea's pale face through the glass insert in the door.

"Can I come in Ms. Helmont?"

Althea leaned her forehead against the doorframe.

"How do I know you're really an agent?" she called out in a shaky voice. "How do I know you're not the disciple Crast warned me about?"

She closed her eyes, hoping the agent would leave even as she feared being left alone.

"We know you must be scared, Althea," another voice called out. "Which is why we're here to help you. We want to make sure Crast can't get to you. We want to make sure you're safe."

There was something in the voice that made Althea reach for the deadbolt. The woman who'd spoken sounded almost as scared and angry as she was.

Opening the door far enough to reveal the Glock in her hand, she surveyed the trio outside.

The female FBI agent was accompanied by a dark-haired man in a suit and tie. A slim, young woman with wavy, chestnut brown hair stood behind him.

The woman's somber blue eyes remained calm as she took in the gun in Althea's trembling hand.

"You're Bridget Bishop, aren't you?" Althea asked, recalling the many pictures of the psychologist she'd seen in the paper and on the news. "You're the one who acted as Crast's witness at Greensville."

Bridget nodded and stepped forward.

"I researched Crast as part of my dissertation," she confirmed. "And yes, I witnessed his execution at his request."

"Then why should I trust you?" Althea spit out, gripping the Glock. "Crast always threatened to send someone for me. He could have sent *you*, for all I know."

The FBI agent shifted her jacket to reveal her own weapon.

"Ms. Helmont, I need you to put away your weapon."

She spoke slowly and clearly as if Althea was a small child.

"As I said, I'm Special Agent Charlie Day, and this is my colleague, Special Agent Hale. Dr. Bishop is here as a consultant."

When Althea didn't budge, Charlie continued.

"We can't force you to speak with us, but I encourage you to hear us out. Your safety could depend on it."

"Please, can we just come in and explain why we're here?" Bridget asked. "Then, if you still want us to leave, we will."

Wishing she had never moved back from Savannah, that she had stayed far away from Crast's hunting grounds, Althea slowly lowered the Glock and stepped back.

"Okay, but you can't stay long. Our Yin Yoga instructor will be here any minute. I've got to figure out what I'm going to do. What I'm going to tell her."

Backing into the spacious studio, Althea kept a safe distance between her and the agents.

"A young woman has been killed and another abducted," Bridget said, standing just inside the door. "We believe the man responsible has some sort of connection to Ernest

Crast."

"I saw the story," Althea said, nodding to the paper she'd dropped on the floor. "They're calling him the Second Strangler after the Shenandoah Valley Strangler. They say he's a copycat who wants to reenact Crast's crimes, but I don't think it's that simple."

Agent Hale stepped forward.

"Ms. Helmont, you said that Crast had threatened you. What did you mean by that?"

Althea cleared her throat as the memories threatened to take over, not wanting the agents to hear the waver in her voice.

"Ernest Crast tried to send me a letter before his execution," she said. "He threatened to send someone to end my life. Someone he called his disciple. It could be *you*, for all I know."

"Do you still have the letter?" Hale asked.

She shook her head.

"I never actually received the original letter," she admitted. "The WPP intercepted it, as they did all my mail back then."

Seeing the disappointment on the agents' faces, she sighed.

"But they gave me a copy so I could read what he'd said," she admitted. "They wanted me to take his threat seriously."

Feeling the usual knot of anger and fear form in her stomach, Althea forced herself to continue.

"They never did find out who this supposed disciple was...or if it was just an empty threat. Which is why they kept me and my kids in the program for so long. And why they tried to stop me from moving back to D.C."

Hot tears threatened behind her eyes.

"But Meg and Richie, they wanted to go to Georgetown like their father," she said, refusing to let herself cry. "They didn't get a chance to know their dad, or even know much about him, but they knew that's where we'd met and...well, they had their hearts set on it and...I couldn't talk them out of it."

Suddenly sure she'd made a terrible mistake, Althea looked up with a stricken expression to meet Bridget's eyes.

"You haven't done anything wrong," the psychologist said quietly. "But you do need to take precautions now. Just in case the man who killed Brooke Nelson really could be this *disciple* the WPP warned you about."

"Precautions?" Althea asked, unable to keep the bitterness out of her words. "You mean I should go back into hiding?"

Her hands balled into fists at her side. Crast had already taken so much from her. And now, after years in the grave, it seemed he wasn't finished with her yet.

"Not hiding, exactly," Hale said. "It's more like strategizing. We'll move you out of range so you can plan your next move in safety. Kind of like a game of chess."

Althea raised a skeptical eyebrow.

"So, I should treat this like a game?" she asked. "Cause from what I remember, I didn't much like Crast's idea of fun."

"You're right," Bridget said, keeping her eyes on Althea's. "This is serious. You have a decision to make. Whatever you choose won't be easy. But we're here to give you that choice."

Crossing to the counter, Althea stuck the Glock back in her purse and pulled out her phone. Whatever she decided to do, she'd need to cancel all scheduled classes for the day.

The sight of Meg and Richie's happy faces on her phone's screensaver felt like a punch in the gut.

What will happen to them if I let something happen to me? I'm the only family they have left. The only one they can count on.

She gripped the phone and turned to Bridget.

"Okay, I'll take *precautions*," she said in a tight voice. "But only until I figure out what to do next."

Bridget nodded, and Althea could see her shoulders relax.

"Good choice," Charlie said, stepping closer. "I've already asked the WPP and the Marshals Service to assign a resource. Deputy Marshal Santino is waiting for my call."

CHAPTER TEN

The insistent ringing of the phone didn't wake Terrance Gage from his alcohol-induced sleep, but it did rouse Sarge from his spot at the end of the bed. Stretching first one leg and then the other, the cat trod up the bed on soft feet until he reached the padded headboard.

Circling around and around next to Gage's bald, motionless head, he meowed plaintively.

"Stop it, Sarge," Gage mumbled without opening his eyes.

He lifted a hand to swipe the cat off the bed, but Sarge was too quick, nimbly stepping to the side as the arm flailed past him without making contact.

Gage groaned as a loud buzz sounded on the bedside table. The phone vibrated intermittently for another ten seconds then fell into an accusing silence.

Pulling a pillow over his head, he tried to sink back into sleepy oblivion, but the effect of the wine was wearing off, and the memories of the night before were seeping in, despite his best efforts to block them out.

She's not still here, is she?

He turned bleary eyes to the recently occupied spot in the bed next to him and stared at it for a long beat as if the woman who'd slept next to him might suddenly reappear.

Nausea rolled through him as he shifted onto his side and peered out into the room, which was lit only by thin lines of sunlight trickling through the closed blinds.

A folder was open on his desk by the window, its contents strewn across the desktop as if blown there by an angry wind.

Groaning again as he imagined Vivian Burke standing over his desk, reading through the file, Gage sat up in bed, prompting Sarge to jump to the floor.

"Did she read through all of it?" he asked Sarge.

The cat stared at him with wide, unblinking eyes as if the question was ridiculous.

"Of course, she went through it all," Gage said in a raw voice. "She's a forensic examiner. Searching for evidence is what she does for a living. Hell, it's likely what she does for fun, too."

Sarge walked to the door, apparently bored with the subject. As Gage let him out into the hallway, he wondered what the cat would say if he could speak.

He'd say I'm an idiot for fooling around with a married woman. Especially one I work with on a regular basis.

The phone began to buzz on the table again, reminding Gage that he had a headache as well as an upset stomach.

"Tell me why I drink wine again?" he called after Sarge, but the cat had disappeared into the kitchen with a disapproving swish of his tiger-striped tail.

Picking up the phone, Gage recognized Charlie's number.

"Finally!" she said when he answered the phone. "I've been trying to reach you all morning."

He held the phone away from his ear with a wince of pain. "What's happened?"

"What's happened is that we've got one woman dead, one missing, and a copycat serial killer on the loose, remember?"

The irritation in Charlie's voice was palpable.

"Some of us got up first thing this morning to work the case," she added. "Thanks to a lead from the WPP, we've managed to locate Althea Helmont. She's in D.C."

Gage felt a spark of interest ignite.

"That's good news. Do you want Bridget Bishop to sit in when you talk to her? She could-"

"We already talked to Althea," Charlie interrupted. "And Bridget was there. She helped us convince Althea to go into protection, again. At least for the time being."

Unsure whether he should feel guilty for not being available when they needed him, or resentful that they'd proceeded without him, Gage didn't respond.

"I tried to call you first," Charlie added after a moment's silence. "You didn't answer, so Hale and I drove out to Wisteria Falls and picked up Bridget. I figured if I was standing there in person, it would be harder for her to refuse."

"Why is Althea in D.C.?" he finally asked. "I thought she'd moved away after...well, after Crast."

Moving into his meticulously organized closet, Gage picked out a navy-blue suit and white shirt.

"Her kids are in college now over at Georgetown, so she moved to D.C. to be close to them," Charlie explained. "I guess she figured Crast was no longer a threat, although apparently she had been warned by the WPP that might not be the case."

"What do you mean?" Gage asked, rifling through a rack of ties. "Are you saying Witness Protection had reason to believe she was in danger before we connected Brooke Nelson's murder to an Ernie Crast wannabe?"

He picked up a pale blue tie and held it against the suit.

"Apparently Crast had sent her a threatening letter before his execution, but I don't have all the details," Charlie confirmed. "I'm waiting for Santino to get here. He'll be joining the task force and personally managing Althea's protection until we find our guy. Hopefully, he can find out more from the WPP."

Gage nodded his silent approval. He'd worked with US Deputy Marshal Vic Santino on more than one case in the past and considered him to be one of the best.

"That's good news. Santino's a valuable asset."

"I agree," Charlie said. "Which is why I've asked him to join us for our first official task force meeting this afternoon. I'm just looking for the right location."

"I'd bet there's an available meeting room at Quantico," Gage said, hoping to avoid the commute into D.C. "How about I take care of the room? Just let me know the time."

Throwing the selected ensemble across his bed, Gage waited for Charlie's okay.

"Fine. Just make sure we have video conference capabilities. I'm betting Chief Fitzgerald and the detectives from the WFPD won't want to make the drive."

Gage was about to hang up when Charlie spoke again.

"Oh, and I think you'd better check the news."

The call dropped as Gage turned to the bed, trying to ignore the rumpled sheets as he pulled on his suit.

I should have just gone to sleep like I'd planned. I shouldn't have had that second and third drink. I should never have made that call.

But the thought of another long night spent in a lonely bed had weakened his resolve to end the impulsive affair before things went too far.

Now he was paying for that weakness with a terrible hangover and a growing sense of unease.

Pushing his troubled love life to the back of his mind, Gage walked out to the living room and switched on the television.

He had it set to a twenty-four-hour news channel as usual. The news feed scrolling across the bottom of the screen prompted another spasm in his already upset stomach.

FBI Task Force Searching for Shenandoah Valley Second Strangler.

A fresh-faced reporter stood in front of FBI Headquarters speaking into a microphone in a solemn voice.

"...the death of D.C. resident Brooke Nelson has been linked to crimes committed by since-executed serial killer Ernest Crast, also known as the Shenandoah Valley Strangler."

Gage cursed under his breath as the reporter continued.

"Sources inside the FBI tell us that a copycat is likely responsible for Nelson's death. The unidentified suspect, which press have dubbed the Second Strangler, is also linked to the abduction of a woman from Wisteria Falls, Virginia last week."

A photo of Libby Palmer appeared on the screen just before Gage turned the television off, his mind whirring with questions as to how the link to Crast had been leaked so quickly.

The pressure would be on from all sides now and the press would be relentless.

Bridget would need to produce a profile of the killer as soon as possible. The sooner they shared it with local law enforcement and the rest of the task force the better.

Heading back into the bedroom for his wallet and sunglasses, Gage was greeted by a lingering scent of perfume.

He feared the temptation to pick up the phone would follow.

But at least tonight I won't be sitting home alone.

The thought did little to improve Gage's mood.

Going to his sister's dinner party was the last thing he felt like doing, but there was little chance of getting out of it.

As Gage crossed through the kitchen toward the garage, his eyes fell on Sarge, who was waiting by the door.

He winced as he thought of the vet appointment he'd promised to make. Anne was determined that the tomcat be neutered before a new batch of kittens was introduced into Stafford County's already overcrowded feline population.

"Sorry, buddy," Gage said as he opened the door to let Sarge slip outside. "But what Anne wants she usually gets."

CHAPTER ELEVEN

Bridget pocketed her newly re-issued FBI security badge and followed Charlie Day out of the entry and reception area toward the BAU offices. She hadn't been back to Quantico for almost two years, but a disorienting sense of déjà vu settled over her when they reached the glass-walled hallway outside Terrance Gage's office.

"We're setting up in Conference Room 3, just to your left," Charlie said, then looked back and smiled. "Although, I guess you know where everything is around here better than I do."

Following Charlie past Gage's closed door, Bridget decided the BAU looked pretty much the same as she'd remembered.

"I'm sure some things around here must have changed while I've been gone," she said as Charlie stopped outside a long room dominated by a sleek conference table. "I know I certainly have."

"I'd say that's a good thing. Change keeps life interesting," Charlie said, pointing toward the conference room. "Now, you go ahead and set up. I'll round up the others."

Stepping into the room, Bridget heard a familiar voice.

"Bridget? Is it really you?"

A man in a white lab coat sat at the end of the table. Bridget gaped at him in surprise, then produced a tentative smile.

"Tony? What are you doing here?"

"Agent Day asked me to attend the initial Second Strangler task force meeting," he said as he stood and walked toward her. "I guess she wants to know what you and I found in Crast's brain. Although, I'm not sure that'll help her catch this copycat killer...if that's what he is."

Tony Yen's youthful face and short, spiky hair hadn't changed much in the years since they'd first partnered up to perform a postmortem study of Ernest Crast's brain.

Bridget knew the forensic neurologist still worked in the Research and Support Unit at the FBI lab in Quantico, but she hadn't expected to see him during her visit. The unexpected encounter prompted a surge of emotions she wasn't sure she was ready to deal with. Not with everything else going on.

"Well, you have held Crast's brain in your hands," she said, trying to keep her voice light. "So maybe she thinks you saw what was inside."

He didn't reply as his reproachful eyes searched hers, perhaps looking for an answer.

Their brief romantic relationship hadn't lasted much longer than their initial research project had, but afterward Tony had referred her to an FBI recruiter, and he'd urged her to join the academy, convinced she was destined for the Behavioral Analysis Unit.

He'd also been first in line to congratulate Bridget when she'd eventually proven him right by becoming one of the youngest agents ever to be accepted into the BAU's elite ranks.

"What happened to you, Bridget?" he asked quietly. "Why'd you just...disappear like that?"

Standing before him now, seeing the hurt on his face, Bridget knew she owed him an apology. Or if not an apology, at least an explanation.

"My father's stroke was...bad. He needed me and I..."

The half-truth stuck in her throat.

Her father's stroke had been upsetting and helping to care for him had taken up much of her time, but Bridget knew her decision to quit the BAU was far more complicated than that.

"I had my reasons for leaving," she finally said. "But I shouldn't have just fallen off the face of the earth. I should have let you know what was going on."

Dropping her eyes, she exhaled.

"It's just, after everything you'd done to help me get into the Bureau...to get into the BAU, I felt guilty...for quitting. Like I'd disappointed you."

Footsteps in the hall caused them both to look around as a tall, thin woman with auburn hair and bright green eyes appeared in the doorway.

"Sorry, am I interrupting something?"

Vivian Burke didn't wait for a reply as she entered the room and took a seat near the head of the table.

The forensic examiner had started working in the FBI's state-of-the-art lab on the Quantico campus around the same time Bridget had moved to the BAU.

They'd worked on the Backroads Butcher task force

together, often butting heads due to their differing styles.

Vivian had made it clear she considered psychology to be a pseudoscience, and that she deemed the analysts who created profiles as little more than hacks.

"Let's talk later," Tony said, sensing Bridget's unease. "I'm just glad you're okay. It's good to see you."

Turning away, he went back to his seat at the far end of the room, leaving Bridget and Vivian facing off across the table.

"So, are you officially back at the BAU, or..."

Vivian let the question die away as if she was already bored with any answer Bridget might give.

"I'm here as a consultant only," Bridget said, trying to stifle the automatic irritation that arose anytime Vivian was in the room. "And just until we catch this guy."

"You sure it's a guy?" Vivian asked, raising a perfectly shaped eyebrow. "Is that what you've come up with in your little *profile*?"

"Of course, it's a man."

Bridget spun around to see Terrance Gage step into the room. He wore a well-tailored navy-blue suit and carried a file stuffed with documents and photos.

Dropping the folder on the conference table, he sank into the chair next to Bridget and pinned Vivian with a hard stare.

"Since when have you heard of a woman who goes around kidnapping other women off the street and strangling them?"

Vivian's green eyes blazed in Gage's direction, but she remained silent as Charlie Day strode into the room and crossed to a computer set up on a pedestal.

"Chief Fitzgerald and Detective Kemp from the Wisteria Falls PD will be joining the meeting via video link," she said, waving in several agents who hovered at the door. "Everyone else grab a seat and let's get started."

As Charlie began to review what they knew about the case thus far, Bridget's eyes were drawn back to Gage.

Her ex-boss appeared tired and his aggressive response to Vivian's question had been out of character. Something was definitely bothering the BAU unit supervisor.

"We've asked former BAU Special Agent Bridget Bishop to consult with the task force due to her past experience with Ernest Crast," Charlie announced after she'd finished her recap. "Bridget, have you managed to pull together a preliminary profile? Do you have any idea who we should be looking for?"

Opening the folder in front of her, Bridget cleared her throat and looked around the room, allowing her eyes to rest briefly on Tony Yen's face before flicking back to Charlie.

"Our unsub is a white male between the ages of twenty-five and thirty-five. He lives alone or has access to an isolated location where he keeps his victims."

Bridget spoke in a modulated, neutral tone, masking her dread as a vision of the killer started to form in her mind.

"Like Crast, the unsub will not willingly dispose of a victim until he has abducted a replacement, and he will always be searching for his next victim."

Picturing Libby Palmer's graduation photo, Bridget's chest tightened with anxiety as she kept reading from her notes.

"The unsub has read about and studied Ernest Crast in the

past and admires his work. He may even have met or corresponded with Crast before his execution."

The room was silent as Bridget sucked in a deep breath.

"The man we're looking for has gone to extraordinary lengths to connect his crimes to Ernest Crast. It's possible he craves the attention and fame Crast received. He may even imagine he is carrying on Crast's legacy by continuing his work."

Vivian Burke raised a hand.

"We tested the tape found on Brooke Nelson's body and matched it to the tape recovered from Crast's last victim," she said when Bridget looked in her direction. "And Crast's fingerprints were recovered from the tape as well. How do you explain that?"

Bridget heard the challenge in the forensic examiner's voice, but she refused to rise to the bait.

"I can't explain it," she admitted. "At least not yet. But from what I know about Crast, it's possible he told someone where he'd hidden his supplies."

Looking at her notes, she thought of the missing fingers.

"Crast would never admit to me he'd kept the body parts taken from the victims as trophies, but I suspect he hid them somewhere before he was arrested."

"You think Crast told our killer where to find this duct tape he used? Any idea why it took so long to turn up?"

Bridget turned to the video call, immediately recognizing Cecil Fitzgerald's weathered face and close-cropped gray hair.

The Wisteria Falls chief of police had been involved in the

highly publicized search for the Shenandoah Valley Strangler, and he didn't look pleased with the idea of a new serial killer causing more death and suffering in his town.

Chief Fitzgerald must be feeling a bit of déjà vu, too.

Vivian raised her hand again.

"Could Crast have had a partner?" she asked. "Someone the police and the Bureau never knew about? Maybe someone who was in jail all this time and just got out?"

This time Cecil fielded the question.

"That's impossible," he said, sounding personally offended. "We found no evidence that anyone else was involved in the abductions or homicides. No other fingerprints, shoe prints, hair, DNA. Nothing to suggest a partner."

"And the victim who survived Crast's attack never saw anyone else while she was being held," Charlie added.

Turning to the timeline in her case file, Bridget considered the possibility Crast had been working with a partner the whole time. Maybe that's why he had gone undetected for so long.

"Crast's first homicide, at least the first we knew about, took place almost twenty years ago," she said. "A partner or accomplice would likely be in his forties by now, maybe older. And if he'd stopped killing all this time, why start again now?"

"Maybe something happened to trigger him," Gage said, without looking at Vivian. "Marriage, divorce, losing a job. Who knows? It's an unlikely scenario, but I don't think we can discount the idea."

Bridget wasn't convinced.

"By the end, Crast was psychotic and delusional," she explained. "He referred to the women he'd killed as *she-devils* and *instruments of the devil.* He believed he'd had a divine calling to murder those women and claimed that Althea Helmont was a succubus who had plotted his destruction."

She wasn't surprised to note more than one skeptical expression on the faces around her. Most people doubted that Crast had been mentally unfit, assuming he'd been faking to try to avoid the death sentence handed down.

But Bridget knew the truth. Ernest Crast had been a monstrous killer. He'd committed terrible acts. But at the time of his execution, he'd also been legally insane.

"What about the letter he wrote to Althea Helmont?" Charlie asked. "He mentioned a disciple who would take revenge on her. Was that just part of his delusion?"

Thinking back to her last interview with Crast before his execution, Bridget frowned.

She'd assumed his threats of retribution and promises of a second coming had been part of his recurrent psychosis, a condition most likely caused by the combined effects of childhood abuse, brain trauma, and years of incarceration.

During that last interview, had he mentioned a disciple who would carry his message? Or was that just her imagination working overtime?

She thought of the threatening letter Crast had sent to Althea Helmont and hesitated.

"Maybe Crast didn't have a partner in crime," she said slowly. "But maybe he did tell someone where he'd hidden his supplies and trophies. Someone he thought would carry on his work after he was gone. In his deluded mind, he may have thought of this person as a disciple."

The room fell quiet for a long beat.

"Any ideas who this disciple could be?" Cecil finally asked.

Bridget ran a hand through her hair and sighed.

"We'll need to work up a list of everyone he had contact with, both before and after he was arrested," she said. "Although I'd be willing to bet this would be someone he corresponded with from prison."

"Okay, so we look at family, friends, cellmates...anyone who wrote to him or visited him in prison," Charlie said, jotting down notes on the pad in front of her. "And I mean anyone. Lawyers, clergymen, doctors. Anyone and everyone is a suspect until they're eliminated."

She looked at Gage and frowned.

"The BAU conducts interviews with inmates down at the state prison in Waverly, right?"

Gage nodded.

"Yes, we have an ongoing offender interview program," he agreed. "We ask serial offenders about their backgrounds and history. It's basically research to find out why people commit violent crimes. The findings are used for training."

"Good, then you must know Warden Pickering over there pretty well," she said. "Call him and get a meeting set. We need you to find out everything you can about anyone Crast was in contact with while he was there."

She turned to Bridget.

"Now, as far as family and friends...his father is still alive, but you were the one person he requested to attend his execution. Do you know why?"

"Odell Crast was abusive," Bridget said, recalling the horror stories Crast had told her about his childhood. "Crast didn't want him at the execution. The only other family he ever talked about to me was his son."

Charlie blinked.

"Crast had a son?"

"Yes. I think the boy was about five or six when Crast was arrested," she said, picturing the photo Crast had shown her during one of their many interviews.

Bridget wondered where the boy was, then realized he'd no longer be a boy.

He'd be a young man by now. Most likely a very angry young man.

CHAPTER TWELVE

D eputy Marshal Vic Santino drove south on I-95 with the windows of his red Chevy pickup open and the radio off, enjoying the strong rush of the wind and the quiet hum of the traffic as he sped toward Quantico and his new assignment.

Glancing at the blue sky overhead, Santino thought of his little boat moored in the dock back in Alexandria, and the lazy afternoon on the Potomac he'd foolishly planned.

Those plans had been scrapped the day before when a fugitive on the U.S. Marshals Most Wanted list had been spotted at a campsite off the Appalachian Trail near Hot Springs, North Carolina.

Santino had headed out with several other deputies, intent on bringing in the fugitive who had since disappeared into the wilderness. He'd been coordinating search efforts with the local rangers that morning when he'd gotten the call summoning him back to Arlington.

The FBI was setting up a task force in D.C. and the lead investigator had specifically requested Santino's assistance.

While he couldn't say he was disappointed to leave the rocky trails, muddy streams, and deer ticks behind, he figured his new assignment on the Second Strangler task force wouldn't be a walk in the park, either.

Seeing the exit for Quantico ahead, Santino merged into the far lane and headed toward the sprawling FBI campus.

Twenty minutes later he'd presented his U.S.M.S credentials in the reception area and was following the directions Charlie Day had left on his voicemail to BAU Conference Room 3.

Knocking on the door, he opened it to see that the room was almost empty. The task force meeting appeared to have taken place without him.

"Deputy Santino, I wasn't sure you'd make it," Charlie Day said as she stood to greet him. "I heard you were somewhere on the Appalachian Trail."

"I got as far as Hot Springs, North Carolina before I was called back," Santino said, stepping further into the room. "We've got a fugitive on the run in the surrounding area, but I hear we have another problem closer to home."

Charlie gestured toward the photos of Brooke Nelson and Libby Palmer displayed on the video conference monitor.

"We're looking for the man who killed one young woman and abducted another," she said. "Crime scene evidence links both crimes to an unexpected suspect."

Santino raised his eyebrows expectantly.

"Fingerprints on the tape used to bind Brooke Nelson belonged to Ernest Crast, the Shenandoah Valley Strangler," Charlie continued. "And the unsub's M.O. appears to be the same as Crast's."

"So, the story in the Post about a Second Strangler in the

Shenandoah Valley was true, then?" he said. "We have a copycat serial killer?"

A voice spoke up behind him.

"Unfortunately, it's not that simple, Deputy Santino."

Turning around, he felt a jolt of pleasure as he saw Bridget Bishop standing in the doorway.

He hadn't seen the psychologist for over a year, but her bright blue eyes and quick smile hadn't changed.

"Bridget, it's good to see you back at Quantico."

"I'm not really back," she said, her smile fading. "Not officially. I'm just here as a consultant. Just until we find the man who abducted Brooke and Libby."

Santino nodded, noting how Bridget had used only the victims' first names, hearing something in her voice that told him she was taking the search for their killer personally.

He knew from working with Bridget in the past that she was good at what she did. The best, really. But her job required her to delve into a psychopathic killers' innermost thoughts and feelings. Being surrounded by that much evil energy was bound to take a toll. Especially on someone as sensitive and intuitive as Bridget seemed to be.

A protective instinct surged through Santino as he noted Bridget's troubled expression. It was a feeling he hadn't felt in years. Not since Maribel had died.

An instant pang of guilt and grief pierced him as it always did when he thought of his late wife.

Her absence hadn't gotten easier to bear over the years as everyone had promised, and lately, he'd become resigned to the fact that it never would.

Catching Bridget's eyes, Santino produced what he hoped was a reassuring smile.

"Don't worry, we're gonna catch this guy, just like we caught the Backroads Butcher," he said with conviction.

Bridget didn't look convinced.

"I'm scared for Althea Helmont," she said, raising worried blue eyes to his. "It's possible Crast may have sent some sort of serial killer disciple after her."

Santino suddenly remembered the call he'd gotten from his contact at the WPP. It hadn't been good news.

"That's right," he said. "Crast wrote a letter to Althea Helmont after she went into hiding. Right before he was executed. It was intercepted by the WPP.

Apparently, in the letter, Crast advised her to keep looking over her shoulder because he was sending someone after her. Someone he referred to as a disciple. Someone who would finish what he'd started."

* * *

Santino brought the Chevy to a stop outside the Healthy Lotus Yoga Studio and surveyed the two men standing outside the door, relieved to see the local officers he'd requested had already arrived and were at their post.

Parking the pickup along the curb under a *No Parking* sign, Santino climbed out and jogged over to the studio entrance, his eyes instinctively darting up and down the street.

He flashed his U.S.M.S. credentials at the officers as the door swung open. Special Agent Tristan Hale stood just inside.

"I thought you must have gotten lost in the woods," Hale complained, pointing to his watch. "I was about to send out a search party."

"I *was* the search party," Santino replied, shaking his head. "And that trail is no joke. I doubt our fugitive knows what he's got himself into. He's probably wishing he was back in custody right about now."

Moving further into the studio, he saw a woman standing beside the reception counter. As she watched him approach with wary eyes, her hand moved stealthily toward her bag.

The hair on the back of Santino's neck stood on end as he realized what was happening.

She's got a gun and she's not afraid to use it.

"Ms. Helmont? I'm Deputy Marshal Vic Santino with the U.S. Marshals Service. I'm going to take you to the safe house where you'll be staying."

Careful not to make any sudden movements, he gestured toward her bag.

"I can't let you bring that gun in your bag to the safe house," he said, reaching out a hand. "But I can keep it safe for you until it's time to go home."

Althea shook her head and took a step backward.

"What if he comes for me and I don't have a gun?"

Santino hooked a thumb toward the door.

"Those two officers will be guarding you until we figure out what's going on. They won't let anything happen to you."

Reaching in the bag, Althea slowly pulled out the gun within. For one pulse-thumping minute, Santino thought she was going to point it at him, but when he stepped forward, she simply handed it over.

He looked down at the semi-automatic Glock in silent approval, then motioned to Hale, who was watching the encounter with one hand on his holster.

"Agent Hale, can you clear Ms. Helmont's weapon and see that it's safely stored for her?"

Once he'd carefully passed the Glock to Hale, Santino turned back to Althea.

"I'm going to need to hang on to your phone, too," he said, bracing himself for her objections. "I know it sucks, but it's policy. If anyone was tracking your phone, they could follow you straight to the safe house."

"But...I'll need to call my kids."

She gripped her phone, holding it against her chest.

"They'll be worried if I just disappear."

"Why don't you go ahead and call them from here?" he suggested. "You can tell them whatever you like. But when we leave here, the phone goes with Agent Hale."

Moving back to the door to give Althea some semblance of privacy, he waited for her to make her calls, trying not to listen in as she told someone on the other end of the line that she'd be out of town for a while.

"You focus on your schoolwork, Meg," he heard her say. "And tell Richie I called. I'll talk to you both soon."

When Althea ended the call and approached the door, Santino was surprised to see that her eyes were dry.

"Okay, let's go," she said, hefting her bag over her shoulder and nodding a stiff goodbye to Hale.

Santino led her outside to his Chevy as the two officers followed behind them and climbed into a nearby SUV.

"The safehouse is in Arlington," he said, once Althea was buckled into the passenger's seat beside him. "So, we're not going very far."

He didn't mention that the house was only a ten-minute drive from his own apartment, or that the pricey property had been owned by a major drug dealer before being seized by the Department of Justice.

The house would be going up for auction as soon as all legal proceedings had been completed, but in the meantime, Santino had gotten approval for the Second Strangler Task Force to use it as a safe house.

Althea's eyes widened in surprise once they'd made their way to Arlington and Santino turned the red Chevy into the long, private driveway.

"This place must be worth a few million," she said in a flat voice. "Isn't it strange how material things don't matter when you're all alone?"

"I know what you mean," Santino found himself saying. "After my wife died, I sold our house...most of our stuff. None of it mattered once I was on my own."

When he climbed back into his Chevy an hour later, Santino waved to Althea, who was staring out the window toward the setting sun. She wore the same stoic expression he imagined was on his own face whenever he thought of Maribel.

It was an expression that left an uneasy feeling in the pit of his stomach as he drove back toward the highway.

CHAPTER THIRTEEN

harlie Day listened to the voice mail from Roger Calloway with growing irritation. The special agent in charge was showing an unusual interest in the Second Strangler Task Force, although Charlie suspected he was motivated by the desire to stifle the growing media coverage rather than his concern over Libby Palmer's safe return.

As she tapped on the little trashcan icon to delete Calloway's offending message, she saw that Vic Santino had also called.

She listened to the message then looked toward Bridget, who was sitting at the conference table pouring over the lab results Vivian Burke had left behind.

"Looks like Santino delivered Althea to the safe house without incident," Charlie said. "He just left a voicemail."

Bridget paused in her work, lifting her head to stare over at Charlie with tired eyes.

"That's a relief."

She rewarded Charlie with a faint half-smile.

"I just hope he can keep her there until we find Crast's copycat. Or should I say his *disciple*?"

"I think we need to ask Deputy Santino for help with

that," Charlie said. "He can access the restricted information in the WPP database. There's bound to be more information about the letter and any efforts they made at the time to locate and identify Crast's disciple if there really was one."

A gleam of interest lit up Bridget's eyes.

"Good idea," she said, leaning back in her chair. "I've been digging through all this paperwork while the information we need is probably in the WPP database."

Lifting her phone again, Charlie was about to tap on Santino's number, then hesitated and looked back at Bridget.

"I've been meaning to ask you something," Charlie said, lowering her voice. "Although feel free to tell me to mind my own business if you want."

Bridget lifted her eyebrows.

"What is it?"

"It's about Deputy Santino," she said, suddenly feeling foolish. "It's just, I wondered if you two were...*you know*."

Bridget stared at her in surprise, then shook her head.

"No, we've worked together, of course, but I don't know anything about him...not *personally*."

It was Charlie's turn to look surprised.

"You're a profiler. I'd have thought you'd try to find out every little detail about the people you work with," Charlie teased. "Especially the ones who look like Vic Santino."

"Just the opposite," Bridget shot back. "I have enough trouble keeping my mind focused when I'm profiling criminals and interviewing victims. I don't need to add the emotional baggage from my co-workers into the mix."

A flush rose in Bridget's cheeks.

"I'm sorry if that sounded terrible. I didn't mean *you*," Bridget added, suddenly flustered. "It's just...I can get too emotionally involved. It's better to keep my distance."

Sensing Bridget's distress, Charlie took a seat beside her.

"We all let our emotions get involved at times," she said, thinking suddenly of Hale. "It's normal."

Bridget dropped her eyes to the paperwork on the table.

"In my case, I'm not so sure it is," she said with a grimace. "According to Faye, I have an empathy problem."

"Who's Faye?" Charlie asked, confused. "And what kind of empathy problem does she think you have?"

Still not meeting Charlie's eyes, Bridget sighed.

"Faye Thackery is my therapist," she explained. "She says I absorb too much of the emotions and energy of the people around me. In my line of work, that can be a problem."

"Psychologists have therapists?" Charlie asked.

Bridget shrugged.

"Some do. Especially those of us who work criminal cases. After everything we hear and see, it's pretty common."

She risked a glance at Charlie.

"Faye helps me figure out all kinds of things."

"Like why you quit the BAU?" Charlie asked, hoping the question wouldn't offend Bridget. "I have been wondering why you left. I mean, you're damn good at the job."

Gathering the paperwork in front of her, Bridget stuck it into the file folder and pushed back her chair.

"I've gone into some pretty dark places over the last ten years," she said stiffly. "I didn't need Faye to tell me I had to quit the BAU if I wanted to sleep through the night again."

Bridget got to her feet.

"And now, I need to get back to Wisteria Falls."

"Right," Charlie said, wishing she'd kept her mouth shut. "And I guess you need a ride."

Checking the clock on the wall, Charlie saw it was inching toward dinner time. Why wasn't Hale back yet?

As she looked toward the door, her eyes stopped on the monitor and Libby Palmer's face staring out at her.

Bridget hesitated beside her.

"You think she's still alive?"

It was the same question Charlie had been asking herself.

"She's only been missing for three days," Charlie said.

"Almost four," Bridget corrected. "If the unsub follows Crast's MO, we have a few more days at most before..."

She faltered as if the words had gotten stuck in her throat.

"Are you going to be okay working this case?" Charlie asked, turning to face Bridget. "I know I'm the one who pressured Gage to bring you in, but if you don't feel up to it, I'll ask him to assign a different analyst."

"I'm the one who interviewed and researched Crast," Bridget said, shaking her head. "And if anyone has the responsibility to figure out what he's done, it's me."

Realizing Bridget hadn't actually answered the question, Charlie frowned. Crast had been the first one to take Bridget into those dark places she was now running from.

And the evil bastard probably knew exactly what he was doing.

Her blood ran cold as a new thought took root in her mind.

"Bridget, you studied how Crast's mind worked...how he thought...do you think it's possible he might have told his disciple to come after you?"

CHAPTER FOURTEEN

Charlie's question seemed to suck all the air out of the room. Bridget opened her mouth to reply and found that she didn't know what to say. The idea that she could be in physical danger had never crossed her mind. Why would Ernest Crast have wished her harm? Why send someone to kill her after all these years?

Maybe because he was a psychotic serial killer who was on some sort of sick mission to kill as many women as possible. Maybe plotting your future death was part of his divine plan.

As usual, the little voice made sense.

Even when Ernest Crast hadn't been suffering from psychosis, he'd been a manipulative killer who'd often tricked his victims into trusting him.

Why wouldn't he have used those same methods to earn Bridget's trust while he waited for the opportunity to act?

"I'm not trying to scare you," Charlie said, reaching out to put a hand on Bridget's arm. "But if you could be in danger-"

"I'm not in danger," Bridget said, her voice coming out sharper than she'd intended. "Now, I need to get home."

Charlie raised an eyebrow but didn't argue.

"I've got to put a call into Agent Calloway first, and then

we can head out," she said, crossing to the door. "I'll be back."

Hearing the door click shut behind Charlie, Bridget dropped her folder onto the table, sending reports and photos spilling out onto the polished wood.

Her eyes fell on a crime scene photo of Brooke Nelson's body discarded in the rocks and weeds outside Moonstone Cavern.

Is that the end Crast intended for me? Was he picturing my dead body when I was sitting across the table interviewing him?

She must have been painfully naïve back then, thinking he posed no threat. Had she learned anything in the years since?

Staring down at Crast's grisly work in the photo, Bridget's mind returned to her visit to Waverly a decade earlier, when she'd witnessed Crast's violent temper firsthand.

Warden Pickering stood on the far side of the security checkpoint talking with the blonde man beside him in a hushed tone.

Emptying her pockets and opening her purse, she was ushered through to the other side by a muscular guard in a tan uniform, wide gun belt, and scuffed black boots.

The warden inclined his head in a greeting as she approached.

"Dr. Bridget Bishop, I want to introduce you to Dr. George Sommerville. He's new to our facility and hasn't had a chance to meet with Ernest Crast yet. I thought he could sit in with you today."

Bridget offered a perfunctory smile, but she feared the long drive down to Waverly had been a waste of time, since Crast was unlikely to share anything new if Dr. Sommerville was in the room.

"Bridget's father helped put Crast on death row," the warden said to Sommerville, who managed to look properly impressed. "I knew Bob Bishop and his partner Harry Kemp back when we were all fresh out of the police academy."

Flashing a wide smile at Bridget, he waved to a guard standing by a metal door. When the door rolled open to reveal a concrete corridor, Warden Pickering motioned for Bridget and Sommerville to proceed.

"Yessir, Bob Bishop and Harry Kemp are two of the good ones," Pickering declared as they stopped at yet another door. "I wouldn't have okayed Bridget's little research project if they weren't."

Bridget's back stiffened. She didn't appreciate her dissertation being downgraded to a little research project when she'd already put in two years of hard work so far.

But the warden didn't seem to notice her chagrin.

"I've got a meeting to get to, but Officer Hoyt will take you two the rest of the way. Y'all have fun."

The warden waved over a young guard with a sandy blonde crewcut and an unfortunate overbite.

"Take Dr. Bishop and Dr. Sommerville into the visiting room and bring in Crast. Give them an hour."

Bridget followed the guard without another word, mentally preparing her questions as she and Sommerville settled into metal folding chairs and waited for the convicted killer to arrive.

"Doesn't this scare you?" Sommerville asked after an awkward moment of silence. "I mean, you do know Crast would break your neck if he had half the chance, don't you?"

"He doesn't see me as a potential victim," Bridget assured the doctor as she studied his handsome features, offended by his condescending tone. "I'm a psychologist conducting research. And in his mind, I could help him achieve his goals."

Sommerville widened his eyes.

"Achieve his goals? You mean like killing more women?"

"According to Crast, he wants to leave a legacy behind. Something that will change the world. I think he's writing a book."

Her words prompted a snort from Sommerville.

"You aren't serious, are you?" he asked, shaking his head. "He's killed seven women and would have killed more if your father hadn't caught him and locked him up like the animal he is."

The sound of heavy footsteps stopped their conversation.

Bridget aimed a resentful glare at Sommerville's blonde head before looking up to greet Crast, who stopped short when he saw her companion.

"Who are you?" he growled at Sommerville.

Stomping forward, he slumped into the chair across from them as Officer Hoyt secured the handcuffs and ankle cuffs, then backed out of the room.

"I'm Dr. Sommerville, the new prison psychologist."

The curt introduction was delivered without a smile.

"And I'm afraid I'm not going to be quite as easy to fool and manipulate as the naïve Dr. Bishop here."

Crast's eyes narrowed in anger as he held Sommerville's gaze.

"You show this woman some respect," Crast ground out between gritted teeth. "I'll bet she's a hell of a lot smarter than some prison quack whose mother never bothered to teach him any manners."

Making a note on the pad he'd brought with him, Sommerville seemed to find the insult amusing.

"You may be right, but we're not here to talk about me. And

since you brought up the subject of mothers, perhaps we should start off by talking about yours," Sommerville said, leaning forward with a smug smile. "How did you get along with your mother?"

Before Bridget knew what had happened, Crast lunged over the table as far as his cuffed hands would allow and smashed his head into Sommerville's nose with a resounding crunch.

Blood spurted onto the wooden table as the unprepared psychologist screamed and crashed back onto the floor.

"Don't you ever mention my mother again, you son of a bitch," Crast bellowed as Officer Hoyt barreled into the room followed by two other guards. "Next time I'll kill you!"

Struggling to break free from the handcuffs, Crast turned to Bridget with wild eyes.

"Don't let him treat you like that, he-"

Crast's words were cut short as one of the guards wrapped an arm around his throat. Ramming his head backward, Crast connected with the guard's chin, then wrenched his head to the side and clamped his teeth down hard on the arm that had loosened around his neck.

Bridget cringed back in her chair as blood trickled down Crast's chin to drop onto Sommerville's notepad.

"You need to get out of here, Dr. Bishop," Officer Hoyt said, appearing at her elbow with a look of concern.

Prodding her toward the open door, he quickly ushered Bridget into the corridor.

"Is Dr. Sommerville okay?" she asked, trying to see past the guard into the room. "Is there something I can do to help?"

But another guard had already materialized behind her, urging her to retreat down the hallway as more guards hurried past them *toward Crast's angry howls.*

Bridget's attention was called back to the conference room by the vibrating phone in her pocket.

Seeing her father's number on the display, Bridget let the call roll to voicemail.

She wasn't in the mood to reassure her father she was safe. She wasn't in the mood for more lies.

Dad knows better than anyone the evil Crast was capable of, and he's smart enough to know that anyone following in his footsteps will be just as dangerous.

Bridget's father had tried to warn her to stay away from Crast, but she'd been insistent that her future career depended on using the serial killer in her dissertation research.

And Crast had jumped at the chance to meet Bob Bishop's daughter. He'd professed to hold no grudge against the man who'd brought his reign of terror in Wisteria Falls to an end.

The serial killer had even confided to Bridget that he was glad his identity and name had been revealed to the public so that his true legacy would live on.

But now Bridget wondered if that had all been an act. Just part of a master plan to take his revenge.

Pacing back and forth in the conference room, she realized Crast must have found it easy to manipulate her. She'd just been too young and foolish to see it at the time.

Somehow, she'd allowed him to get inside her head. The twisted images and memories he'd left behind had been torturing her ever since.

And now it seemed clear that hers wasn't the only mind he'd been manipulating from his cell on death row.

He'd managed to create a killer to do his bidding. A disciple to continue the deadly work he'd started. A second strangler who might be coming for Bridget next.

* * *

Bridget was still pacing when Charlie flung the door open. The FBI agent's gray eyes flashed with frustration as she stepped inside the conference room and held up her phone.

"I'm sorry, Bridget, but Calloway is insisting on a call and I'm still waiting for Hale to get here. I know you need to get back to Wisteria Falls so I'm thinking we should–"

"I can take Bridget home," a deep voice interrupted.

Vic Santino appeared in the doorway.

"I wanted to hear about the profile she's come up with, anyway. Maybe she can fill me in on the way...if she's willing."

He looked toward Bridget with a hopeful expression. It was the same expression Hank often wore when he was waiting by the door before his morning walk.

"Yes, she's willing," Charlie said before Bridget could respond. "Unless she wants to call an Uber."

Once again picking up the contents of her folder, Bridget followed Santino out to his pickup truck, relieved to finally leave the suffocating conference room and the prison-like walls of the FBI building behind.

Exiting Quantico, Santino steered the Chevy toward the

interstate, then glanced over at Bridget, who was still clutching her folder against her chest.

"You want to put that in the back?" he asked, nodding to the thick file. "It'll take a while to get you home."

Bridget shook her head, but she lowered the file to her lap and relaxed back against the seat.

"You have your profile in there?"

"Yes, but a profile isn't very helpful without a manageable pool of suspects," Bridget explained as they merged onto the interstate heading west. "Which is why we're compiling a list of everyone who came in contact with Crast before his execution. Then we'll use my profile to narrow down that list."

Keeping his eyes on the traffic ahead, Santino frowned.

"What about the letter Crast sent to Althea Helmont? If you got a chance to study that, could it help you figure out who this disciple might be?"

Bridget turned to him with wide eyes.

"Would the WPP have kept the letter all this time?" she asked. "It's been almost eight years."

"I'm not sure," he admitted. "But I'll make a few calls tonight and see what I can find out."

As Santino brushed a dark strand of hair off his forehead, Bridget noted the simple silver band on his ring finger.

Stifling an unexpected pang of disappointment, she looked down at the folder in her lap, her mind returning to her earlier conversation with Charlie.

"Hey, you okay?" Santino asked. "Cause if you're not up for this...well, the BAU could assign a different analyst."

"I wish everyone would quit asking me if I'm *okay*," she insisted, turning her face away so he couldn't see the doubt written across it. "I'm *fine*."

After a short silence, Santino cleared his throat.

"It's just that you don't seem fine," he tried again. "If something about the case is bothering you, you can tell me."

Keeping her eyes toward the window and the stream of traffic beyond, Bridget sighed.

"It's just something Charlie asked me earlier," she said, feeling her stomach tighten. "Something I hadn't considered."

She fidgeted with the folder on her lap, not sure she should say anything to Santino. Not sure her fear made any sense.

"Okay, so what did Charlie ask you?" he prodded.

"She asked if Crast's disciple might come after *me*."

Santino's startled expression revealed his surprise.

"Charlie thinks since I researched Crast, that he might..."

"No," he interjected. "Our unsub's not going to come after an ex-FBI agent with a gun and team of people by her side."

He sounded confident.

"Our unsub is a coward at heart. I'm sure of that."

His words echoed Bridget's earlier sentiment.

"Yes, you're probably right," she said, feeling a bit better. "I guess I'm being paranoid. It's a hazard of the job."

Giving her a long sideways look, Santino seemed satisfied with her answer.

"Okay, now that we've got that settled, we need to keep our focus on finding this Second Strangler. If we're lucky, we may still have a chance to save Libby Palmer."

But as Bridget looked toward the east and the darkening sky, she had the unsettling feeling that their time was running out.

CHAPTER FIFTEEN

The disciple merged his sedan into the line of traffic behind the red Chevy pickup, carefully using his blinker and sticking to the speed limit. He didn't want to attract undue attention as he followed Bridget Bishop and her armed companion toward Wisteria Falls.

He'd been watching the entrance to the Healthy Lotus Yoga studio that morning, as he'd done most days for the last few weeks.

The feds had arrived first, even before Althea Helmont, parking across the street from the studio, giving the disciple a perfect view of the action from his position in an empty office on the third floor above them.

Watching with binoculars as Althea had scurried down the sidewalk toward her studio, he could see by the set of her shoulders and turn of her head that she'd spotted the vehicle parked under a *No Parking* sign.

He'd been startled to see Bridget Bishop step out of the unmarked vehicle accompanied by an attractive blonde woman and a dark-haired man, both carrying guns in holsters under their jackets. He hadn't known the psychologist had returned to her job as an analyst with the

FBI.

Bridget had quickly disappeared into the yoga studio, only to leave again with the female agent a short time later, but the disciple had remained in the empty office, his gaze trained on the door as additional police had arrived.

He'd wanted to find out where they were taking Althea Helmont. His whole plan depended on it. So, he had settled in, prepared to wait.

When the red Chevy pulled up, the disciple hadn't taken much notice until it had parked under the same *No Parking* sign the FBI agent had chosen and a leanly muscled man stepped out wearing a lightweight jacket over a black t-shirt and jeans.

Deciding the newcomer's casual clothes, tousled hair, and shadow of a beard probably meant he wasn't standard FBI, the disciple had watched him flash his credentials at the cop outside the studio door and disappear inside.

Unable to sit still any longer, he'd returned his binoculars to his backpack and jogged down the stairs, slipping out onto the sidewalk.

He'd kept his baseball cap pulled down low over his eyes and the collar of his jacket turned up as he walked to the corner and waited for the crosswalk light to turn green.

Making sure to keep his gait casual, he'd passed behind the red Chevy, tucking a small, black locator tag into the truck bed as he passed by. He'd continued past the vehicle, glancing back through the windshield.

A khaki green bulletproof vest emblazoned with the words U.S. Marshal rested in the passenger's seat, eliciting a smile from the disciple as he crossed in front of the Chevy and jogged across the street, heading toward the black sedan he'd parked around the corner.

The locator tag had shown up on his phone within minutes, leading first to a pricey property in Arlington, where he imagined Althea Helmont was holed up, and then down I-95 toward Quantico.

He'd been tempted to follow the tag to the FBI campus but had lost his nerve after he'd pictured a S.W.A.T. team waiting for him at the Quantico exit.

When he'd seen the locator tag on the move again just as the sun was starting to set, he knew where it was headed.

He's taking Bridget home. He's taking her back to Wisteria Falls.

It hadn't been hard to spot the Chevy shortly after it had merged onto I-66. Now only a few car lengths behind the pickup, the disciple allowed himself to relax.

Reaching toward the passenger's seat, he ran his hand over the cover of the handbook his mentor had bequeathed him.

The feel of the leather under his fingers comforted him.

The handbook held the key to his past and his future. All the answers he needed were inside, just as his mentor had promised when he'd given it to the disciple for safe keeping.

He'd now read the handbook from cover to cover so many times that the leather was worn, and the ink had faded where he'd traced his finger over his favorite words again and again.

Although the disciple had already memorized nearly every line, he still liked to flip through the dog-eared pages and read the hand-written words.

Catching a glimpse of the red Chevy up ahead, the disciple felt his pulse quicken as he made out the outline of Bridget Bishop's head in the passenger's seat.

The woman who played a starring role in the handbook was right in front of him. He'd learned everything about her from the explicit details within its pages.

It was clear his mentor had been obsessed with Bridget Bishop from the first time he'd met her, transfixed by what he'd described in the book as her *untainted innocence*, which he longed to possess and devour.

"Only by taking her life will her spirit stay with me unto death and beyond, even to the second coming."

The disciple's voice trembled with anticipation and need as he murmured the final words written about Bridget Bishop in the handbook.

Lowering his foot on the pedal, he passed the slow-moving car in front of him, wanting to keep the pickup in sight as the exit to Wisteria Falls approached.

His heart thumped faster in his chest as the Chevy pulled off the exit onto Landsend Road. Following at a safe distance in the sedan, he realized the deputy marshal was sure to see the vehicle if he looked in his rearview mirror.

Maybe he's running the plates on the front of the car right now.

The disciple sucked in a deep breath, forcing himself to stay calm as he steered the sedan into the Gas & Go parking lot.

He couldn't follow the pickup any further. He couldn't risk being seen or questioned. Not when he was so close to the scene of his latest abduction.

Remembering that Libby Palmer was waiting for him in the darkened room, he watched Bridget Bishop ride off with her U.S. Marshal bodyguard.

I can't lose focus now. I have to check on my latest catch.

He needed to make sure the girl was still safely bound, just as he'd left her. He couldn't risk making the same mistake his mentor had made with Althea Helmont.

If the girl escapes and runs away, the second coming we have planned will turn into a second execution.

As he looked up at the Gas & Go sign, he decided he might even take Libby some food and water. He planned to keep her a few more days, at least, and he could use some food to refuel as well. The next few days would be busy.

Now that his abduction of Brooke Nelson and Libby Palmer had made the world take notice, it was almost time to carry out the second part of the plan.

Retribution against the woman whose escape and betrayal had led to his mentor's capture and execution was long overdue.

CHAPTER SIXTEEN

A lthea Helmont stared eastward into the star-filled sky with a heavy heart. Meg and Richie were close by, but now beyond her reach, living their lives as usual, oblivious to the unnamed and unseen danger their mother had been living in fear of most of their lives.

Going to great lengths to shield her children from the terror Crast had represented, Althea had moved with them to Savannah to live in ignorant bliss for more than a decade.

It wasn't until Meg had started looking through a secret cache of old photos that Althea had broken down and told them the truth about her ordeal in the Shenandoah Valley.

They'd both been too young to remember the day their young, newly widowed mother had vanished from their lives, only to return ten days later, bruised, battered, and determined never to be a victim again.

The twins had grown used to their vigilant, overly protective mother who obsessively doubled-checked that doors were locked, and windows were closed.

They'd pushed aside Althea's warnings about returning to D.C. to attend their father's alma mater in Georgetown, sure that any threat Ernest Crast may have once posed had died along with him.

Knowing that her only options were to lose Meg and Richie or join them, Althea had followed her children back to the city of her nightmares, telling herself it had been long enough, refusing to let Ernest Crast ruin any more of the life he'd tried to take from her.

I *was so young when Crast took me. Not much older than Meg is now. Not much older than Libby Palmer, either.*

Althea leaned her forehead against the cool windowpane, closing her eyes against the darkness, reliving the fateful day she'd encountered Ernest Crast beside Rose River Falls.

Althea threw back her head and sighed, reveling in the warmth of the sun on her face and the wind in her long, loose hair as she stood by her old white Volvo in the Dark Hollow Falls parking lot.

It had been so long since she'd taken a day away from the twins, away from the diapers and the crying and the constant demands for her time and attention, that she hardly knew what to do with herself.

She'd been stuck in an endless cycle of washing, cleaning, and feeding ever since Richard's accident, with little time to grieve his death, and little energy to do anything but survive another day.

The idea of leaving the twins with a sitter for the day to go hiking in the nearby Shenandoah National Park had seemed impossible when a fellow mother she'd met at the local park had called, inviting Althea to join her on a rare day out.

But after much cajoling, she'd agreed, and had even begun to look forward to the physical and mental freedom of a day spent outside her house and free from the responsibilities within it.

Checking her watch, Althea saw that it was almost noon. Her hiking partner was already an hour late and precious minutes were quickly ticking away. She pulled out her phone but could see right away she had no reception.

Worried she may be waiting at the wrong milepost marker, Althea dropped her lightweight backpack on the ground and dug through it until she found the crumpled map she and Richard had used the one time they ventured into the national park on their own.

Yes, she was definitely at Milepost 49.5, and yes, she would have to get going if she wanted to make the five-mile loop up to Rose River Falls and back before it was time to head home to the twins.

"I must have wished too hard when I was wishing for some alone time," she murmured to herself as she started walking.

Heading along Skyline Drive, she turned onto a horse trail leading uphill toward the falls, stopping short when a deer came crashing through the underbrush only a few feet away.

Althea yelped in surprise, then watched in awe as the deer stared over at her with fearless eyes before it continued on into the trees.

She followed a shallow stream until she spotted the Dark Hollow Falls trail ahead. A group of hikers had gathered in the adjacent parking lot, and Althea moved past them with a friendly nod, uninterested in starting a conversation with strangers as she headed downhill toward the waterfall.

By this time Althea's legs were growing tired, and she wondered how she'd ever get back up the hill on the return trip.

Resting at the overlook for the lower falls, Althea took in the rushing water as it made its way down seventy feet of rocks and boulders into the pooled water below.

As she looked toward the trail ahead, she considered turning around and retracing her steps, but the uphill view behind her convinced her to keep heading downhill.

After what seemed like ages the trail began its steep incline along the Rose River, causing Althea's untrained legs to tremble underneath her as she finally stood next to the waterfall.

Lowering herself onto a wide, smooth boulder, Althea shrugged off her backpack and closed her eyes.

She listened to the rush of the water and the distant sound of the other hikers at the bottom of the waterfall, relishing the opportunity to rest in the peaceful place without any fear of interruption.

The trip back to her Volvo wouldn't take long. The trail loop had brought her back close to the parking lot where she'd started, and as the soothing sun beat down, Althea allowed herself to drift off.

She jerked awake as the sun began to set in the west. The sounds of voices from below had stopped, and there was no one left on the trail or standing on the outlook.

Pushing her stiff body into a seated position, Althea stretched her back and looked around just as the man's shadow fell over her.

"You out here all alone?" he asked, hovering over her.

"My friends are around here somewhere," she said instinctively, hearing something in his voice that set her senses on full alert.

Scooting back on the big rock, she got to her feet and clambered down onto the trail, eager to put distance between herself and the man who was staring at her with feverish interest.

"I didn't see anybody else on my way up here," he said, following after her. "You sure your friends didn't leave you behind?"

"They'll be waiting for me at my car, I guess," she said, struggling to keep the tremor out of her voice as he blocked her path with his big body, preventing her from continuing her uphill climb toward the end of the loop.

He reached out a big hand and grabbed for her arm just as Althea bolted away, running downhill, retracing her steps the way she'd come, her heart pounding and her breath coming in sharp gasps.

"Come back here, woman," the man called out, sounding both amused and angry. "I wasn't done talking to you."

Hearing his heavy shoes pounding down the trail behind her, Althea screamed out in fear, hoping a park ranger might hear her.

As she turned to look over her shoulder, her foot lost its grip on the slippery riverbank, sending her tumbling over the rocks and grass until she came to a stop in the shallow water.

"You're gonna kill yourself like that," the man said as he again reached out a hand and dragged her out of the water.

He wrapped a big arm around her throat before she could scream again, dragging her down the incline toward the fire road ahead as she kicked and clawed at his arms and legs.

Suddenly they were next to a beat-up old car parked along the deserted dirt road. The man popped open the trunk and forced her inside before slamming the lid.

Moments later the car was bumping along the road as Althea screamed in fear and rage. Soon the bumping stopped, and the wheels rolled along smoothly, letting her know they were on the highway, heading to who knew where.

Forcing herself to stop screaming, Althea tried to think.

What did the man want with her? What was he planning to do?

She suddenly remembered the reports on the news about the women who'd been disappearing, only to turn up dead a few weeks later. Women from small towns in the Shenandoah Valley. Young women like her.

The realization that he was going to kill her turned her blood to ice. She retched up the scant remains of the apple and protein bar she'd eaten in the car on the drive over, then lay whimpering in the dark as she thought of little Meg and Richie waiting for her at the sitter's house.

Her twins would be orphans, just like she'd been.

Althea had grown up in the foster system, moving from place to place, never having a permanent home of her own. She couldn't let that happen to her children. She couldn't leave them on their own.

By the time the car came to a stop and the man wrenched open the trunk, Althea had vowed to do whatever was necessary to survive. No matter what it took, she would find a way to get back to her children alive.

"No more screaming," the man said, pointing the muzzle of a gun into the trunk. "There's people around here, and I'll have to kill you now if you make too much of a fuss."

Resisting the temptation to lift her leg and kick the gun out of his hand, Althea nodded. She didn't resist as he hefted her out of the trunk and carried her toward the back door of a rundown farmhouse.

Once they were inside, he pulled out a roll of bright blue duct tape and waved it in front of her face.

"You try to run away, and I'll tie you up with this, you hear?"

Althea forced herself to nod.

"Please don't kill me," she choked out, her mouth too dry to speak above a whisper. "I'm a mother. I have children waiting for me."

"What kind of mother are you going out on your own and leaving your kids behind?" he growled down at her. "Women who run around deserve what they get. That's what Mama always told me, and she was a righteous woman. Not like you."

Grabbing her arm, he pushed Althea toward an open door leading down into a cellar. She opened her mouth to scream, then closed it again as Meg and Richie's little faces hovered in her mind.

She needed to be smart. And she'd have to be patient.

If she bided her time, eventually the madman would make a mistake. And when he did, she'd be ready.

Althea blinked as headlights appeared in the street below, dragging her mind back to the opulent safehouse. Back to the new nightmare she found herself in.

Her eyes followed a black sedan with dark tinted windows as it continued past the house and turned the corner.

Was there really a disciple out there waiting to take her away? Was Crast's strange, sinister threat to end her life about to be fulfilled?

She thought of the malevolent message Crast had written for her. It was etched into her brain. A permanent scar that impacted every decision she'd made since.

Rest not, you instrument of the devil, lest you be taken in the night. The second coming is close at hand. My disciple will come to end your life, as you have ended mine.

Had it been a scheme Crast had devised to ensure she never forgot him? To make sure she lived in a state of constant fear?

Or was there truly a disciple out there?

Had Crast recruited some sort of serial killer in training who was willing and able to enact his diabolical plan?

If so, Althea wasn't about to let Crast have the last word, even from his grave. She'd outwait him and outwit him, again.

Once more she had to be patient and bide her time.

CHAPTER SEVENTEEN

A light spring rain started to patter on the roof as Bridget opened the door and waited for Hank to run inside. The Irish setter had been thrilled to see her on Jacey's doorstep, and he'd taken off across the yard with Bridget chasing after him before she'd been able to properly thank her neighbor for dog sitting.

Looking back with a wave, she saw Jacey straining her neck to get a good look at Santino, who now stood on the porch surveying Fern Creek Road with an intense, alert expression.

"I thought you said the unsub wouldn't come after an ex-FBI agent with a gun," she said, crossing her arms over her chest. "So, why are you scanning the street as if you expect us to be ambushed at any minute?"

A flush of color filled Santino's cheeks.

"Just a habit, I guess," he said with a sideways grin. "I like to be aware of my surroundings. Just in case."

"Okay, well, thanks for the ride home."

Feeling suddenly awkward as she turned back to the door, Bridget wondered if he expected her to invite him inside.

That would be the polite thing to do, but maybe not the

best idea, considering the files of work waiting on the kitchen table.

She thought of the Felix Arnett report and sighed.

"You want to come in?" she asked, surprising herself with the invitation.

Santino seemed surprised, too.

"Uh, sure," he said, heading through the open door. "I can check around and make sure everything's safe if you want."

He stopped short when he saw Hank standing in the middle of the living room.

"Although this big guy would have probably let us know if anyone was in here."

Bending over, he stuck out a hand to Hank, who sniffed it politely before nuzzling against it.

"Hank's not much of a guard dog," Bridget admitted. "He likes meeting new people too much for that, which is kind of strange considering his background."

Santino ruffled Hank's fur as he looked up at Bridget.

"Most setters are pretty friendly, aren't they?" he asked.

"Yes, but Hank's a rescue. He was half-starved and flea-bitten, not to mention missing some fur when they rescued him from a bad breeder along with a few dozen other puppies."

She tried not to think of the miserable state of the animals she'd seen at the rescue center where her friend Daphne had been volunteering.

"Poor Hank was as weak as a kitten, but he still managed to wag his tail when he saw me. I ended up taking him home that day and we've been inseparable since."

Looking back at her, Santino produced a knowing smile.

"I had you pegged correctly," he said. "You're a sucker for a sob story, aren't you? But don't worry, you're safe, I won't bore you with mine."

Bridget tried to look indignant, then laughed.

"I can be pretty tough when the situation calls for it," she protested, wondering just what his sob story would be if he trusted her enough to tell her.

Her eyes fell to the silver band on Santino's finger, and she suddenly wondered if whoever had put it there was waiting at home for him.

Lifting her gaze, she caught him staring at her with an amused expression, and she felt a flush of heat work its way up her neck and into her cheeks as his eyes met hers.

The moment was broken by a knock on the door.

"Bridget? You in there?"

Daphne Finch knocked again as Bridget winced.

"That's a friend of mine," she said with an apologetic shrug.

Crossing to the door, she pulled it open halfway.

"What are you doing here?" Bridget asked, trying to shield Santino from her friend's curious eyes. "I'm a little busy."

"Hey, there!" Daphne called, slipping past her to offer a red-tipped hand to Santino. "I'm Bridget's best friend, Daphne Finch, and who are you?"

Santino hesitated, looking to Bridget as if seeking rescue.

"This is Deputy Marshal Vic Santino," Bridget said, inserting herself between them. "He's a...colleague of mine."

Turning back to the door, Daphne called out in a loud

drawl.

"Come on in here, Ginny! What are you doing hanging around outside, girl?"

A small blonde girl with big green eyes appeared.

"I was waiting for an invitation, Mom," the girl said in a weary voice. "Like you should have done."

Daphne took no note of her daughter's reprimand as she continued eyeing Santino as if sizing him up for a new suit.

"Are you two heading out on a date?"

The question earned a glare from Bridget, who suddenly realized Daphne looked as if she were the one dressed for a night on the town.

The ex-beauty queen's tall, thin figure was wrapped in a short black skirt, silky red blouse, and stiletto ankle boots. Her naturally blonde hair was slicked back from her face, and she'd lined her sea-green eyes with charcoal black liner.

Bridget felt suddenly dull and dowdy next to her.

"No, we're not going out," Bridget said between gritted teeth. "I told you we're just colleagues. Deputy Santino was kind enough to give me a ride home from...a meeting."

She tripped over the words, not wanting to admit that she'd been out to Quantico. Not trusting Daphne to keep the information to herself.

"Well, if you aren't going to make the most of a Saturday night, I might as well," Daphne said. "Which is why I was hoping you could watch Ginny for me. My sitter backed out at the last minute."

Looking over at six-year-old Ginny, who was a miniature version of her mother, only with pigtails, a gap between her front teeth, and much more sensible clothes, Bridget raised her eyebrows and clasped her hands.

"Would I get to order in pizza and eat that chocolate chip ice cream in my freezer?" she asked with a teasing smile.

Ginny nodded enthusiastically, her small face breaking into an excited grin.

"And you can watch lots of cartoons, too!" Ginny added with a giggle. "And play with Hank!"

At the sound of his name, the Irish setter appeared at the kitchen doorway, apparently eager for his dinner.

"Why don't we feed Hank first, and then we'll order the pizza?" Bridget said, waving Daphne toward the door. "And your mommy will be back before you know it."

"You're a lifesaver, Bridge," Daphne called over her shoulder, halfway out the door. "I'll be back by midnight."

Bridget nodded, knowing full well Daphne was unlikely to show up until the following morning, but playing along for Ginny's sake.

Waiting for the door to close, she turned to Santino, who was still standing in the middle of the room.

"You know, I'm a big fan of pizza and ice cream, too," he said, giving her his best hopeful Hank smile.

"You don't need to get home?" she asked.

"I'm good," he said simply. "Unless you'd rather I go?"

She ignored the rush of pleasure his words provoked.

"No, Ginny and I would enjoy your company," she said, feeling a little giddy as she headed into the kitchen to prepare Hank's food. "You two can start up the cartoons if you like."

The sight of the Felix Arnett files on the kitchen table dampened her mood, but she averted her eyes and gave Hank his dinner, then ordered the pizza.

She was just opening a new bottle of wine when Santino appeared in the doorway, looking relaxed and content.

"Ginny's a smart girl," he said, letting the door swing shut behind him. "She has good taste in cartoons."

Bridget grinned and poured a long splash of the deep red liquid into a wine glass, feeling more at ease with him than she had all day.

"What do you expect, of course, she's got good taste, she's my goddaughter," Bridget teased. "Although her mother's taste might be a bit questionable."

She motioned to a second wine glass on the counter and raised an eyebrow. When he nodded, she poured the cabernet into the glass and handed it to him.

"I take it Daphne's a bit of a free spirit?"

"That's a diplomatic way of phrasing it," Bridget said, deciding she liked Santino more than she should. "Let's just say Daphne doesn't always look before she leaps."

Taking a long sip of the wine, Santino leaned against the counter next to Bridget, his arm so close to hers that she imagined she could feel the warmth of his skin.

Bridget had just decided she would ask Santino about the silver wedding band when Ginny appeared at the kitchen door.

"When's the pizza gonna get here?" Ginny asked, rubbing her stomach for dramatic effect.

"It should be here shortly," Santino said. "I'd say we have

enough time to watch another cartoon."

He'd just led Ginny back into the living room when Bridget's phone buzzed in her pocket.

The call was from Terrance Gage.

Bridget hesitated, then thumbed *Accept* on the display to answer the call.

"Warden Pickering has agreed to let you speak to Judd Landry on Monday morning," Gage said. "He moved into the cell next to Crast on death row just before the execution."

"I remember Landry," Bridget said with a shudder. "He killed that family down in Richmond."

She pictured the man's yellowish eyes and greasy hair.

"I believe his death sentence was converted to life without parole when the death penalty was repealed in Virginia."

"That's right," Gage said. "Now, you get your questions ready for Monday. Hopefully, Crast told Landry something we don't already know."

Ending the call, Bridget turned around to see Santino standing in the doorway, a worried look on his face.

"You heard any of that?" she asked.

He nodded but hooked a thumb toward the door.

"That'll wait," he said. "Ginny won't. The pizza's here."

CHAPTER EIGHTEEN

Charlie Day turned on the Expedition's windshield wipers as they reached Old Mill Highway. The rain was coming down in a slow drizzle. It lent a grayish cast to the Sunday morning, seeming to match Hale's mood. His easy smile of the previous day had been replaced by a tired scowl.

Pulling his Glock out of its holster, Hale retracted the slide just far enough to peek inside. Apparently satisfied there was a round in the chamber, he slid it back into place and re-holstered his weapon with a soft grunt.

"You think you're going to need that?" Charlie asked, keeping her eyes on the uneven country road ahead.

"I doubt Odell Crast is going to come at us with both barrels blazing," Hale replied tersely. "But if he does, I'll be ready."

Wondering what had happened to put her passenger in such a foul mood, Charlie glanced over at his profile, taking in the freshly clean-shaven jaw and brooding eyes.

"Did you read through Bridget Bishop's research notes on Odell?" Hale asked, staring out the rain-spattered window. "If everything Crast told her was true, his father was almost as much of a monster as he was."

Charlie thought back to the nauseating description of Crast's childhood and upbringing. His claims of abuse were hard to read and went a long way in explaining how the man had grown into a cold-blooded killer.

"Is that what's gotten to you?" she asked. "You don't want to spend your Sunday morning interviewing a child abuser?"

"Oh, no, I'm looking forward to this," Hale said, sitting up straight as an old farmhouse came into view. "I just hope this old man tries something, cause I'm-"

Holding up a hand to stop him from finishing his sentence, Charlie shot Hale a warning look.

"Odell Crast isn't worth blowing up your career, *Halo*, so get over yourself and get ready to do your job."

The use of his undercover nickname usually irritated Hale, but this time it seemed to snap him out of his belligerent mood. He sighed and relaxed back into the seat.

"We both know Odell was abusive, but that's not why we're here," she reminded him. "We need to find out what he knows about his grandson. Or anyone who may have come around here expressing an unhealthy interest in his son's crimes."

Hale rubbed at his smooth chin with a nervous hand.

"What I can't understand is how Odell didn't know what his own son was up to," he said. "Crast even held some of the women out here, didn't he? How could he not have known?"

"Odell was in jail when Crast killed his victims," Charlie said, slowing as they reached the turn-off to the farm. "He'd gotten caught passing bad checks. I'm thinking it was probably the first time Crast had been living on his own."

Pulling the big SUV onto a narrow dirt lane, Charlie bumped slowly toward the dilapidated farmhouse, her eyes scanning the sagging porch and dirt-encrusted windows for signs of life.

"Bridget's notes mentioned Crast's fixation on leaving a legacy behind," she said, letting the SUV idle. "Apparently, he told Bridget he wanted to *leave his mark* on the world."

"Like some kind of dog on a tree," Hale muttered.

Charlie ignored the comment as she tried to decide where to park the big vehicle.

"Bridget said the legacy obsession had been passed down from his father," she continued. "Perhaps it's a way to get the old guy talking."

Hale pointed toward an overgrown patch of ground by the side of the house. Muddy tire tracks cut it in half.

"I say we go around back. The tracks look fresh."

Steering the Expedition gingerly over the uneven yard, Charlie followed the tracks around the house.

She brought the SUV to a stop in the muddy courtyard between the back porch and a weathered wooden barn.

A dented pickup truck rested on blocks inside the barn. Two booted feet stuck out from underneath it.

"Let's surprise him while he's got his hands full," Hale said, pulling open the door before Charlie could respond.

Jumping out after him, she felt her new boots sink into a muddy puddle. Dirty water soaked the bottom of her pants legs, causing her to curse under her breath as she trudged toward Hale, who had miraculously made it across the courtyard without having to splash through any puddles.

"You folks know how to read?" a voice called out. "Cause there's a *No Trespassing* sign on the fence just as clear as day."

Looking down at the legs sticking out from under the truck, and then at her own muddy boots, Charlie felt her temper start to rise.

"Mr. Odell Crast? I'm Special Agent Charlie Day with the FBI, and I've got Special Agent Tristan Hale with me. We'd like to ask you some questions."

"FBI agents know how to read, don't they?" the voice called out again. "Cause that sign doesn't change depending on who's looking at it."

Resisting the urge to aim a muddy boot at the feet in front of her, Charlie glanced at Hale.

"Actually, Odell, I'm not sure I do know how to read," Hale said, crossing to stand beside the concrete block holding up the truck's left front wheel. "Maybe that sign is telling me to use that old sledgehammer over there to knock out this block."

He dropped a big hand on the truck's hood with a loud bang, causing the whole vehicle to vibrate.

"What the hell are you doing?"

The man attached to the legs wrestled himself out from under the truck with a great deal of effort.

Puffing from the exertion, he sat up and glared at Hale, before turning to Charlie.

"You two will want to talk to my lawyer," he said in a wounded voice. "I have nothing to say."

"How about we just take you in on suspicion of first-degree murder then?" Hale said, earning a swift look of alarm from Charlie. "We figure you look good for those women who've gone missing around here. Like father, like son, right?"

"Hold on, now," Odell said, rolling onto his knees and then pushing himself painfully to his feet. "You know I've got nothing to do with what happened to those women."

Hale snorted.

"Just like you had nothing to do with what your son did all those years ago?" he asked, incredulous. "You don't think you hold some responsibility for raising a serial killer?"

Waving away the question, Odell turned toward the farmhouse, his white hair caked with dirt and sticking up in the back from being under the truck.

"We just want to ask you a few questions about your grandson," Charlie called. "You tell us what you know about Colby, and we'll leave you in peace."

"Which is more than what your son did for those women," Hale added under his breath.

Charlie motioned for Hale to be quiet, then tried again.

"When's the last time you saw your grandson, Odell?" she asked in a low voice. "Do you know where he is now?"

A sudden stillness fell over the man's big body.

"They took that boy away from me a long while back," he said, not turning around. "I haven't seen him since."

"I read the reports on what you'd done to Ernest," Charlie said, struggling to keep the reproach out of her voice. "He'd been beaten...starved...kept down in the cellar for days at a time. Is that what you were doing to Colby? Is that why they took him away from you?"

Shuffling around to face them, Odell narrowed his eyes.

"Who's been filling your head with those stories?" he asked. "Those are all just lies Ernie told to try to get out of prison."

In the gray morning light, his broad face and blazing eyes looked disturbingly like the pictures Charlie had seen of Crast.

"So, why'd they take Colby, then?" Hale demanded.

"That wasn't my fault," he protested. "That child's mother was the one who caused this whole mess. She up and left Ernie. That's what drove him crazy. He loved that silly girl, and she went and broke his heart."

Charlie hesitated. She hadn't seen anything about Colby's birth mother in any of the files. Had Crast once been married and in love?

Seeing the look of doubt on Charlie's face, Odell sneered.

"Oh, they didn't tell you the real story about Ernie, did they? How his mama was touched in the head, always spouting off about the devil and some such. And how his wife ran off and left him and his kid. That's what made him go off and kill those girls if you want to know the truth."

He adjusted the saggy waistband of his jeans.

"It wasn't anything to do with *me*."

"Then where's Colby?" Hale asked, his voice cold. "If you were such a great grandfather, why'd they take away your grandson? Who will carry on your legacy without him?"

The old man fixed Hale with a bitter stare.

"I tried to keep him here, but they claimed he was in

danger. They said there were plenty of vigilantes out there wanting revenge on the son of the Shenandoah Valley Strangler."

Rubbing at the grizzled whiskers on his chin, Odell adopted a whiny tone that set Charlie's nerves on edge.

"Even the press wouldn't leave us alone. Kept coming around. As did Ernie's groupies. Finally, social services just up and took Colby. Said it was for his own good."

"Groupies?" Charlie and Hale both asked at the same time.

Odell shrugged.

"Groupies, crazies. I don't know what you'd call them. Once you're on the news the nut jobs seem to come out of the woodwork, I guess. They wanted to see the place where those women died. Wanted to see the serial killer's kid."

A suspicious gleam came into his eyes.

"Why are you trying to find Colby anyway?" Odell asked. "You don't think he had something to do with those two girls going missing, do you?"

"Is that what *you* think?" Hale shot back. "Do you think your grandson is capable of homicide?"

Odell's mouth tightened and he again turned to go.

"One more question," Charlie called out. "Did your son leave anything around here when he went to prison?"

A firm shake of Odell's head was his only answer.

"Well then, do you know where he might hide something if he didn't want anyone to find it?" Charlie asked.

She looked around the ramshackle barn, seeing no obvious hiding place where Crast would have felt safe leaving his souvenirs or tools.

"Did he have a place around here he'd used in the past? A hideout or fort, maybe?"

Looking over his shoulder, Odell met Charlie's eyes.

"You should ask those cops who arrested him," he said. "Detective Bishop and Detective Kemp. They went through all his stuff. Took most of it with them. Probably sold it over at the pawn shop. They always seemed shifty to me."

Odell stepped out into the rain and headed for the house.

"Can we look around the property?" Charlie called, chasing after him. "Maybe even take a peek inside the house?"

Shaking his head, Odell laughed.

"You think I'm stupid enough to let you two plant some sort of evidence to use against me?" he asked, stopping to stand in the rain. "Next thing you know you'll be accusing *me* of taking those girls and I'll be sitting in jail."

"We can come back with a warrant," Charlie called, knowing it was an empty threat as he vanished into the house.

They had no evidence linking Odell Crast to any crime. No reason to believe the Second Strangler could be hiding inside the old house or behind the barn.

Stomping back to the car, Charlie felt the time ticking away with every wasted step and every lead that led nowhere.

"I'll call Gage and let him know we didn't have any luck tracking down Colby Crast," she said, pulling out her phone.

She needed to do something to take her mind off the fact that they were still no closer to finding Libby Palmer.

Charlie watched the rain trickle like tears down the window beside her as the phone rang again and again. Just as she was ready to hang up, a woman's voice sounded in her ear.

"Hello?"

Charlie hesitated and looked down at the display, thinking she'd called the wrong number.

"Hello?"

Recognizing Vivian Burke's distinctive tone, Charlie cleared her throat.

"Is Gage there?" she asked, her mouth suddenly dry.

"He's in the shower," Vivian said. "Can I give him a message for you?"

Charlie raised her eyebrows at the question.

Yes, tell him he shouldn't fool around with married women.

She decided to keep the thought to herself.

"No, that's fine. I'll talk to him later."

She pressed *End Call* and dropped the phone in her lap before Vivian could reply.

"Who was that?" Hale asked, sensing Charlie's agitation.

"If it is who I think it was, I'd say it's trouble."

CHAPTER NINETEEN

The disciple stomped his wet boots on the hardpacked dirt outside the thick wooden door and tried to shake the rain off his jacket. Sheltering under the sprawling branch of an overhanging swamp willow tree, he stuck the big key in the old lock and turned it with slippery fingers.

Dripping rainwater onto the worn wooden floor as he stepped inside, he shouldered the door closed behind him.

He was halfway across the room when the voice spoke.

"You left the key in the lock. You're getting careless."

The disciple froze, then looked back as if expecting to see the owner of the voice behind him, but the room was empty.

Impatient to get on with his work, he hurried back toward the door, tripped over a loose floorboard, and crashed down onto one knee.

Pain shot through him as the jagged wood sliced through his jeans, piercing his skin.

Scrambling back to his feet, he looked down at the torn cloth and sticky crimson smear which now marred the floor.

"There's no use crying over spilled blood," he muttered numbly, reciting words memorized from the handbook. "Not even when it's mine."

Retrieving the key, he gripped it in his hand and crossed to the narrow wooden door on the far wall.

The throbbing in his knee grew worse as the disciple leaned forward to unlock it. Gritting his teeth against the pain, he pushed the door open and limped onto the small landing.

He saw the girl on the stairs just as the metal bar smashed into the side of his head. Arms flailing wildly in the air, he toppled over the wobbly railing and crashed onto the wooden floor ten feet below.

Looking up through blurry eyes, he saw the girl standing on the landing looking down at him, a strip of blue duct tape dangling from one wrist, and the thin metal bar from the bedframe still clutched in her fist.

He tried to call out to her, but all the breath had been knocked from his lungs, and only a faint wheeze escaped.

"You let your guard down, didn't you? Now you have to pay for your carelessness. Just as I had to pay with my life."

The voice echoed through the disciple's mind as he rolled over onto his side and clutched at his throbbing head.

"Get up and go after her! She's going to get away."

Recoiling at the angry words, the disciple pushed himself to his knees, swaying as a wave of dizziness swept through him.

"Come back here," he rasped as he staggered to his feet and grabbed for the railing. "Come back here you evil bitch!"

Forcing one foot up at a time, he slowly ascended the stairs, growing stronger and steadier with each step, willing the flood of adrenaline and anger to propel him to the top.

The dented metal bar had been discarded on the landing. He kicked it down the stairs as he approached the door, listening to the metallic *clink, clink, clink* it made on the way down.

Taking the gun out of his waistband, he held it in front of him before quickly stepping through the door.

The sparsely furnished room was empty. Only the small table altar of bones stood as witness to his mistake.

The disciple blinked in confusion as he lifted a hand to his head. His skin felt warm and sticky under his fingers.

Pulling back his hand, he saw that it was covered in blood.

Rage surged through him. He spun around, his eyes darting to each corner of the room before settling on the only window, which had been boarded up long ago.

The bottom board was hanging askew.

The disciple bolted forward, wrenched the board off, and threw it to the floor, creating a gap big enough to stick his head through, but not wide enough for his shoulders.

Straining to see past the profusion of branches and greenery blocking his view, he managed to catch only patchy glimpses of the gloomy gray sky.

She couldn't have gotten through here. It isn't possible.

He drew his head into the room and turned slowly around.

A glance at the door confirmed it was still locked, and a pat of his pocket reassured him that the key rested inside.

There was only one key, he was sure of that. He'd installed the lock in the old door himself after the voice had urged him to secure their hiding place.

Blood dripped from his knee and trickled down his face as

he limped across the floor to stand in front of the built-in cupboard running across the side wall.

Resting his ear against the wood, he listened.

The faintest inhale of breath reached him as an ugly smile spread over his face.

He gripped the gun tighter in his hand, then decided it wouldn't be necessary. Sticking the gun back into the waistband of his pants, he inhaled deeply, put one hand on the cabinet's handle, and jerked it open.

Libby Palmer screamed as he reached in and grabbed her around the throat, yanking her toward him with the strength of unbridled fury.

"You tried to...fool me," he gasped out. "You...tried to...kill me. Now, you get...what you...deserve."

Oblivious to the throbbing in his aching head, and the pain shooting up from his knee, the disciple squeezed and squeezed until the screaming stopped.

Only when Libby lay motionless beneath him did the disciple release his cramped hands.

Listening to the silence, he realized he was once again alone. He hadn't followed the plan. He hadn't taken the next woman before disposing of the one beneath him.

"I had no choice," he said, his voice cracking on the words. "She tricked me. She tried to kill me. I had to do it."

But there was no answering voice to reassure him that he was still on the right path. The path of the mentor.

He was alone.

"I'll fix this," he muttered, getting to his feet. "Don't you worry. I'm going to fix this if it's the last thing I do."

* * *

Three newly prepared bones had been added to the collection on the altar as the disciple locked the door behind him and began to drag the black garbage bag toward the sedan.

Still furious with himself for being careless, and unsettled by the sudden disruption of his plan, he was eager to dispose of the girl's body and move on to the next task on his list.

The voice had been unusually quiet as he'd boiled, scraped, and cleaned the bones, and the disciple was beginning to worry his mentor might have deserted him for good.

"I'm going to be more careful," he said into the empty interior of the car as he headed toward the river. "I'm going to make everything right. I promise."

Steering the sedan onto the riverbank, he stopped and climbed out. Looking around, he wondered if he was far enough away from his hideout to be safe.

Should he drive further to dump the girl's body? Or would that risk him being pulled over and possibly having the car searched? He listened for the voice to guide him.

The voice had never been wrong. He'd trusted it this far. There was no going back now. He'd have to move on with the plan written in the handbook.

He'd have to find Althea Helmont right away.

Hefting the black bag out of the trunk, he dragged it over the uneven ground, catching the plastic on the jagged rocks and branches along the shore.

By the time he pushed the bag into the murky depths of

the river, several rips had opened up, exposing glimpses of pale flesh and dark curls.

He picked up a thick branch and prodded the bag, pushing it further into the river, wishing he'd thought to add rocks to weigh it down.

Turning away in panic at the sound of rustling in the bushes behind him, he saw a raccoon ambling through the overgrown grass, likely on its way home from a night of scavenging.

The startled animal stopped to stare at him, its beady eyes alert behind a black mask of fur, its ringed tail bristling over a plump, gray body.

Apparently deciding the disciple presented no imminent threat, the raccoon continued on its way.

Looking back, the disciple saw that the garbage bag had already disappeared under the surface of the river.

He ran to the car and jumped in, heading straight for the highway, mentally calculating how long it would take him to get to Arlington.

Looking down at the passenger's seat, he realized too late that he'd left the handbook back at the hideout.

It doesn't matter. It's all written in my mind now.

But the absence of the handbook nagged at him as he drove east on I-66, and by the time he arrived at the elegant house north of Arlington Boulevard, he was in a heightened state of agitation, sure that something terrible was about to happen.

He forced himself to cruise by the house slowly enough to see one man stationed outside in an unmarked car, while another stood by the front door talking on the phone.

With a start, he realized the man on the porch was the same man he'd followed toward Wisteria Falls the other evening. The man who'd driven Bridget home.

Keeping his eyes straight ahead, the disciple drove out of the neighborhood and back toward the highway, his hands clenched around the steering wheel in a steel grip.

It would be too difficult to take Althea while she was being guarded by the U.S. Marshals. He'd have to bide his time.

The woman who'd caused his mentor's downfall would get what she deserved eventually.

In the meantime, there was an empty room to fill. He would have to move on to the next name on the list in the handbook.

He would have to move on to Bridget Bishop.

CHAPTER TWENTY

Monday morning brought clear blue skies, giving no hint of the rain which had fallen the day before. A sprinkling of yellow wildflowers dotted the landscape along the highway as Bridget stared out the window of Gage's Navigator.

"When's the last time you drove down to Waverly?" Gage asked, switching lanes to pass the semi in front of them. "You ever go back after they put Crast down?"

Dragging her mind away from the list of questions she planned to ask Judd Landry, Bridget glanced at Gage.

"They didn't *put him down*," she chided. "That makes it sound like he was a sick animal at the vet."

"He *was* a sick animal," Gage said, unrepentant. "Only I doubt they had a veterinarian there to do the honors."

Bridget rolled her eyes, figuring it was a waste of time to talk to Gage about capital punishment.

He'd made his position clear when Virginia had abolished the death penalty in the state, and Bridget wasn't about to waste her time and energy arguing about it now.

She had more pressing concerns on her mind. Like what she should ask the man who'd been Crast's neighbor on death row.

"No, I haven't been back to the state prison since the last time I interviewed Crast there," she admitted. "It was the last time we spoke, actually. When I went to Greensville for his execution, we didn't have a chance to talk before...well, before they carried out the sentence."

Gage nodded and turned his attention to the congested traffic ahead while Bridget went back to her brooding.

She propped her head against the window as the final meeting she had with Crast replayed behind her closed eyes.

Crast was already handcuffed in place by the time Bridget entered the visiting room. His bloodshot eyes fell on her with a feverish eagerness that frightened her.

She'd suspected he was suffering another bout of psychosis when she'd received his latest letter, but the manic gleam in his eyes confirmed it.

"You wanna watch a man die?" he asked before she'd had a chance to sit down. "I think you might enjoy it."

Ignoring the question, Bridget held up the letter he'd sent.

"I got your letter," she said. "And I have to say I'm a little worried. It sounds like you may be hearing voices, again."

Crast shook his head.

"Mama's in here," he said, leaning forward as if he was sharing a secret. "She told me they're going to kill me. She said you might like to watch. That's why I asked Warden Pickering to put you as my witness."

Bridget studied his broad, coarse face. Her stomach dropped as she realized what he was saying.

"I can't do that," she said quickly. "Is there someone else who-"

"You're the only one I trust," he said, looking at the door behind her with a gleam of suspicion in his eyes. "There's no one else."

Swallowing hard, Bridget looked away.

"I've spoken to your lawyer," she said, still not meeting his gaze. "I gave him my written opinion on your current mental health issues. If the appeals court finds you unfit, they may stay your execution."

She didn't add that her opinion also stated there was no way to determine if he'd been mentally competent during the commission of his crimes. Acute psychosis had plagued him off and on over the years, but she had no proof that these episodes had coincided with the murders.

Lowering his voice, he'd produced an unnerving smile.

"If they do kill me, I'll have the last laugh," he said, raising his eyebrows. "I've got a little surprise in the works."

"Okay, we're here, you ready for this?"

Gage put a hand on Bridget's arm.

"Bridget, did you hear me? Are you ready?"

She shook away the echoing memory of Crast's words, looking up to see they'd turned into the prison's parking lot.

"I'm as ready as I'll ever be."

Following Gage's smooth, shiny head into the prison, she was startled to see Warden Pickering looking the same as he always had. Eight years hadn't had much impact.

"Good to see you, Agent Gage," the warden said, grabbing Gage's hand and pumping it up and down before turning to Bridget. "And Dr. Bishop. It's been a while."

Bridget stood nervously beside the men as they made small talk, discussing the warden's imminent retirement and the recent changes to the prison now that the death penalty had been abolished in the state.

"We still get the worst of the worst," Pickering complained. "Only now, we don't get to send them off to Greensville. Once they arrive, they're here for good."

Waving over a stone-faced guard, Pickering sent them off toward the maximum-security unit to meet with Judd Landry.

"I think I should speak to him on my own," Bridget said as they followed the guard through a metal and concrete maze of hallways and locked doors.

"You sure you want to do that?" Gage asked. "He's a psychopath with nothing to lose. He could turn nasty."

Bridget hesitated. She would prefer to have Gage with her. His reassuring presence would make the unpleasant task more palatable. But Judd Landry was likely to be combative if he had an audience watching his performance.

Best to have a private, one-to-one chat.

She looked back at Gage as the door to the visiting room closed behind her, hoping she hadn't made a mistake, then turned to face Landry, who was seated at one of several tables in the room, his hands and legs uncuffed.

"Looks like we got this place all to ourselves," Landry said, closing one eye in a lecherous wink as Bridget crossed to the table. "Just you, me, and Officer Friendly over there."

Twisting around, Bridget saw the stone-faced guard positioned at the door. She didn't recognize him from her previous visits to the prison but was relieved to have him there, nonetheless.

She allowed her shoulders to relax as she studied Landry, who she'd only seen before in photos shown on the news or plastered in the paper.

The convicted murderer was tall, thin, and greasy looking, with a beak-like nose and a blackened front tooth.

He sprawled in his chair as if indifferent to Bridget's presence, but his eyes followed her every move, and his pupils were dilated, giving away his keen interest.

"Thank you for agreeing to meet with me, Mr. Landry. I'm Dr. Bridget Bishop, and I have a few questions for you about Ernest Crast."

"Are you one of those women who get off on convicts?" Landry asked, licking his thin, cracked lips. "Cause I'm allowed conjugal visits under certain circumstances."

Shuddering at the man's leering smile, which revealed a lower row of jagged, yellowed teeth, Bridget tried again.

"I have a few questions for you about Ernest Crast."

This time Landry scowled.

"Why waste my time talking about a dead man?" he asked, shaking his head in disapproval. "That bastard's been gone for years. He's not coming back, so everybody needs to move on."

"I can see where you're coming from," Bridget said. "But my questions are relevant to a current investigation. If you cooperate, your efforts could be raised to the parole board."

Landry scoffed.

"Parole board? Lady, you should have done your

homework. I'm not ever gonna be eligible for parole. So, nothing I do, for good or evil, makes a damn bit of difference in here."

"It may not make a bit of difference in here," Bridget said. "But it could make a lot of difference to someone out there."

Her eyes flashed as she studied Landry.

"All I want to know is if Ernest Crast talked to you about anyone while he was in here."

When Landry didn't respond, Bridget continued.

"Did Crast ever mention a partner or a helper of any kind?"

Lifting a hand to scrub his grizzled chin, Landry shrugged.

"He was always writing letters and getting fan mail from crazies. He loved that kind of stuff. Sometimes he'd read letters out loud like he was proud some wacko looked up to him. Like he was the leader of some kind of cult."

Bridget's pulse jumped at the phrase.

"He thought the people who wrote him letters looked up to him?" she asked. "Did he say they were his followers?"

She decided to take a chance.

"Did he call them disciples?"

A frown creased Landry's forehead.

"He did talk about religious-type stuff all the time, but I don't remember anything like that."

He crossed bony arms over his chest.

"Usually, he just ranted about women. He said they were all *instruments of the devil* and crap like that. Said the women he killed had gotten what they deserved. Although I think he was close to his mama. Always talked about her. And about *you.*"

The leer returned to his face, and he leaned forward again.

"He bragged about you all the time," Landry sneered. "He always said he had his own personal shrink. Seemed like he had the hots for you pretty bad. Can't say I blame him."

An uncomfortable flush filled Bridget's face and she instinctively leaned back, trying to put as much distance between her and Landry as possible.

The gesture wasn't lost on the killer.

"You think you're too good for me, don't you?" he said, his eyes narrowing. "But you aren't all that. You weren't even the only shrink Crast talked to. He spent way more time with Dr. Sommerville than he ever spent with you."

Bridget blinked in surprise.

"Crast willingly talked with Dr. Sommerville?" she asked, thinking back to the disastrous first meeting between Crast and the prison psychologist. "Do you know what they talked about?"

"Ask him yourself if you want to know," Landry muttered. "He still works here. His office is just down the hall."

* * *

Bridget and Gage followed Warden Pickering down another hallway, their shoes clicking in unison like marching soldiers against the slick floor as they went.

"You're lucky to find Dr. Sommerville in his office today," the warden said over his shoulder. "He's made quite a name for himself in the corrections community. Tours all over the place giving lectures on mental health initiatives for inmates."

"Thanks for letting me take a little of his time," Bridget said as they reached the psychologist's office. "I'll just stick my head in while you two finish catching up."

She didn't wait for a reply as she knocked on the closed door, then pushed it open.

Dr. Sommerville looked up from his desk with a prepared smile. The smile faltered when he saw Bridget in the doorway.

"Dr. Bishop," he said, rising from his desk. "What a pleasant surprise. What brings you back to Waverly?"

"I was just interviewing an inmate about a current case," she said vaguely, studying his even features. "I see your nose healed up nicely."

A confused frown creased the psychologist's forehead.

"The day we met, Crast headbutted you in the nose," she reminded him. "I figured it was broken, but you couldn't tell now by looking at you."

Irritation flickered under the surface, but Sommerville managed to conjure up another weak smile.

"I'd forgotten all about that," he said wryly. "I got to know Ernest Crast fairly well after an admittedly rough start."

"I wasn't aware," Bridget said. "He never mentioned meeting with you when I was conducting my research on trauma in serial killers. We could have compared notes."

Sommerville cocked his head.

"We still could, if you'd like," he offered. "I read the paper you wrote with Tony Yen. The correlation between brain trauma in the frontal cortex and violent crime fascinates me."

"That paper was mostly Tony's work," she admitted with a blush of pleasure. "He's a genius. The autopsy of Crast's brain was his work, of course...since he's a neurologist."

Bridget realized she was rambling.

"Anyway, I'm sure you're busy, but now that I know you and Crast had sessions together, I was wondering if he'd ever talked about someone he was communicating with. Someone he may have referred to as a disciple?"

Detecting a faint tightening of his jaw, Bridget felt sure Sommerville was about to answer in the affirmative.

"No, that doesn't ring a bell," he said instead.

Bridget tried to mask her disappointment as Sommerville crossed to a file cabinet and began to rifle through it.

"It looks as if the file on Crast has been archived," he said after several fruitless minutes of searching. "I can ask for it to be retrieved if you want to go through it. It could take a while."

"That would be great," Bridget said as she crossed to the door. "And please, let me know if you remember anything else in the meantime."

Walking back to the car with Gage ten minutes later, Bridget decided Sommerville knew more than he'd let on. But she had the distinct impression that she wouldn't be hearing back from the prison psychologist any time soon.

CHAPTER TWENTY-ONE

Terrance Gage steered his Navigator out of the prison's parking lot and settled in for the long drive up to Quantico, satisfied he and Bridget would have plenty of time to discuss her return to the BAU after the scheduled Second Strangler task force meeting that afternoon.

He'd made the mistake of checking his voicemail while he'd waited for Bridget to conduct her interview with Landry, and had gotten an earful from Anne, who was furious at him for missing her dinner party on Saturday.

Stewing over his sister's pronouncement that she'd made Sarge a vet appointment for the following day, Gage wanted time to think through the situation before he made any promises. The two-hour drive should give him that chance.

But just when he'd started to relax, Vivian called.

"Feel free to take it," Bridget said, spotting the caller's name on the Navigator's big display. "It won't bother me."

Gage hesitated, his finger hovering over the hands-free button. Catching Bridget's questioning look out of the corner of his eye, he inhaled deeply and answered the call.

"Vivian, how are you?" he said in a painfully cheerful voice. "Bridget Bishop and I are driving toward Quantico now.

Will we see you at the task force meeting this afternoon?"

He held his breath, listening to what sounded like dead air.

"Vivian, you still there?" he asked, hoping she'd hung up.

"I'm here."

Her voice was curt.

"And yes, I'll be at the meeting this afternoon. I was calling to confirm the meeting location."

Exhaling in relief, Gage glanced at Bridget with a smile.

"It's the same conference room as last time," he said. "BAU Conference Room 3. See you there."

He disconnected the call before Vivian could say anything else. He'd have to deal with the fallout later.

"Did Charlie forget to include the location when she sent out the meeting request?" Bridget asked, sounding concerned.

"No, the location was on there," Gage quickly assured her. "I guess Vivian must have missed it."

Hoping Bridget wouldn't call Charlie to ask, he winced as he thought of the agent's call the day before.

Vivian had assured him Charlie had no idea she was the one who had answered his phone, but Gage had his doubts.

Charlie Day is no fool. I wish I could say the same for myself.

He glanced over at Bridget, sure she'd be staring back at him with accusing eyes, but she'd already gone back to reading through her file and making notes in preparation for the meeting, apparently no longer thinking of Vivian's awkward call or Gage's strange reaction to it.

Once again berating himself for carrying on an illicit affair and risking his reputation with his fellow agents and colleagues, Gage promised himself he'd end things with Vivian as soon as he had the opportunity.

And when Vivian walked into the BAU Conference Room later that afternoon with green eyes blazing and her mouth set in an angry red line, Gage could see she was having second thoughts about their relationship as well.

Averting his gaze, he turned around to see Charlie Day staring at him from across the table, her clear gray eyes filled with questions as they flicked to Vivian, then back to him.

"Thank you all for coming," Charlie said, her attention turning to the meeting at hand. "Please take your seats. Deputy Marshal Vic Santino has some important information to share with the task force."

All eyes turned to the front of the room where Santino stood beside the oversized smartboard mounted on the wall. He held a tiny remote in one hand.

An image of a handwritten letter appeared on the screen. Gage's eyes widened as he realized he was looking at a letter Crast must have written before his execution.

"I was able to retrieve this letter from the U.S. Marshals Witness Protection Program archives," Santino said as he zoomed in on the image. "As you can see, the letter was written to Althea Helmont, his last victim, and signed by Ernest Crast."

He gestured toward the back of the room.

"I've already given the original letter to the task force's forensic examiner, Vivian Burke, who will be working with the FBI lab to test the document for fingerprints or DNA that can confirm Crast actually handled the letter."

"And we've got a handwriting expert looking at it as well," Vivian added from her position against the back wall. "It will be compared against verified samples of Crast's handwriting."

Gage glanced away as Vivian turned in his direction.

"Is there doubt then that Crast actually wrote the letter?" Gage asked Santino.

"Chain of custody is in question," Santino admitted. "We aren't sure how the WPP obtained the letter in the first place."

He pressed the remote and pointed to the screen.

An image of an envelope appeared next to the letter. Althea Helmont's name was written in blue ink, and an address had been added below.

But there was no return address and no postmark.

"The letter was never mailed?" Gage asked.

"It doesn't look like it," Santino replied. "But somehow it found its way to the WPP, and then into the archives."

Squinting up toward the smartboard, Gage couldn't quite make out the words. He dug in his pocket for his new reading glasses, sliding them on as Vivian spoke again.

"Deputy Santino, there are a few people in the room who can't see the smartboard. Would you mind reading the relevant parts of the letter aloud, so the entire task force knows what we're dealing with here?"

A flush of embarrassment heated Gage's cheeks he imagined Vivian staring in his direction. Taking off his glasses, he thrust them back into his pocket.

"Sure," Santino said, clearing his throat. "The main part

we're interested in is at the end of the letter."

Gage felt his embarrassment turn to dread as Santino's deep voice filled the room.

"Rest not, you instrument of the devil, lest you be taken in the night. The second coming is close at hand. My disciple will come to end your life, as you have ended mine."

* * *

Gage's nerves were still on edge as he and Bridget merged back onto the interstate heading toward Wisteria Falls.

"I know you said you didn't want to talk about it, but I have to at least try to get you to come back to the BAU," Gage said. "After all the time you've put in, and the success that you had with your last case..."

Holding up a hand to silence him, Bridget exhaled.

"I don't want to talk about the Backroads Butcher case," she said. "Not with this new investigation going on. Maybe not ever. I need to move on from that. And from the BAU."

"You've been exposed to some pretty disturbing situations," Gage said slowly. "I get it. We all have our battle scars from this job. But it often means we come out stronger once we've had time to heal. We develop thicker skin."

Bridget shook her head.

"You keep telling yourself that, Gage. But I don't buy it."

She opened the folder on her lap, revealing Libby Palmer's graduation photo.

"For now, you and I need to stay focused on finding Libby," she added. "If the disciple Crast mentioned in his letter really is the Second Strangler, we have to assume he'll follow Crast's M.O. He'll already be looking for another victim. Someone to replace Libby before he kills her."

Gage knew she was right. They had a day or two at best to stop another abduction. If they didn't manage to catch Crast's disciple soon, another woman would go missing, and Libby Palmer's body would be discarded somewhere for them to find.

"Besides, I can't come back to the BAU now, anyway. I already have a job," Bridget said, lifting her chin. "I hadn't been sitting around twiddling my thumbs when you came to find me in Wisteria Falls, you know."

She closed the folder on her lap and crossed her arms defensively over her chest.

"I'm working on a local case. A homicide."

"Right," Gage said. "I didn't know Wisteria Falls' homicide rate was so high."

Bridget shrugged.

"It's no different than every other town," she said. "There are good people and bad people wherever you go."

He nodded but didn't reply, sensing she wanted to say more.

"What's strange with this case, is that the bad guy...the man I've been hired to evaluate, the man who is accused of shooting his wife in the head...doesn't seem so bad."

She looked at Gage with a perplexed frown.

"If I didn't know what he'd done, and if I looked at his history, and talked to his family and friends, I'd think Felix Arnett was a pretty good guy."

"So, this Felix Arnett guy is your client?" Gage asked.

Bridget shook her head.

"No, the Commonwealth prosecutor is my client. That's the problem," she admitted. "I'm supposed to write and submit a report as to Felix Arnett's mental fitness to stand trial."

"Sounds pretty straightforward to me," Gage said. "So, what's the problem?"

Biting her bottom lip, Bridget considered the question.

"Felix has no prior history. There was no indication of trouble in the marriage. Everything was normal. Then all of a sudden, the neighbors heard gunshots and called the police. *Two* gunshots."

She turned to him.

"But the CSI team didn't find any bullets at the scene," she said slowly as if doubting her own words. "Then the medical examiner went in and pulled a 9mm bullet out of Whitney Arnett's head. Ballistics confirmed it had been fired from the gun seen in Felix's hand before the WFPD shot him."

"Looks like the identity of the shooter and the cause of death seem pretty clear," Gage said. "So, I'm guessing it's the manner of death that's bothering you? You think instead of intentional homicide, it was some kind of accident?"

Bridget lifted her hands in frustration.

"I don't know what I think. But based on my evaluation, Felix Arnett isn't capable of coldblooded murder. And I'm wondering what happened to the second bullet. It was never recovered."

Gage opened his mouth to ask more questions, then closed

it again, knowing Bridget well enough to know she'd have gone through all possibilities by now.

But he had the feeling she was telling him about the case because she wanted a second opinion. Someone to tell her if she was missing something.

"Why not ask the FBI lab to review the evidence in the case?" he suggested. "Maybe they could even send out an evidence response team to go over the crime scene again. That is if the prosecutor and the local PD would support the Bureau's involvement."

"They might," Bridget said thoughtfully. "Although the lead detective, Harry Kemp, can be pretty territorial when it comes to outside assistance. He partnered with my father for years, and his attitude could really drive dad crazy."

Sitting forward in her seat, Bridget gave a resolute nod.

"But, I think you're right," she said. "I'm going to ask Chief Fitzgerald to call in the Bureau to review the case. I wouldn't feel right turning in my evaluation otherwise."

"Well, I'm glad you think I'm right about something," Gage said, pleased with himself. "It's a step in the right direction. Who knows what I could be right about next time?"

CHAPTER TWENTY-TWO

Opal Fitzgerald knocked twice on the conference room door, then opened it without waiting for a reply. Her husband looked up from the table with a start, his eyes taking in her companions with a wary gleam as he hefted himself off his chair and moved toward them.

"I wasn't expecting visitors this afternoon, Opal," he said, raising one gray-speckled eyebrow. "Much less three of you."

"I'm not a *visitor*, I'm your *wife*, Mr. Chief of Police," she shot back, placing both hands on her generous hips. "But as for these two, I found them hanging around in the lobby."

Bridget Bishop blushed as Opal turned to her with a smile.

"Don't you worry, Bridget, Cecil will remember his manners eventually," she teased. "You know, old men can be forgetful."

"I'm sorry to bother you, Chief," Bridget said, gesturing back toward her companion. "You remember Special Agent Terrance Gage from the FBI's Behavioral Analysis Unit?"

Cecil Fitzgerald nodded and offered a hand.

"Of course, it's good to see you, Bridget, and you, Agent Gage," the police chief said. "But I'm having a meeting here with Ms. Reardon about the Arnett case. I believe that's why

Opal stopped by, as well."

Opal looked toward the conference table to where Liz Reardon was sitting, surrounded by stacks of documents and open file folders.

Despite the mess on the table, the prosecutor looked remarkably calm and collected. Not a hair was out of place in her sleek, polished bob, and her wide, hazel eyes were alert and curious as she stood and crossed the room.

"How'd you know I wanted to see this woman, Opal?" Liz said in her usual honey-smooth drawl.

Gliding past Opal on four-inch heels, the prosecutor stopped in front of Bridget.

"I hope your visit here today means you have that report ready, Dr. Bishop," she said. "Cecil and I were just talking about the case we're going to present to the grand jury."

"You better hurry up and do it," Opal said, unable to resist adding in her two cents worth. "I don't like the idea of that man roaming around town as free as you please."

Liz's back stiffened, but she kept her eyes on Bridget.

"No, I haven't completed my report. That's actually why I stopped by," Bridget said, glancing at Cecil. "You see, my findings are concerning. Which is why I'm recommending that Chief Fitzgerald invite the FBI in to review the evidence and the crime scene to make sure nothing's been missed."

Her words hung in the room for a long beat.

"You're recommending what?" Cecil finally asked, just as Opal was about to speak. "You think I should ask the feds to come in here and stick their noses in-"

Suddenly looking up into Gage's hard face, Cecil paused.

"Look, I mean no disrespect," he said, holding up both hands in supplication. "But I've got enough trouble in this town right now without inviting in more. I'm already working with the feds on the Second Strangler case, so-"

"So, it shouldn't be much of a stretch to ask the FBI lab to look into this other homicide," Gage said. "From what Bridget shared with me, you've got a few holes in your case."

Liz Reardon looked around at Cecil, obviously confused by the comment, but Opal knew just what Gage was talking about.

From his immediate response, so did Cecil.

"Witnesses are notoriously unreliable," he protested. "We don't know for sure there really were two gunshots."

"But the jurors are bound to have doubts," Opal murmured to herself, hoping she'd said it loud enough for Cecil to hear.

Raising a well-manicured hand, Liz turned to Gage.

"Hold on now, Agent Gage. You're saying you want us to call in the FBI to review a homicide just because of one little discrepancy in a witness' testimony?"

Bridget shook her head.

"That's just the part we need the FBI to help with," she clarified. "But I'm having a hard time matching up my psychological evaluation of Felix Arnett with his supposed actions the night his wife died."

She met Cecil's eyes and held them.

"Opal told me that you worked with Felix in the past. That you thought he was a good kid. And I can't find anyone who's seen him lose his temper or witnessed any acts of violence or instability in the past."

Pointing to the files spread out on the conference table, Bridget frowned.

"The photos of the scene don't reflect the expected actions of a non-violent man or the usual fate of a happy marriage."

"Sometimes people's actions can't be explained," Liz sputtered. "Just because we don't understand it, doesn't mean it didn't happen."

Bridget sighed and shook her head.

"My whole career has been spent trying to figure out why some people do terrible things," she said. "I've stood face to face with serial killers and delved into their brains, literally, to try to find answers."

Sucking in a deep breath, she looked around the room.

"What I've found, is that there always is a reason. No matter how bizarre, ugly, or frightening it may be...there is a reason. If I'm going to submit a report with my name on it, I need to find out Felix Arnett's reason."

Opal flicked her eyes to Cecil. She could see by the set of his jaw that her husband was softening toward the idea.

"It wouldn't take long to get a response team out here to go over the crime scene again," Gage added. "And then you could send your evidence over to the lab."

He raised an eyebrow in Liz's direction.

"It would look good in front of the jury if it comes to that."

All eyes were trained on Cecil as he turned to Opal, clearly seeking her advice.

"If Bridget still has questions about the case, I guess you should call in some help," she said with a sigh. "Especially since one of your officers put the suspect in the hospital."

But the thought that an FBI response team would soon be crawling over the scene and examining every fact and trace of evidence caused a pang of unease in Opal's midsection.

She knew full well that if Felix hadn't shot his wife as the responding officers had assumed when they'd arrived, the rest of the events of that evening could be called into question.

Harry Kemp had investigated the shooting after the fact, and he'd determine the officer had followed all protocols.

But there were always questions. And Detective Kemp had been known to cut a few corners in his time.

"Okay, now that we have that settled," Gage said, "it means Bridget can focus on the Second Strangler case while she waits for the feedback on the Arnett investigation."

At the mention of Brooke Nelson's killer, Opal turned to face Gage and Bridget, her voice thick with indignation.

"What it means is that your task force needs to find that monster before he puts another girl on my autopsy table."

CHAPTER TWENTY-THREE

B ridget arrived home with just enough time to feed Hank and change clothes before she had to leave again for her six o'clock appointment with Faye Thackery. The psychotherapist's home-based office was only a few miles away. As Bridget climbed into the old Ford Explorer she'd had since college, she wondered if it was about time to invest in an upgraded model, but the little voice quickly dismissed the idea.

No need to get rid of something that's still perfectly serviceable.

Pulling up outside Faye Thackery's newly renovated bungalow, Bridget felt the usual nervous tension settle into her shoulders and back.

The therapy sessions had proven to be more of a challenge than Bridget had anticipated. But fear and anxiety were emotions to be faced and conquered, so when she'd started avoiding the people, places, and activities she loved after the Backroads Butcher case, she'd known it was time to seek professional help.

Hank ran down the sidewalk eagerly, remembering the treats Faye always seemed to have close at hand, while Bridget dragged her feet, not sure she was ready for another emotional session.

Following Hank around to the office entrance on the side of the bungalow, Bridget knocked softly, counted to ten, then began backing up the walkway, already anticipating the safety of the Explorer's well-worn interior.

"Bridget?"

Faye stood behind her on the driveway, her short, silvery hair agleam in the light of the setting sun, her delicate features arranged in a pleased smile.

"I ran out for some tea," she said, holding up a shopping bag in one small hand. "I know you love chamomile, and I used the last bit of leaves earlier today."

Shooing Bridget and Hank back toward the door, Faye followed close behind them as if she feared Bridget would make a run for it.

"Go on in. It isn't locked."

Bridget turned to gape at Faye in disbelief.

"You left your door unlocked?" she asked. "With the Second Strangler running around Wisteria Falls?"

"We can't live our lives in fear," Faye admonished as she brushed past Bridget to push open the door. "Besides, Wisteria Falls is a safe town, for the most part."

Wondering where Faye had gotten that idea, Bridget stepped into the small reception area and stared around, half expecting someone to be standing in the shadows.

But the shadows disappeared as Faye flipped on the light. Prodding Bridget toward the cozy room where she held her sessions, she crossed to the teapot in the corner.

While the therapist busied herself making tea, Bridget took

a seat on the plush sofa. She surveyed the peaceful room with appreciative eyes as Hank made himself comfortable on the soft Moroccan rug at her feet.

The smooth oak floor, white paneled wooden walls, and vaulted ceiling with exposed oak beams lent a forest-like feel to the space which Bridget found strangely comforting.

If only we didn't have to talk about me and my issues, I'd love to come over here all the time to hang out with Faye.

Faye was already delivering the tea and settling into the chair across from her with a notebook and pen in hand.

It was too late to back out now.

"So, how have you been sleeping?" Faye asked before taking a sip of steaming tea. "Still having the same nightmares?"

Bridget picked up her teacup and blew on the hot liquid inside, glad to have something to occupy her eyes and hands as she considered the question.

"Sometimes I'm not sure if they're nightmares or just memories," Bridget admitted. "But yes, I'm still having trouble sleeping. Especially now that I'm consulting with the BAU on the Second Strangler case."

Taking a tiny drink of her tea, Bridget raised her eyes to Faye, who was staring at her with a startled expression.

"How did that happen?" she asked. "Going back to work with the BAU, even as a consultant, is a pretty big step."

"I didn't want to," Bridget said. "But I felt obligated by the unusual circumstances. You see, the case is linked to Ernest Crast. And since I'm the only analyst who's studied him..."

Her voice faltered into a sigh. She'd already shared her life history in detail with Faye, including the years spent working on her dissertation and studying Crast, so there was little need to rehash the reasoning behind her involvement in the case.

"Facing your fears is usually better than avoiding them," Faye reminded her. "Although I imagine it's been difficult."

A surge of resentment worked its way through Bridget as she watched Faye take another sip of the Chamomile tea.

Difficult? Is that how she sees it? How would she possibly know what it's like to face a serial killer? To see his eviscerated victims firsthand. To think you may be next on his list.

Faye had spent her professional life helping everyday women manage everyday problems. She had no idea what kind of evil was truly out there.

"Yes, it has been difficult," Bridget managed to say. "But I'm dealing with it. It's getting better. *I'm* getting better."

You know that's not true. Is that your plan to get out of therapy? To act like you've miraculously been healed?

The little voice sounded disappointed.

Haven't you learned that sometimes the only way to get to the other side of the fire is to go straight through it?

* * *

Bridget drove home on autopilot, her tired mind replaying the events of the day as the white Explorer sped through town. She turned onto Fern Creek Road just as full darkness settled over the quiet street.

Her stomach rumbled as she pulled into the driveway,

reminding her she had nothing in the house to eat.

Ushering Hank inside, she dished food into his bowl, then stood in front of the refrigerator, gazing mournfully at the near-empty shelves, contemplating her options.

Order pizza again, or go to the grocery like a responsible adult?

She was leaning toward the pizza option when she heard a knock on the front door.

An irrational fear that the disciple had tracked her down was soon replaced by relief when she heard a deep voice.

"Bridget, you in there? It's me, Santino."

Something fluttered to life in her empty stomach as she opened the door to find Santino standing on the porch.

"I know I should have called first, but the number I had for you must be an old one," he said with a rueful smile. "When I got a no-longer-in-service message, I thought I'd take a chance and drive over."

"My number changed when I left the Bureau," Bridget said, stepping back to let him in. "I'll give you my new one so you can call next time instead of driving all the way out here."

Santino stood awkwardly in the middle of the room as if unsure what he'd come for.

"Was there something you wanted to tell me?" Bridget asked with a frown. "Is everything all right? Has there been a break in the case?"

Rubbing at the dark stubble on his jaw, Santino hesitated. Before he could answer, Hank appeared in the doorway.

The Irish setter's tail started to wag as soon as he caught sight of Santino, and he trotted over to allow the deputy marshal to bend over and ruffle his fur.

"We didn't get a chance to talk today at the task force meeting," Santino said, looking up at Bridget. "I guess I was a little worried after our conversation over the weekend, and I thought I should check on you."

"Worried about what, exactly?" Bridget asked.

A flush of color worked its way up Santino's neck.

"You're the one who asked me if I thought Crast might come after you," he said. "Once I started thinking about it, and when I couldn't reach you on the phone, I guess I let my imagination run a little wild. Especially after I saw this."

He reached in his pocket and pulled out a piece of paper. As he unfolded it, Bridget saw it was a letter.

"The letter to Althea wasn't the only letter the WPP had in their archives," he said, his eyes meeting hers. "There was a dozen or more. One was addressed to you."

Bridget looked down at the letter in his hand.

"Don't worry, this is just a photocopy," he assured her. "The original has been sent over to the lab with the others."

Staring down at the paper, Bridget realized she didn't want to read it. Didn't want to be drawn back into Ernest Crast's dark, twisted mind. Not yet.

"I'll read that later," she said, plucking the paper out of his hand and tucking it into her own pocket. "But now, I'm starving. I need to get something to eat."

Santino nodded as if he understood.

"Okay, no pressure," he said. "I've already emailed digital copies of all the letters for you to review. There may be something in those to help you with your profile."

He frowned and rubbed at his stubble again as if trying to calculate a mental math equation.

"How confident are you that our Second Strangler is this disciple Crast mentioned in his letters?" he asked.

Bridget shrugged.

"Profiling isn't an exact science," she said. "It's a strategy. A way to describe a killer through the identified connections and links between his or her victims, M.O., and signature. These factors help to determine motivation, meaning the killer's reason for killing."

"And you think the Second Strangler's reason for killing is some type of twisted loyalty to Ernest Crast?"

She nodded.

"Based on the connections and links we've made thus far in the case, I'd say it's possible."

Seeing the doubt in his eyes, she tried to think of a way to explain it in common terms.

"If our killer believes he's following orders from Crast, he's likely suffering from a psychotic disorder. Hearing voices. Having delusions. It could even have started off as a shared psychotic disorder, like in a cult, where both the leader and followers suffer under shared delusions of what is occurring around them."

A gleam of understanding shone in Santino's eyes.

"So, this guy could be suffering a psychotic break tied to his interaction with Crast? He could be hearing voices and suffering delusions that revolve around Crast and his crimes?"

"Exactly," Bridget said. "At least, that's my theory so far, but it is just a theory. We need to keep an open mind. There are other possible motives and other possible theories."

Santino looked intrigued.

"Any of those you'd like to share with me?" he asked. "Maybe over dinner somewhere?"

The fluttering and rumbling going on inside Bridget's stomach intensified.

"The weather's nice, so we could go somewhere that has outdoor seating," he added. "Somewhere Hank could go, too."

Tempted by the idea, Bridget wavered.

"I really should get started looking through those letters," she said. "And I haven't checked in with Charlie and Hale to find out if they've had luck tracking down Colby Crast."

Santino stiffened and averted his eyes, putting Bridget's well-honed senses on alert.

"Is there something about Colby Crast you aren't telling me?" she asked. "Something you're hiding?"

His silence told her she was on to something.

"I can't help with the investigation if I don't have all the information," she protested. "If you know something about Crast's son, please tell me."

"All I know is that Colby's file has been sealed and we're having a hard time getting it unsealed," he said. "It's likely just the usual red-tape around protective services cases and sealed adoption proceedings."

Bridget raised her eyebrows.

"So, Coby was officially adopted after he was taken away from Odell Crast?" she asked.

"Listen, I can't tell you any more than I know," he said, sounding suddenly tired. "But I can feed you if you'll let me."

He took a few steps toward the door, earning a curious look from Hank, who had heard his name being mentioned.

"Oh, alright," Bridget said, smiling at the similar hopeful expression on both of their faces. "Let's go eat."

CHAPTER TWENTY-FOUR

A silvery sliver of moon shown in the sky over Fern Creek Road as the black sedan glided silently down the winding street. Passing the red brick house with the wraparound porch and white shutters, the disciple saw Bridget Bishop appear at the door, a vision called forth from a dream.

"That's her. She's the chosen one."

The voice was back.

Relief rolled through the disciple's body as he realized he'd been forgiven. He was no longer alone.

"I've come for her," he said into the hush of the car's interior. "I'll take her tonight. I'll do it just as you wanted."

But the thrill of anticipation abruptly ended as he saw the red Chevy pickup parked on the side of the road.

Looking in his rearview mirror, the disciple saw a man follow Bridget down the porch steps.

It's that damn deputy marshal again. He must know she's next on the list. Why else would he come to this lousy town to guard her?

He continued to the end of the street, making his way onto Landsend Road before circling back around.

By the time he drove past the red brick house again, the

lights in the window were off and the red pickup was gone.

"You let her get away. You screwed up again."

Shaking his head at the contemptuous words, the disciple pulled out his phone and brandished it like a sword.

"I can track him!" he cried out. "I know how."

He opened the app on his phone, his eyes searching the little map on the display for the tracker he'd thrown into the back of the pickup. But the locator dot on the app had disappeared.

Either the deputy marshal had discovered the tracker and disabled it or the battery inside the little device had died.

Throwing down the phone, the disciple drove to the end of the street in a blind fury, his hands gripping the steering wheel as he listened for his mentor to tell him what to do next.

Headlights lit up the street in front of him as he stopped at the stop sign. He caught a glimpse of a woman's face in the oncoming car as it drove past him.

A flash of red brake lights lit up his rearview mirror, and he looked back to see the car turning into a driveway.

Bridget's next-door neighbor had come home.

He strained to see the small figure climbing out of the car, making out a petite woman with a long, dark braid. She was carrying in a bag of groceries, her hands full and her guard down, but by the time the disciple could react, the woman had disappeared into her house, shutting the door behind her.

Banging his hands on the steering wheel, the disciple impulsively turned left, heading toward an empty field behind the row of houses.

The sedan's wheels bumped over the curb and onto the field, cutting through the overgrown grass as the disciple steered the vehicle along a high wooden fence that separated the field from the backyards on Fern Creek Road.

"If anyone sees you here, they'll know you're up to no good."

Too nervous to respond to the voice, the disciple continued bouncing along the field until he saw the back of the red brick house on the other side.

Bringing the car to a halt beside the fence, he climbed out and mounted the hood, sticking his head over the top to peer into the backyard.

The house was still and dark, and the backyard was covered in shadows, the only light coming from the sliver of moon and a sprinkling of stars overhead.

As he was just about to hoist himself up and over the fence, the disciple remembered the gun in the deputy marshal's holster, and the lean, strong muscles under his jacket.

The man was likely an expert marksman and a trained fighter. If he caught him coming over the fence, he'd easily take him out before his feet could even touch the ground.

Hearing a door open and footsteps on pavement, the disciple ducked down behind the fence and held his breath. The sound was coming from the house next door.

He peered through a crack in the fence as a small woman with a long braid carried a bag of trash toward a gray, plastic garbage can.

"Stay in the house, Pixie!" the woman called out, shutting the door behind her, then struggling to shove the bulging bag into the plastic container.

The disciple listened for the voice, not sure what his mentor would want him to do now, but the only sound he heard was the woman's angry muttering as she wrestled with the bag.

Estimating the distance between the fence and the woman, the disciple figured he could easily scale the fence and have his arm around her throat before she knew what was happening.

"That's what you thought that first time and you almost got killed. You almost got caught. You want to end up like me?"

Fear flashed through him at the thought of being seen and captured. He had to be careful. He couldn't afford any more mistakes.

He watched as the woman trudged toward the porch, her hands now free and her yapping dog making a racket on the other side of the back door.

I waited too long. Now it's too late.

His eyes flicked back to the red brick house in front of him.

Bridget Bishop is the chosen one. It's her turn next.

But as he lowered himself back to the ground, he heard a soft voice drift through the still night air. It sounded like it was coming from the house next door.

"Come on, Pixie, time for your walk!"

Checking that his gun was in his waistband, the disciple inhaled deeply and smiled.

"I think I know how to get Bridget Bishop's attention," he muttered, making his way along the fence, heading back toward Fern Creek Road.

CHAPTER TWENTY-FIVE

Jacey Wallace opened her front door and waited for Pixie to run out onto the porch. The miniature teacup Yorkie was high strung and energetic even at night, and she'd found it best to give the tiny dog a final walk around the block before putting her to bed.

Looking up at the waning crescent moon hanging in the sky, Jacey followed Pixie down the walkway, trying not to think of the empty bed that would be waiting for her that evening.

Her husband Parker had come home several months ago to announce he'd gotten an offer for a dream job in Denver. Jacey had already started planning her ski-lodge wardrobe when he'd informed her that he'd be going alone.

"This is a once-in-a-lifetime opportunity, and I can't afford to have you holding me back."

His callous words had severed something deep inside her, simultaneously ending both her marriage and her childhood fantasies of a happily-ever-after.

Parker had granted Jacey full custody of Pixie, which wasn't surprising since he'd never had any patience for the little dog or her high-pitched yapping, and now Jacey's life revolved around the precocious little canine's schedule.

She was up at eight for nibbles and a morning walk, followed by grooming and a mid-morning snack. Then a late lunch and an afternoon nap preceded dinner and another walk before bed. It was all very regimented, just as Pixie preferred.

But Jacey had begun to yearn for some human company to spice up her routine, and as she passed Bridget Bishop's red brick house, she wondered again who the dangerous-looking man in the red pickup truck had been.

He was just as intriguing as the FBI agent who'd stopped Pixie's mad dash for freedom a few days before, and Jacey decided she might have to start hanging around Bridget's house more often.

Tugging against her lead, Pixie pulled Jacey down the sidewalk, then stopped to yap at something in the shadow of a sprawling oak tree.

"Come on, girl," Jacey urged, suddenly realizing that she and the little Yorkie were alone on the empty street. "Let's get home and get to bed."

But Pixie continued to yap toward the darkness beyond the sidewalk, her tiny body stiff with excitement.

Bending down to scoop up the little dog, Jacey heard a rustling sound in the bushes behind the tree.

Probably just a cat or a squirrel. Or maybe a raccoon.

She turned to go, ignoring Pixie's protests as she walked back toward her house. Once she'd passed Bridget's driveway, she set the dog down and let her run for the door.

Jacey made it halfway up the walkway to the porch before

she noticed her side gate was unlatched.

"Now, how did *that* happen?"

Opening the front door to allow Pixie to scurry inside the house, Jacey closed it after the little dog before stomping around to the side yard.

She'd already started to close the gate when she saw the garbage can lid had fallen off. Narrowing her eyes, she studied the backyard, now wondering if Pixie really had seen a raccoon.

A rake had been propped against the fence, and Jacey picked it up, holding it out in front of her as she stalked toward the garbage can.

Turning the prongs down, she used the rake to poke at the can, hoping to scare away any scavengers.

When nothing jumped out at her, she moved closer and peered inside. Seeing only the garbage bag she'd forced in earlier, Jacey sighed and leaned the rake against the can.

As she leaned over to pick up the lid, an arm wrapped around her throat, and a hand settled over her mouth. She grabbed for the rake, but her hand found only air as she was jerked back against a rock-hard body.

Lifting one leg, she smashed her foot back against a solid knee. Again and again, she kicked, prompting the man behind her to grunt in pain.

"Stop fighting or I'll break your neck," he hissed in her ear.

But Jacey had seen the news. She knew all about the Second Strangler. She'd read all the stories about Brooke Nelson and Libby Palmer. There was no way she was going to let the man take her without a fight.

A wave of dizziness swirled through her as the unseen man tightened his arm around her neck

Using the last of her strength, Jacey wrenched her head back, loosening the man's grip, giving her the opportunity to sink her teeth into the hand covering her face.

The warm, metallic rush of blood filled her mouth, and she retched and tried to twist away.

"You're...dead," the man panted as he dragged her toward the back gate. "You...shouldn't have...done that."

He unbolted the latch and shouldered open the wooden gate as Jacey teetered on the edge of unconsciousness.

A faint, familiar sound reached her ears just as the gate swung shut behind her. It was the high-pitched sound of Pixie's bark. The yapping that Parker had always hated.

But it brought a ghost of a smile to Jacey's lips.

Pixie's okay. She's safe inside the house.

But her relief was short-lived as she saw the black sedan parked against the fence.

Too weak to scream or struggle, she watched through half-closed eyes as the man lifted her up and dumped her into the trunk. Leaning over her, he picked up a roll of bright blue duct tape and wrapped it around and around her ankles, before moving up to secure her wrists.

Blood from his wounded hand dripped onto the duct tape, smearing her skin and clothes as he worked.

She winced as he slammed the lid shut, then listened to his footsteps as he crunched through the grass and leaves to the front of the car.

Suddenly the engine roared to life, and the car was bumping along over the uneven ground as Jacey lay listlessly in the darkness, willing herself to think, willing her body to move.

Sucking in several long, deep breaths, the oxygen began to work its way through Jacey's body again as the car sped further and further away from Fern Creek Road.

She pulled her knees up to her chest and used her bound hands to pry the blood-soaked tape off of her ankles.

As she started working to free her wrists, the car came to a sudden stop. Jacey froze as a door shut and then the trunk lid opened, revealing the dark sky and the crescent moon above.

Rough hands reached into the trunk and dragged her out as Jacey feigned unconsciousness. As the man dropped her onto the ground, she risked a look around, using the dim moonlight to make out a thick cluster of trees and bushes at the edge of a murky pond.

Knowing she may never have another chance, Jacey kicked out at the man's feet, knocking him off balance, before scrambling up and running toward a scraggly forest of pine and poplar trees.

Adrenaline and desperation gave her the energy to reach the trees before the man could catch up to her.

"Come back here!" he screamed, his voice trembling with rage. "There's nowhere to run!"

But Jacey was already running through the dark forest, not caring that her arms were tied in front of her. Not caring that she didn't know where she was going.

All she knew was that if she wanted to live, she needed to

get away from the madman behind her.

After what seemed like hours of running through the darkness of the forest, the trees gave way to flat, soggy ground.

Jacey slowed and looked down at her muddy shoes, realizing she'd reached the bank of a wide river.

"It's the Shenandoah," she murmured in a numb whisper, staring blankly at the moonlight reflecting off the water. "It must be."

Moving swiftly along the riverbank, she was just starting to believe she might escape when she heard someone crashing through the forest behind her.

Jacey dropped to the ground, realizing she had only minutes to find a place to hide before the man would emerge from the woods. Scanning the riverbank, she could see no bushes or foliage to use as a possible hiding spot.

Tree branches snapped behind her and she heard a man's voice in the distance. It sounded like he was talking to someone, and his voice was growing closer,

Sucking in a deep breath, she stepped into the water.

CHAPTER TWENTY-SIX

Bridget woke with a headache after indulging in one too many glasses of wine the night before. She and Santino had enjoyed dinner at the Wisteria Falls Café, sitting on the restaurant's small porch and sipping a glass of merlot until the staff had come out to say it was time to lock up.

Slipping into faded jeans and an oversized t-shirt, Bridget snapped on Hank's lead and followed him out the front door.

She always took the dog for a walk first thing in the morning, enjoying the quiet, calm of the sleepy neighborhood as it was coming to life.

The sound of frantic yapping drew Hank's attention as they passed Jacey's house. The setter tugged Bridget up the walkway, his eyes alert, and his body tense.

"Come on, Hank, we haven't been invited," she said, pulling on his lead. "Let's go."

Reluctantly Hank retreated down the walkway, following Bridget along the sidewalk for another few yards before stopping to let loose a sharp series of barks.

Suddenly charging toward the fence, Hank jerked the lead from Bridget's hand as he cut across the grass, heading straight toward the open side gate.

"Heel, Hank!" Bridget cried out in alarm. "Heel, boy!"

But Hank wasn't listening as he continued on through the gate, ignoring Bridget's commands.

Running after him into Jacey's backyard, Bridget grabbed up the dog's lead and turned to him with an accusing glare.

"Just what do you think you're doing?" she scolded.

Her disapproval turned into dismay when she saw the sticky, brownish-red smears on the trash can.

"Is that what I think it is?" she asked Hank, stooping to inspect the gray plastic bin. "Is that blood?"

Dread seeped through her as she followed a trail of trampled grass toward the back gate.

The outline of a bloody handprint was visible on the wood.

Pushing open the gate, she saw tire tracks in the patchy, muddy grass. A strip of bright blue duct tape had been discarded beside them.

Bridget stood still, momentarily stunned. Then the faint sound of Pixie's frantic barks reached her, drawing her eyes toward the house.

"Jacey!" she cried out, sprinting across the yard to the back porch. "Jacey? Are you there? Jacey?"

Pounding on the back door, she listened, then tried the doorknob, which twisted easily in her hand.

Cursing the small-town habit of leaving doors unlocked, Bridget pushed open the door a few inches, anticipating Pixie's attempt at escape.

She grabbed up the Yorkie in one hand as the little dog charged toward her, then looked around the darkened kitchen.

"Jacey?" she called, stepping into the room, and pulling Hank in after her. "Jacey, it's Bridget. Are you in here?"

Sensing she was speaking to an empty house, Bridget quickly checked all the rooms, growing increasingly frantic.

A cell phone had been left charging on the bedside table, and her purse was hanging on a hook by the front door, her car keys beside it.

It was clear that Jacey had left the house unexpectedly.

Pulling out her phone, Bridget bypassed 911 and called Cecil Fitzgerald directly, her breath starting to come in gasps as she worked out what must have happened.

"Bridget, this is a surprise," the chief said, "What can I-"

"My next-door neighbor is missing," Bridget said, trying to keep the panic out of her voice. "There's blood...lots of blood. And her purse and keys are still here. It looks like she's been abducted. You've got to send someone out here *now*."

Her voice cracked as she held Pixie tighter against her chest.

"You've got to hurry, Chief Fitzgerald. I think the Second Strangler took her. I think he has Jacey."

* * *

Harry Kemp pulled up to the curb in an unmarked cruiser, his gray, receding hairline damp with sweat despite the mild morning temperatures, and his eyes hidden behind mirrored sunglasses.

Throwing down the cigarette he'd been smoking, he

crushed it under the worn heel of his shoe before walking toward the house at a leisurely pace that suggested he was in no hurry to respond to Bridget's call.

The detective was followed by two uniformed officers in a patrol car, who immediately jumped out and began to cordon off the area outside Jacey's house.

"Detective Kemp, we've got to organize a search party," Bridget said, jogging down the front steps to meet him halfway. "We can't know how long Jacey's been gone, but there are tire tracks behind the house leading-"

"There may not be a need for that," Kemp interjected in a grim tone. "I'm sorry to have to tell you this, Bridget, but a body was pulled out of the Shenandoah River this morning."

Bridget shook her head, not sure she understood what he was saying, unable to believe what she was hearing.

"Responding officers verified it was a white female with dark hair," he said. "Which pretty much matches the description you gave to Chief Fitzgerald. Blue duct tape had been used to restrain the body."

Turning away to hide the tears in her eyes, Bridget knew Jacey's death was all her fault. The disciple must have been coming after her, just as she'd feared.

He must have gotten the wrong house. He mistook Jacey for me.

A heavy hand fell on her shoulder.

"You want me to call your dad?" Kemp asked. "He could be over here in a jiffy if you need someone to-"

"No," Bridget said with a tell-tale sniffle, gesturing to her red-rimmed eyes. "I don't want him to see me like this."

She tried to think through what she should do next.

"We need to call Special Agent Charlie Day," she finally said. "She's the lead investigator on the Second Strangler task force, and she'll need to call out an emergency response team to manage the crime scene."

Kemp shook his big head in protest.

"Oh no, you don't," he said, pulling a pack of cigarettes out of his pocket and tapping one into his hand. "Chief Fitzgerald already told me you're trying to get the feds to take over the Arnett investigation, and now you want to just hand over this scene before we're even sure this new Strangler was involved?"

"I'm sure," Bridget said, a flush of anger rising in her cheeks. "And this isn't about *handing over* anything. It's about making sure we catch the bastard who took Jacey before he hurts anyone else."

Disdain twisted Kemp's sagging features into a grimace.

"Until Cecil says otherwise, this is *my* scene. And I'm not calling in the FBI or anybody else until we determine what happened and who has jurisdiction."

Swallowing back her objections, Bridget decided she'd have to take up the matter with Cecil. Talking to Kemp would just be a waste of time.

As she turned away, a familiar, high-pitched voice reached her ears, causing her to look toward the street.

Daphne Finch's blonde head was visible in the growing crowd of neighbors and onlookers who had started to gather.

Crossing to the police barricade, which had been set up at the bottom of Jacey's driveway, Bridget motioned for the officers to let Daphne through.

"She's with me," Bridget said, then spotted little Ginny behind her mother. "They both are."

"What in the Sam Hill is going on here?" Daphne asked as Bridget led her and Ginny up the walkway and away from the gathered crowd. "I was taking Ginny to school and saw all this in front of your house. I near about had a heart attack."

A lump formed in Bridget's throat as she tried to explain. She hugged Pixie against her chest, somehow feeling she at least owed it to Jacey to take care of the Yorkie now that she'd failed her in every other way.

"Could I hold her?"

Ginny was looking up at Pixie with adoring eyes.

"Sure, you can," Bridget said, bending over to lower the tiny dog into Ginny's outstretched arms. "Just don't let her down. We don't want her running away."

Cuddling Pixie against her small body, Ginny followed Bridget and Daphne toward the house.

"My neighbor Jacey Wallace was abducted last night," Bridget said in a hushed tone. "And a body was found in the Shenandoah River this morning."

Daphne's green eyes widened in shock.

"I think it was the Second Strangler," Bridget added in a strained voice. "And I think he was coming after me."

CHAPTER TWENTY-SEVEN

C harlie sped along Landsend Road, her foot on the floor of the Expedition with Hale riding shotgun beside her. She'd been in Calloway's office, briefing him on the task force's progress, when Bridget had left a frantic voicemail about her neighbor being abducted.

The psychologist's anguished words echoed again and again in Charlie's head as she drove toward Wisteria Falls.

"The Second Strangler...the disciple...was here, in my neighborhood. He abducted my neighbor, and they've...they've found a body. We need a response team here right away."

By the time the Expedition skidded around the corner onto Fern Creek Road, a sizable crowd had gathered outside the crime scene.

Police vehicles with flashing lights, a news crew with a satellite truck, and a throng of excited spectators had congregated in the winding street.

"There's space behind the cruiser," Hale said, pointing to the curb behind a black and white Ford Interceptor with a bar of lights flashing on the top.

Before they could climb out of the Expedition, a big man

with gray hair and mirrored sunglasses rapped on the window.

Charlie recognized him from previous encounters as Detective Harry Kemp, an old-school detective with a chip on his shoulder the size of Montana.

"You can't park there," he bellowed, throwing a lit cigarette to the ground as he spoke. "Move this tank out of here."

Putting a hand on Hale's arm to restrain him, Charlie rolled down the window and produced her badge.

"Special Agent Charlie Day with the FBI Washington field office," she said in a cool voice. "I'm here at the request of Dr. Bridget Bishop. That's her house right there."

"And this is a crime scene if you haven't noticed," the man said with a scowl, although he'd lowered his voice. "And Bridget Bishop isn't in charge of my crime scene."

Hale leaned over to pin Kemp with unfriendly eyes.

"Is Chief Fitzgerald here, Detective?" he asked. "Because he also asked us to come by, and I'd hate to keep him waiting."

Hale's bluff didn't work.

"Cecil is at another scene," Kemp said, crossing his arms over his chest. "But I'll let him know you two stopped by."

Turning on his heel, Kemp strode back toward the house, leaving the stale smell of cigarettes behind.

Before Charlie could put the SUV in reverse, Hale reached out a big hand and switched off the engine.

"Let him send a tow truck," he muttered. "We're not going anywhere until we talk to Bridget."

He opened the door and climbed out, then circled around to stand next to Charlie.

Seconds later Bridget emerged from the red brick house and headed across the lawn toward them, her face pale and drawn in the bright morning light.

"Thank goodness you're here."

She looked back in the direction Kemp had gone as if she feared being overheard.

"We've got to get Chief Fitzgerald to call in a response team. There's biological evidence in the backyard that could lead us straight to the man who abducted Jacey."

Putting a firm hand on Bridget's arm, Charlie propelled her back toward the red brick house.

"If this really is the work of Crast's disciple, he was likely coming after *you*," she said, keeping her voice low. "Which means you need to stay out of sight until we figure out what's going on."

Bridget shook off Charlie's hand.

"We're wasting time," she said, a frustrated frown creasing her forehead. "We need to test that blood, and the handprint, and the tire tracks so that-"

"Let's just slow down," Charlie urged, hearing the underlying panic in Bridget's voice. "First, I'd like to speak with Chief Fitzgerald. If we can get the local PD's cooperation, it would make things a lot easier. I don't want to go bulldozing into the scene without first trying to work it out amicably."

A deep voice sounded behind her.

"I'm glad to hear that, Agent Day. But just what is it we

need to work out?"

Spinning around, Charlie saw that the Wisteria Falls chief of police had finally arrived.

"Cecil, I didn't see you pull up," she said, gesturing toward Hale. "I don't think you've met Special Agent Tristan Hale in person yet, have you?"

Before Cecil could respond, Bridget stepped forward.

"We don't have time to waste on formalities and bureaucracy," she insisted. "A serial killer is out there and he's escalating. He's taken two women in one week, and he's progressed from abducting women on the street to hunting them down in their homes."

All eyes turned to her.

"He's taking risks. He's made mistakes. He's left evidence behind. That means he's losing control. He's going off-script. Anyone he comes across now could be in serious danger."

"And you're saying this is the same guy who abducted Brooke Nelson and Libby Palmer?" Cecil asked.

Bridget nodded.

"That's exactly what I'm saying. And if you don't believe me, maybe you'll believe your own eyes."

Pulling out her phone, Bridget tapped on an app and waited for it to load.

"This is video from my security system. I have cameras in the front and back of the house. They're motion activated."

She held out the phone as a black and white video began to play on the little display. Charlie stared at the image of a long wooden fence. Her eyes narrowed as she made out a man's head. He peered over the fence, looking toward the camera.

"That's our guy," Bridget said, tapping a finger on the display to pause the video. "That's the Second Strangler."

"It's too far away," Cecil protested, squinting at the screen. "The picture isn't clear enough to make a positive identification. Could be half the men in town if you ask me."

Bridget exhaled in frustration.

"I'm not saying we can make an I.D. using this video alone. But if you compare it to the video that captured Brook Nelson's abduction, you'll see the resemblance. It's the same guy."

Turning to see Detective Kemp stomping toward them, Charlie braced herself for another round of sparring. But Cecil held up a hand before Kemp could speak.

"The FBI Second Strangler task force will be handling the investigation into this scene, Kemp," he said brusquely. "As well as the scene down by the river where the body was found. No use making a fuss. It's been decided."

Kemp's face turned a dull red, but he didn't argue.

"Agent Day is leading the task force and she'll coordinate resources. For now, keep both scenes secured and the press out while waiting for the Bureau's investigators to arrive."

But Kemp had already turned and was walking away.

Relieved to have the belligerent man out of the way, Charlie turned back to Bridget.

"I'll get an evidence response team out here," she assured her. "But in the meantime, I need you to go home and pack a bag. You shouldn't stay here on your own. Not until the Strangler is identified and in custody."

Charlie heard Bridget's sharp intake of breath and

prepared for an argument, but the psychologist only nodded.

"You're right," she said. "There's no way I can stare out at Jacey's empty house all day without going crazy. I'll go pack."

*   *   *

Once Bridget had disappeared into the red brick house, Charlie motioned to Hale.

"Ask Cecil to assign two uniforms to keep an eye on Bridget's house," she said. "No telling what the Strangler will do next. We can't give him another chance to get to Bridget."

"Will do, boss," Hale said dryly. "But we've got a problem. I'm being told there's going to be a delay getting the evidence response team out here."

Charlie's eyes flashed with irritation as Hale held up his hand in supplication.

"Don't shoot *me*, I'm only the messenger," he said. "All I was told is it's a resource issue and they're working on it."

Pulling her phone from her pocket, Charlie tapped on Calloway's number. It was the SAC's responsibility to make sure his agents had immediate access to a response team when needed, wasn't it?

She started speaking as soon as Calloway answered.

"I just jumped through hoops to get the local chief of police out here to let us handle this crime scene, and now I'm being told we don't have the resources."

"And I'm doing my best to get you a team out there as fast

as possible," Calloway snapped back. "You sit tight and keep the scene secure until the ERT arrives."

Realizing he'd ended the call, Charlie dropped the phone back in her pocket and turned to Hale.

"The response team's ETA is unknown," she admitted. "And we need to get over to the river."

She checked her watch.

"Opal is probably already there waiting to collect the body."

Looking toward Bridget's house, Charlie saw a small blonde girl appear in the window. The girl held a tiny dog in her arms as she looked out with wide, worried eyes.

Charlie lifted her hand in a friendly wave, but the child stepped back, letting the curtains fall back into place.

Thirty minutes later Charlie watched as a boxy white truck with an oversized FBI logo on the side pulled up to the curb.

The doors swung open, and several agents jumped out, moving with a sense of urgency that Charlie appreciated.

"Sorry for the delay," a woman in an FBI jacket, black jeans, and protective gloves called as she unloaded several bags of equipment. "You want to take us back to the scene?"

Pointing the team through the side gate, Charlie and Hale followed behind, watching at a distance as the technicians began their inch-by-inch search of the crime scene.

"Excuse me."

The voice was cool and familiar.

Charlie turned to see Vivian Burke standing behind her.

"I've been sent to collect blood samples to take back to the lab," she said, looking bored. "Field work is not usually my thing, but according to Calloway, your field office is short-staffed, so, unfortunately...here I am."

Watching as Vivian crossed to the fence and began setting up her supplies, Charlie wondered what Terrance Gage saw in the cold, condescending woman.

The thought of Gage sent her reaching for her phone again.

Now that the response team had arrived, she and Hale could go over to the river and see what Opal had discovered.

She listened to the phone ring again and again. She considered just hanging up but decided to leave a message.

"Get up and get dressed," she ordered, hoping Gage would check his messages for once. "We need you to meet us down by the Shenandoah River. The Second Strangler had a busy night."

CHAPTER TWENTY-EIGHT

Ignoring the buzzing of his phone on the bedside table, Terrance Gage dropped his feet onto the floor and willed his stomach and head to stop spinning. As he heaved himself up and off the bed, the room tilted on its axis.

He took a tentative step toward the bathroom, then realized he'd better hurry. Seconds later he was retching into the sink, his stomach expelling the last vestiges of red wine he'd consumed the night before in a futile effort to erase Vivian Burke from his mind.

Another round of buzzing from the bedroom reminded him of the multiple calls from Vivian and his sister Anne, which he'd ignored in his alcohol-induced indifference.

Both women were likely to be fuming this morning.

Turning on the shower, he didn't wait for the water to heat up, but instead stepped right in, letting the icy water stream over his hairless head and wide shoulders without even gritting his teeth.

Now fully awake and freshly showered, he wrapped a towel around his midsection and ventured out to the living room.

An empty bottle of wine sat next to a profusion of greasy fast-food wrappers and used napkins. His stomach lurched again as he collected the trash and carried it to the kitchen.

Dumping the evidence of his late-night binge in the garbage can, he turned on the coffee machine and opened the cabinet.

He was reaching for the box of instant oatmeal when he heard scratching at the back door.

Sarge slipped inside as soon as Gage pulled the door open. The tomcat crossed to his bowl and stared morosely into its empty depths before blinking up at Gage with tired eyes.

"Hard night for you, too, big guy?"

Gage poured food in the cat's bowl and then set about making himself oatmeal and coffee.

Once he'd forced the oatmeal down, hoping the sticky substance might soak up any wine left in his stomach, he carried his cup of coffee into the walk-in closet and surveyed the racks of suits and ties.

Picking out a dark gray suit and lavender tie, he got dressed, then checked his reflection in the mirror. Other than the suspiciously puffy eyes, he didn't look half bad.

When he walked back into the bedroom, Gage knew he couldn't ignore his phone any longer. He couldn't afford to just hide away. He needed to get to work.

He had to face Vivian and deal with the mess he'd made.

The first voicemail he listened to from the forensic examiner made his blood run cold.

"I've run the DNA tests from the blue duct tape on Brooke Nelson's body," she said without greeting or preamble. "I found DNA from at least three contributors. Call me back."

Not bothering to listen to the other voicemails, Gage called

Vivian's number, eager to hear if any of the DNA contributors had a match in CODIS."

"You're alive," Vivian said as soon as she answered the call. "I was beginning to think you must have keeled over in that big, lonely house of yours."

"I've been busy," Gage said, determined not to let her goading get to him. "But I just heard your voicemail about the DNA tests on the duct tape. You said you found DNA for three people on the tape? Did you get a match in CODIS?"

Vivian snorted.

"It isn't that easy," she said. "I said we had at least three contributors in the sample I tested. But it was a mixed sample, meaning it contained DNA from multiple sources, and it was a very small quantity."

"Okay, but was there a match in CODIS?"

She paused, and Gage imagined she was purposely drawing out the suspense. That she enjoyed making him wait.

"The only match I got in CODIS was for Ernest Crast," she admitted. "Tests confirmed that Crast's DNA and the DNA on the duct tape share a significant number of genetic markers."

"How significant?"

She sighed as if he wasn't likely to understand the details.

"We performed a Y-DNA test. It was a conclusive match."

"So, it couldn't be from anyone else?" he prodded. "You're absolutely sure?"

Vivian sighed again.

"The DNA profile had to be Crast...or someone in his direct paternal ancestral line."

"What do you mean by *direct paternal ancestral line*?"

He suspected he knew what she was about to say.

"The Y chromosome passes down virtually unchanged from father to son," Vivian explained. "So, technically, the DNA profile on the tape that matched the profile for Crast in CODIS could have been from Crast's father or his son."

Gage was still trying to make sense of what she'd said when Vivian spoke again.

"So, you just called about the DNA tests?" she asked. "You aren't curious about where I am and what I'm doing?"

"I don't have time for mind games right now, Vivian," he said impatiently. "I need to find Ernest Crast's son."

He was about to end the call when he heard a siren wail in the background.

"I'm next door to Bridget Bishop's house," she said softly. "I'm collecting blood from the crime scene at her neighbor's house. It looks to me like the Second Strangler decided to pay her a visit, but he got the wrong address."

* * *

Gage left Sarge sleeping in a patch of sunlight on the kitchen floor as he went out to his Navigator and climbed inside.

As he backed down the driveway and headed for the highway, he decided to call Vic Santino, hoping the deputy marshal had been able to dig up more information on Colby Crast since the last time they'd talked.

Santino answered on the second ring.

"You have any luck tracking down Colby Crast?" Gage

asked. "We've got results back verifying the blue duct tape does have Crast's DNA. Either that or the DNA is a match to his father or his son."

Santino didn't respond right away.

"I'm still waiting for more information from my contact at the WPP," the deputy marshal finally said. "But if you want to meet up, I can fill you in on what I know so far."

"I'm actually on my way out to Wisteria Falls," Gage said, checking his watch. "I'm driving out to the crime scene."

There was another pause on Santino's end.

"Crime scene?"

Merging onto the highway, Gage navigated past a slow-moving minivan, then pressed his foot to the floor.

"Don't tell me you haven't heard about the abduction in Bridget's neighborhood. I thought I was the last to know."

"No, I've sort of been out of touch this morning managing some protection services errands," he said evasively. "Is Bridget okay? What's happened?'

Gage wasn't sure he knew all the details himself, but he filled Santino in the best he could as he continued to speed west on the interstate.

"I'm going right past the Arlington exit," he said, checking the road signs ahead. "I could swing by and pick you up if you want to ride along. You could fill me in on what you know about Colby Crast along the way."

Santino was quick to agree, and Gage soon pulled up outside a trendy apartment complex. The deputy marshal was already standing by the curb.

Climbing into the passenger's seat, he seemed agitated, his

usual cool, laidback demeanor replaced by nervous energy.

"I tried to reach Bridget but she didn't answer," he said as he clicked on his seatbelt. "Are you sure she's okay?"

"Charlie said she was upset but unharmed," Gage confirmed, pulling back into traffic. "I think she's going to stay somewhere else until we bring this guy in."

He noted Santino's hands clenched into fists on his lap.

"Is everything okay?" Gage asked. "Did something happen to Althea Helmont?"

Santino shook his head, but his face remained tense.

"Althea is safe for now," he said. "I went by the safehouse this morning. She's doing as well as can be expected, although she's eager for us to catch the Strangler, of course."

Realizing he wasn't going to elaborate, Gage decided to move on to the reason he'd called Santino in the first place.

"Okay, so what did you find out about Colby Crast?"

"Not a lot," Santino admitted. "Not yet. But I'm expecting a call back from a legal liaison at the WPP at any time. She's petitioning to get access to the sealed adoption records."

Leaning back in his seat, he crossed his arms over his chest.

"So far, all we really know is that Colby was adopted by a family out of state," he said. "The adoption record was sealed by the judge at the time, which is standard practice in the protection program. But we've had push back getting authorization to review the files."

"How old would Colby be now?" Gage asked.

"Twenty-two," Santino answered. "About the same age as Althea Helmont's twins. A little older."

His voice was hard. Gage had the feeling the search for the Second Strangler had become personal for the deputy marshal over the last few days.

"The DNA test indicated Crast or someone in his direct paternal line could have come in contact with the tape," Gage said. "And we're looking for Colby. But, what about his father? I know Charlie and Hale talked to him and he was uncooperative..."

"Odell Crast must be seventy years old by now," Santino said, rubbing at the dark stubble on his chin. "From what I've read in the files, he always was a mean son-of-a-bitch."

Gage shrugged.

"He's old, but maybe he's not working alone. Maybe Odell's the one directing this disciple and convincing him that Crast wants him to kill. Maybe he's the one giving him orders."

"I say we get a warrant to search Odell Crast's farm," Santino said. "I have a feeling any plans Crast made begin and end at the place he called home."

CHAPTER TWENTY-NINE

Bridget stood in her old bedroom unpacking her overnight bag. Something about the little room she'd grown up in still felt safe and familiar, even though Paloma had redecorated it several times over the years since Bridget had moved away to college, leaving the house on Maplewood Drive behind.

The sunshine yellow walls of her childhood had been muted to an eggshell white, and the battered bunkbeds she and Daphne had used for countless sleepovers had long since been dismantled, but the essence of the room remained.

Something about it still felt like home to Bridget, even when the rest of the house felt like Paloma.

I can still feel mom in here. Her presence, her energy...it's never faded away. Not in this room. Not for me.

A soft knock sounded on the doorframe.

"You doing okay in here? Hank and I were worried."

Bob Bishop stood in the hall with Hank at his heels. He caught Bridget's forlorn expression before she could hide it.

"Nothing for either of you to worry about, Dad."

Crossing the room, she rested a hand on his arm.

"I'm fine," she assured him. "Just a little shaken up."

"I worry about you, Bridget," he said, putting a warm hand over hers. "I always have. Ever since your mother…"

A flash of pain crossed his face, deepening the fine lines and wrinkles left behind by years of work and worry.

"You're so much like her, you know. Strong and independent. But too soft-hearted for your own good."

He sighed and walked to the bed, sinking down on it as if too weary to stand, pulling Bridget down to sit next to him.

"Edith always took on everyone else's burdens," he said softly. "It was her fatal mistake, in the end…"

He was silent for a long moment, then shook his head and glanced up at Bridget, as if confused. He could still get muddled at times. It was a lingering effect of his stroke and one that worried Bridget more than she let on.

"You don't talk about Mom much, anymore," she said, unable to ignore the pang of resentment that had arisen at the rare sound of her mother's name on his lips. "Why not?"

The question hung between them in the little room as her father seemed to consider the question. When he spoke, his voice was thick with emotion.

"The kind of love your mother and I had…well, it's rare. Not many people find that one true love in their lives. But when you do, and when it's taken from you, it leaves a terrible void."

He cleared his throat, about to continue, when Paloma's voice made them both jump.

"I was wondering where you two had gone," she said in a stiff voice. "Angelo has stopped by to check on Bridget."

Concern that Paloma may have overheard her father's

comments, was replaced by a more pressing worry.

"How does Angelo know I'm here? I came here to..."

She faltered, not wanting to use the word *hide*, but not sure what else to call it. Suddenly not sure what she was doing.

Why did I let the disciple chase me out of my own home?

"I came here to get away from...*everyone*," she finally said, unable to hide her anger. "And that includes *reporters*."

Paloma huffed.

"Angelo is part of the family," she protested. "And he's concerned about you. After all, you are seeing each other now."

"We're not *seeing each other*," she objected. "And what else have you told Angelo about what's going on?"

Before Paloma could answer, she turned to her father.

"What about you, Dad?" she asked. "Did you tell Angelo anything Kemp shared with you about the case? Is that how he's getting information for his Second Strangler articles?"

"Unfortunately, my source wants to remain anonymous."

Angelo Molina appeared in the doorway behind his aunt. He wore an apologetic smile.

"But I assure you, your father has shared nothing with me other than his concern for your safety," he added. "Although I'd love to hear your take on what happened to your neighbor."

"Let's leave Bridget to unpack," Bob said. "She's had a rough morning and doesn't need us making it any harder."

Rising to his feet, he ushered Paloma and Angelo back down the hall. Closing the door behind them, Bridget sat down next to Hank, pulling his warm body against her.

Worried voices drifted down the hall from the living room, and from the kitchen she heard Pixie's high-pitched bark followed by Ginny's girlish giggle.

Daphne had agreed to take the miniature Yorkie in for the time being. At least until Jacey's next of kin was notified and other arrangements were made.

For now, everything was up in the air.

Jacey's body was likely still on the riverbank of the Shenandoah as Opal Fitzgerald and her team examined the scene and the body in situ.

Once the M.E. was satisfied she'd gotten all the pictures, video, and evidence needed, Bridget knew the remains would be taken to the medical examiner's office for autopsy.

Parker will be notified. I doubt their divorce is even finalized, so he'll be considered Jacey's next of kin. He'll make the decisions about Pixie and the house and...

Frustration surged through Bridget at the thought of Jacey's arrogant ex-husband standing over her neighbor's dead body before callously deciding how to dispose of her belongings.

Getting to her feet, Bridget crossed to the door and quietly pulled it open. She needed to get out of the crowded house before she suffocated from the grief and the guilt.

She needed to do something to make amends to Jacey.

The least she could do was stand beside her and bear witness to what she'd suffered. If she went to the river, she might be able to identify her neighbor's body.

It's the least I can do for her now that she's gone.

* * *

Bridget and Hank drove along Landsend Road until they reached the turnoff for Shoreline Trail.

Following a narrow gravel road that skirted alongside the nature trail, they soon reached a grassy clearing next to a wide, slow-flowing river.

"That's the Shenandoah, Hank," Bridget said, bringing the Explorer to a slow-rolling stop. "The water out there flows up to the Potomac, and then down through D.C., and all the way out to the ocean. Isn't that something?"

Hank stared at her as if considering the question, then turned curious eyes toward a cluster of cars and people gathered further up the riverbank.

Following his gaze, Bridger was surprised to see Terrance Gage's shiny head in the crowd. Vic Santino stood beside him.

Bridget opened the door and climbed out of the SUV, allowing Hank to jump out behind her.

As they made their way over the uneven ground, Bridget scanned the riverbank ahead, spotting the medical examiner's white tent just beyond a slight bend.

"Bridget? What are you doing here?"

Santino was striding toward her, his eyes searching her face.

"Are you sure you want to-"

"I need to see Jacey," she said, not meeting his eyes as she continued walking. "I owe her that."

Falling into step beside her, he tried to take her arm, but she shook off his hand.

"What are you talking about, Bridget?' he asked. "You don't think this is somehow your fault, do you?"

"She was targeted because of me," Bridget insisted, heading straight toward the tent. "And now I need to do what I can to...to make this right."

But she knew that nothing she could do would ever fix what had happened. Nothing could bring back the dead, although sometimes they seemed to stay with you. Whether you wanted them to or not.

"Bridget?"

This time the voice belonged to Gage.

"You can't just go in there," he called out.

But Bridget had already flashed her badge and ducked under the crime scene tape, moving resolutely toward the tent.

As she approached the flap, Opal appeared.

"Bridget?"

Her eyes were wide in her round face.

"Honey, you shouldn't be here," she said, putting a hand on Bridget's arm. "You don't want to see this."

"No, it's not what I want," Bridget said. "But that doesn't really matter. It's the right thing to do."

Blocking Bridget's entry, Opal shook her head.

"You don't understand. There's been a mistake."

Bridget blinked.

"What mistake? What are you talking about?"

"The woman in there couldn't be your neighbor," Opal said quietly. "Not if she only went missing last night."

A rush of dizziness washed over Bridget.

"The woman we pulled out of the river has been in the water for several days."

Opal cleared her throat.

"If I had to guess, I'd say we've found Libby Palmer."

Her words hit Bridget like a bucket of ice water.

"Libby Palmer?" she said, trying to look over Opal's shoulder. "The Second Strangler killed Libby Palmer already? He dumped her body here?"

"We don't have confirmation it's her yet," Opal warned. "But based on my examination, I'd say it's highly likely."

She lowered her voice and leaned forward.

"Cause of death appears to be manual strangulation," she said. "The woman's arms and legs were wrapped in blue duct tape, and the ring finger on her left hand is missing."

Bridget nodded, struggling to rein in her emotions.

She was relieved that Jacey's body wasn't in the tent. But devastated that Libby Palmer had been killed. There would be no bringing her back to her mother. No second chance.

And the disciple must still have Jacey.

The thought sent a chill down Bridget's back.

We could find her body next.

CHAPTER THIRTY

Santino's eyes returned to Bridget Bishop's dark fall of chestnut hair as she spoke to Opal Fitzgerald outside the white medical examiner's tent. He was eager to know what she was saying to the M.E. but sensed his uninvited interference wouldn't be appreciated.

"What is Bridget doing here?"

Spinning around, Santino saw Charlie Day approaching.

The FBI agent charged past him toward Bridget and Opal, obviously less concerned than Santino had been about interrupting their private conversation.

Santino took the opportunity to step up behind Charlie and listen in as Bridget turned around, her face flushed and her blue eyes wide.

"What's going on?" Charlie demanded, looking first to Opal and then to Bridget. "You both look like you've seen a ghost."

Putting one hand on Bridget's elbow and one on Charlie's, Opal guided the women toward the side of the tent and out of earshot of the reporters and onlookers who had gathered.

Santino followed closely behind. He looked around to see Gage and Hale heading in their direction.

The two men joined the growing circle around Bridget.

"Opal says that the woman they found by the river wasn't Jacey Wallace," Bridget said bluntly. "It's Libby Palmer."

A surprised silence descended on the little group.

"Are you sure?" Charlie finally asked in Opal's direction.

"The body has been in the water at least forty-eight hours," Opal explained. "So, it couldn't be Bridget's neighbor."

Gage cleared his throat.

"And you're sure it's Libby Palmer?"

"She can't be sure until she gets a positive identification from next of kin," Bridget cut in. "But based on the missing person photo and the fact that Libby was abducted not far from here...it's her."

The frustration in her voice was palpable.

"The cause of death appears to be manual strangulation," she added. "And her left ring finger is missing. So, it looks like we were right about who took her. It's the Second Strangler."

"I'm sorry," Santino said. "I know how much you wanted to find Libby before it was too late."

Bridget met his eyes and held his gaze. Before she could reply, Charlie spoke up.

"I hate to be the one to state the obvious, but Jacey Wallace is still out there somewhere. Which means we've got to mobilize forces to find her," she said. "I plan on pulling together a search party and combing the area."

Hale nodded.

"So far, the Strangler has stayed close to Wisteria Falls,

and close to the river," he said. "I think we concentrate on searching along the Shenandoah first."

"And while we're coordinating the search, we'll have the lab analyze the evidence taken from the abduction site," Charlie added. "With the track marks and tape we found behind Jacy's house, and the blood on the fence, we have a lot to work with."

Reaching out a hand, Bridget gripped Charlie's arm.

"The Strangler didn't stick to Crast's M.O. this time. He killed Libby Palmer *before* he'd abducted Jacey," she said, her voice somber. "I'm thinking he made mistakes and left evidence behind because he was in a panic to take someone as soon as possible."

She looked at the other faces around her.

"He's escalating. Which means we don't have much time to find Jacey before he kills her, too."

Charlie nodded.

"We'll do everything we can, I promise you that."

She started to walk away, but Gage stopped her.

"One more thing," he said. "The lab confirmed DNA on the duct tape collected from the Brooke Nelson scene is a match to Crast or someone in his direct paternal line. Which means his son or his father could have handled the tape."

Santino noted Bridget's frown, although neither Charlie nor Hale seemed surprised.

"I suggest you get a warrant for Odell Crast's farm as soon as possible," Gage added. "If you tell the judge that DNA on the tape could belong to Odell, it should do the trick."

Watching Charlie and Hale disappear back into the crowd,

Santino felt a buzz in his pocket.

His pulse picked up as he saw the text.

Judge Bingham will see you this afternoon regarding the emergency petition on the Colby Crast records. Don't be late.

Checking his watch, Santino turned to Gage.

"I've got to get to the federal courthouse by four."

"What's the rush?" Gage asked. "Is this about Colby Crast?"

Santino nodded, already backing toward Gage's Navigator.

"The judge has agreed to see me about the petition to unseal the adoption records," Santino confirmed. "With any luck, we'll know where Crast's son is by tonight."

* * *

Santino's head was reeling as he jogged down the courthouse steps. He'd made it into downtown D.C. in record time and had dashed into the judge's chambers with a few minutes to spare.

Judge Bingham had been in a generous mood, and Santino suspected the jurist had watched enough prime time television dramas to be properly impressed by the DNA profile match the FBI lab had uncovered.

Armed with his approved petition in hand, Santino had ducked into the clerk's office just before closing, leaving with a thin file of photocopied records.

He'd scanned through enough of the records and notes to send him racing toward the Metro. He needed to get back to Arlington and pick up his truck.

Taking a seat on the train, he flipped through the documents in the file again, reading through a condensed version of Colby Crast's short but eventful life history, as documented by the U.S. legal system.

The first document in the folder was Colby's birth certificate. It listed Ernest Crast as Colby's father and eighteen-year-old Norma Jenkins as his mother.

The next document was a petition by child protective services to remove five-year-old Colby from his father's custody due to Ernest Crast's arrest and indictment on multiple first-degree murder charges.

The petition referred to Crast's late wife but didn't mention Norma Jenkins by name or explain how she'd died.

A court order placing Colby in Odell Crast's care followed. His new address was listed on Old Mill Highway.

After that Santino read through a printout from the Witness Protection Services database which documented various stages of review and approval before Colby was accepted into the witness protection program.

The reason given for his placement in the program was the risk of retaliation and harassment as a result of his father's conviction of multiple felony homicides.

Following the printout was a certificate showing Colby Crast's legal adoption by the Darnell family of Orlando, Florida when he was eight years old.

Apparently, he'd lived happily in Orlando for over a decade as Colby Darnell before applying to Georgetown University. A copy of his acceptance letter was the final document in the file.

Santino had already done the mental calculation. Colby Crast had returned to the D.C. area before Brooke Nelson had been abducted. And according to the school's registrar, he was currently living in a dorm which was only a fifteen-minute drive from the safehouse where Althea was staying.

As he made his way into his apartment, Santino checked his Glock, then retrieved more ammunition from his safe.

If he was going to seek out a serial killer's son, he would need to be ready for all possibilities.

He considered calling Gage and asking the BAU agent to go with him to the dorm. It could be good to have a profiler with him to try to determine if Colby was being honest.

But in the end, Santino decided it would be best to go on his own. A deputy marshal in jeans and a casual jacket making a few inquiries was less likely to draw attention than a federal agent in a fancy suit and tie.

He figured he'd made the right call when no one seemed to notice him walking into the dorm and heading up the stairs to room 211.

The door was open, so Santino stuck his head inside.

A young man with shaggy, strawberry blonde hair and a plain, broad face looked up.

"Colby Darnell?"

The man frowned but nodded.

"Yep, I'm Colby. Who are you?"

"I'm Deputy Vic Santino with the U.S. Marshals Service," he said. "And I'd like to ask you a few questions about your father."

"My father?" Colby asked suspiciously. "He's in Orlando.

What do you want with him?"

As Colby stood, Santino saw that the young man was tall. Taller than his own six-foot frame by several inches. And Colby's shoulders and arms were thick with muscles as if he worked out often.

He was definitely old enough and strong enough to overpower and strangle the women who'd been attacked by the Second Strangler.

"Not your adopted father," Santino replied, keeping his voice low. "I'm talking about-"

Colby put up a hand and strode forward.

Santino was reaching for his gun when he realized that Colby was only closing the door.

"No one around here knows anything about my background, or my biological father," Colby said, sounding scared. "And I don't want them to know."

Watching a range of emotions play over the young man's coarse face, Santino felt the stirrings of sympathy.

From what he'd read in Colby's file, Crast's son had escaped a life straight out of a Dickensian nightmare. But eventually, he'd found a haven with a normal, average family and was going to one of the best colleges in the country.

He wouldn't appreciate a U.S. Marshal showing up and threatening all that. But then, why move so close to the scene of Crast's crimes in the first place if you were trying to hide your past?

"I figured the FBI would come by here eventually," Colby said. "After the articles in the paper said there was evidence linking the abductions to the Shenandoah Valley Strangler murders, I knew it would just be a matter of time before someone might think I was involved."

"And are you involved?" Santino asked, still primed to reach for his weapon if needed. "Do you know who abducted and killed Brooke Nelson and Libby Palmer?"

A worried gleam entered Colby's eyes.

"Libby Palmer is dead?" he asked. "Did they find her body?"

Santino studied Colby's face, trying to read his emotions. He wasn't sure what he was seeing. Worry? Or was it guilt?

"When were you last in Wisteria Falls?" Santino asked. "When was the last time you went home?"

The question appeared to anger Colby. His neck turned red, and then the flush of color began working its way upward.

"My home is in Orlando with my new family," he said, raising his voice. "Ernest Crast is dead, and so is my connection to Wisteria Falls. If I never go back there again it'll be too soon."

Hearing a threat of tears in the young man's voice, Santino hesitated, giving him a chance to regain his composure.

"I'm not here to cause trouble," Santino said, keeping his eyes on Colby's hands. "But two women have died, and I'm sure you'll soon see in the papers that another woman has been abducted."

A stricken look settled over Colby's face. His knees gave way, and he sank heavily onto the bed.

"He's taken another woman?" he muttered numbly.

"Yes, and we need to find her before he kills her, too."

Colby looked up at Santino with the same small, close-set

eyes he'd seen in Ernest Crast's mugshot.

But there was no fire of hate or rage in Colby's eyes.

Instead, Santino saw fear and sadness.

A terrible sadness that had been a decade in the making.

"Do you know who is doing this?" Santino asked. "If there's anything you can tell me. If you or your grandfather–"

The mention of Odell Crast provoked an instant reaction.

Colby shot off the bed, his broad face creasing into a mask of anguish.

"I don't know anything about that old man," he said, turning away from Santino. "I don't want to know anything about him. He's as much of a monster as my father ever was."

"I can't begin to understand everything you've been through, Colby. But I'm going to need you to talk to the agents working on the case," Santino said, keeping his voice calm. "They need to know anything and everything you can remember about your father that might help us figure out who's abducting these women."

When Colby didn't turn around or respond, he tried again.

"I can drive you over there now if you'd like."

Colby shook his head.

"I have class now," he said, wiping at his eyes with a big hand. "But maybe after...if you can give me the address."

Santino hesitated, then nodded.

He wasn't sure Colby was being completely honest, but he didn't think the young man was the psychotic killer who'd abducted Jacey Wallace only the night before.

There was no evidence linking him to any crime other than the DNA he carried in his blood. Another troublesome legacy his father had passed down to him.

At this point, he had no reason to doubt that Colby was being sincere. Of course, it wouldn't hurt to ask for surveillance on the young man, just to be sure.

Leaving his card and the address of the FBI's Washington field office with Colby, Santino walked back to where he'd parked the Chevy against the curb.

He groaned as he saw the parking ticket, then stuck it in his pocket as he climbed into the driver's seat and merged back into traffic heading toward Arlington.

Althea Helmont was getting antsy. He'd stop by and see her on the way home. He need to make sure she stayed safely tucked away. At least until the Second Strangler was found.

CHAPTER THIRTY-ONE

A lively fire bathed the sumptuous living room in a soft, golden glow as Althea Helmont huddled miserably on the plush leather sofa. She'd spent another day in isolated luxury and had hated every minute of it.

Hearing a soft knock at the front door, she jumped up just as a key turned in the lock.

"When am I getting out of here?" she demanded before Santino could offer up a greeting. "I want my phone back. I want to talk to Meg and Richie. I need to know they're okay."

She fell silent as Santino stepped into the light. His grim expression didn't bode well.

"What's happened?" she asked, watching with wary eyes as he crossed the room and flipped on the television.

Navigating to a local news channel, he stepped back so that Althea could see the screen.

The headline turned Althea's blood cold.

Body of Second Strangler Victim Found in Shenandoah River.

A doleful reporter stood next to a wide river. She faced the camera at an angle, allowing the viewers to see the police cars, crime scene tape, and medical examiner's tent in the background behind her.

"Authorities have reason to believe the latest homicide may be related to the abduction and murder of Brooke Nelson, and the disappearance of Libby Palmer," the reporter said into a handheld microphone. "Identity of the victim is being withheld pending notification to next of kin."

Santino turned to her and sighed.

"I wanted you to see why you can't leave this house. Not yet," he said. "I don't want you to end up in that river next."

Anger surged through her.

"So, this maniac gets to run around freely while I'm locked away?" she fumed. "Do you or the FBI even have any leads, yet? Do you know who could be doing this?"

Santino hesitated, as if unsure how much to tell her.

"Don't you dare hold back information from me," she cried out. "I have a right to know what's going on. If I feel like I'm being stone-walled, I'll walk out of here right now."

Turning toward the window, Althea wondered if she had the nerve to make good on her threat.

Is the Second Strangler waiting for me out there? Hoping I'll slip up and show my face? Or is he miles away in Wisteria Falls looking for a new victim right now?

She let her shoulders drop and turned back to face Santino.

"We're doing everything we can to catch this guy," he assured her before she could say anything else. "We've been interviewing everyone Crast knew, analyzing DNA evidence, organizing search parties. We won't leave a stone unturned. I promise you that."

As she listened to him talking, she noticed a piece of paper had fallen out of his pocket.

Bending over, she picked it up.

She was about to hand it to him when she realized what it was. It was a parking ticket.

The violation location printed on the ticket caught her eye.

"What were you doing outside the dorms in Georgetown?" she asked with a frown. "Were you interviewing Meg and Richie?"

Her heart began to hammer in her chest.

"They don't know what Crast did to me," she said, feeling hot tears of rage build up behind her eyes. "I couldn't stand for them to know."

"It's okay," Santino said, stepping forward to put a comforting hand on her arm. "It'll all be okay."

Wrenching her arm away, she stepped back to glare at him.

"No, it's not okay!" she shouted. "What he did to me wasn't *okay*. What I've suffered every day since isn't *okay!*"

Whirling around, she crossed to the fireplace, staring into the flames with unseeing eyes.

"You have no idea what it's like. To be locked up in darkness. To be held prisoner by a madman."

Her voice broke, and a sob escaped.

"You couldn't possibly understand how it feels to fight to stay alive when all you want is to die so that the pain will end."

When she spoke again, her voice was hard. Brittle with pain. But she was once again in control.

"Now, what were you doing in Georgetown?"

The question filled the room and Althea waited, hoping Santino would answer truthfully.

"I was interviewing Ernest Crast's son," he admitted. "He's a young man now. A student at the school."

A jolt of panic ran down Althea's body at his words.

"Colby Crast is a student at Georgetown?" she said in disbelief. "He's going to the same school as Meg and Richie?"

"Well, he's been living under witness protection," Santino explained. "And he had nothing to do with his father's crimes, of course. He was a child. As much a victim as anyone else Crast hurt and abused."

But Althea wasn't listening. Her mind was working through the facts. Turning over the risks and possibilities.

Did Colby Crast know who Meg and Richie were? Had he started attending the school to be close to them? To seek some sort of revenge on the woman who'd testified against his father and sent him to the death chamber?

"He's not a child anymore," Althea said aloud, although she was talking more to herself than to Santino. "He's old enough to do harm. He's old enough to seek revenge."

Santino shook his head.

"I talked to Colby," he said, looking concerned. "I could see right away that he's not like his father. He's been raised by a good family, and now he appears to be a good student. He doesn't seem to pose a threat to you or your children."

When she didn't respond, he sighed.

"Look, I'm going to put surveillance on him just to be sure," he said. "Just until we catch the Second Strangler."

Althea cocked her head.

"Surveillance? When?"

The question seemed to throw Santino.

"I'm not sure how quickly I can get it arranged," he admitted. "Likely I can have someone watching him as early as tomorrow."

He hesitated, then cleared his throat.

"Of course, the other option is to have your children come stay with you here."

"No!" she spit out as fury filled her. "I refuse to have my children hide away while Crast's kid gets to walk free."

Clenching her hands into fists, she raised them in the air.

"When Crast took me, I made a vow to escape. For my children's sake," she said, her voice bitter with the memory. "I did what I had to do, and when the time came, I ran. I made it back to them. I didn't go through all that so that they could live in fear."

Santino stared at her with cautious eyes, as if he expected her to lunge at him at any minute.

Good. Let him be afraid. I'm tired of being the prey. It's about time I become the hunter.

She lowered her fists and unclenched her hands, deciding it may be best to use stealth instead of raw strength.

"I'm sorry if I reacted badly," she said, dropping her eyes. "But I'm worried for my children."

"Of course," Santino replied. "And I'll do everything in my power to make sure you and your children are protected."

After she closed the door behind Santino, Althea leaned her back against it, trying to think.

The fact that Colby Crast was at the same school as her son and daughter, and that he had moved back to the area just before the killings began, couldn't be a coincidence.

She was done sitting around waiting for Crast's threat to come true. Done hiding away.

Hurrying toward the bedroom, she picked up her purse.

Ripping out the custom-made lining along the bottom without hesitation, she retrieved the compact, lightweight Ruger she had always kept as a back-up to her bigger Glock.

She didn't have to check the chamber, already confident that it was loaded and ready to go.

After her escape from Crast, Althea had quickly purchased a variety of weapons for self-defense and had sought out expert training on the care, handling, and use of her multiple guns.

She'd been preparing for this day for years, and now that it had come, she was ready.

All she had to do was wait for the guard outside to take a bathroom break and she could slip past him.

Of course, it wouldn't take long for him to raise the alarm, but by then, she'd be halfway to Georgetown.

CHAPTER THIRTY-TWO

B ridget walked along the river's edge, looking down at the rushes and sedges waving over the water. A light breeze lifted her hair and fluttered Hank's floppy ears as he walked beside her with muddy paws.

Zipping up her lightweight jacket, she listened to the muted sound of calling voices in the distance and the gentle buzz of insects on the water's shimmering surface.

If she hadn't been searching for her missing neighbor's body, she thought she might enjoy the peaceful surroundings.

As it was, her feet were getting wet and sore, and the setting sun was taking the warmth of the day with it as it sank deeper and deeper into the Shenandoah River.

"Over here, Bridget!"

Charlie Day stood fifty yards up the riverbank, her golden blonde hair set alight by the setting sun.

The FBI agent waved her arms as if Bridget might not be able to see her, motioning for her to join the rest of the search party as they approached a small gathering of trees ahead.

Looking past Charlie, Bridget saw Cecil Fitzgerald plodding down the riverbank toward the group. She winced when she saw that Harry Kemp was with him.

She didn't need another run-in with her father's ex-partner. If they were going to find Jacey, they'd need all available resources working together.

They didn't need the WFPD detective creating tension with his pointless power struggles and combativeness.

Walking up the bank toward Charlie, Bridget noticed a group of reporters standing behind the crime scene tape which marked off the restricted search area.

She surreptitiously scanned the group and was relieved not to see Angelo Molina in the crowd.

As her eyes moved on to the throng of onlookers who'd congregated behind the reporters, she was surprised to see a familiar face.

Felix Arnett stood quietly at the edge of the crowd. His dark hair framed an ashen face, his translucent skin appeared ghost-like in the waning light.

Lifting a hand in greeting, she caught his eye and waved, but he only stared at her for a long beat, then turned and disappeared back into the crowd.

What is Felix doing out here anyway?

The question hovered in her mind unanswered as she watched the medical examiner's van bump over the grass toward the Shoreline nature trail.

Opal must have completed her examination of Libby's body. The next step would be the medical examiner's office and Opal's cold, metal table.

As the van reached the gravel road that ran parallel to the nature trail, a voice called out. The van jerked to a stop.

All eyes turned toward a man in a yellow jacket standing by the river. He raised his hand and yelled again.

"I've found something!" he called. "It's a body."

Charlie was the first to make a dash toward the man, followed by Hale and the Cecil, who didn't quite reach the running stage but made a valiant effort.

Bridget and Hank shot across the grassy riverbank, reaching the man in the yellow jacket just as Charlie arrived out of breath.

"Down there," the man pointed, his voice high-pitched and breathless. "Just at the edge of the river grass there."

Catching sight of a long black object twisting in the water, Bridget thought at first she was seeing a snake.

She cried out in shock when she realized she was looking at Jacey Wallace's long black braid.

It was attached to a body half-in and half-out of the river.

Without thinking, Bridget plunged into the water, her shoes sinking into the muck, the water quickly rising up to her knees.

She grabbed a limp arm floating on the surface. Remnants of blue duct tape clung to it.

"Help me get her out!" she screamed back at the people on shore as Hank began to bark in distress.

Suddenly Charlie and Hale were beside her.

Charlie lifted Jacey's other arm while Hale grabbed her ankles. Within seconds that had her laid out on the riverbank.

Instinctively checking for a pulse, even as she told herself it was already too late, Bridget dropped her head to hide her welling eyes.

As she started to pull her hand away, she felt a faint, erratic pulse under her fingers.

"She's got a pulse!"

The words echoed through the dusky air, prompting a gasp and then a cheer to roll through the crowd behind them.

Opal appeared as if by magic, her face serious but calm as she checked Jacey's vital signs, then wrapped a white sheet around her motionless body, careful not to cover her face.

"Call an ambulance!" Opal cried out, and then hands were helping Bridget to her feet.

She looked around to see Cecil beside her, his eyes as wide and disbelieving as her own.

"She must have gotten away," Bridget managed to say, though her throat was sore from yelling. "She must have hidden from him in the rushes."

"And now maybe we'll have a witness," Cecil added with a grim nod. "Maybe now we'll find out who this Second Strangler is after all."

* * *

Red and white flashing lights lit up the dark riverbank as the stretcher was loaded into the ambulance and the doors slammed shut.

Watching as the lights faded into the night, Bridget looked down at her filthy, sodden shoes and sighed.

She'd never been so relieved and worried at the same time.

Although Jacey Wallace was still alive, and the paramedics had seemed hopeful she would survive her ordeal, Bridget knew there would likely be another abduction soon.

"Now that Libby is dead and Jacey has escaped, the disciple is all alone. He'll be desperate to take another woman," she warned Charlie, who was standing beside her looking shell-shocked in her mud-splattered suit. "He could try something as soon as tonight."

"We could release a special bulletin to the public," Charlie suggested in a weary voice.

Although Jacey had been found and whisked away to the hospital, the FBI response team was just getting started with their job of examining the scene and collecting crucial evidence.

It was going to be a late night, and the conditions around the river at night would make things difficult.

"If Jacey comes around, we might even be able to get a description out with the bulletin," Bridget added, trying to sound hopeful.

But as Charlie walked away, Bridget couldn't help feeling as if she were in the middle of a terrible nightmare.

Crast's disciple, the man terrorizing the community as the Second Strangler, was still out there. And most likely, he was looking for her. Why else would he have gone to Jacey's house?

This isn't a nightmare. It's real...but you'll find him.

The little voice had been silent all day, but now it spoke up loud and clear. It even sounded mad.

Of course, she knew the voice that sounded so much like her mother was just a figment of her imagination. Didn't she?

Or is it a delusion? Am I psychotic like Crast and his disciple?

Psychosis wasn't always obvious. Not always accompanied by ranting and raving like in the movies.

Some people suffered psychosis without anyone noticing much more than a bit of unusual behavior.

And usually, the people suffering psychosis were so caught up in their delusions, so totally convinced in the world their mind had created, that they never suspect it wasn't real.

Not until things begin to unravel.

Bridget feared that once the disciple's delusions were challenged, he would become even more dangerous. He could try to take down everyone around him.

Her mind was still whirring with the possibilities as she walked back toward the road.

She wished she could go home and take a warm shower. She'd love to change into clean dry clothes and order a pizza. Maybe have a glass of red wine.

The thought of wine brought thoughts of Vic Santino with it. Unfortunately, Santino wasn't around for a repeat of the other night, and her house was off-limits for the time being anyway.

She'd have to go back to her father's house and face his questions. Face his wife and her nephew.

Looking around for her Explorer, Bridget couldn't see it anywhere, then remembered she'd lent it out to the search effort. A group of volunteers had likely taken it to look further down the river. Who knew when they would be back?

"Your father's sick with worry, you know."

Bridget turned to see Harry Kemp behind her.

"He asked me to check on you," Kemp added. "I've already called and let him know you're here and you're safe."

Guilt congealed in Bridget's chest as she pictured her father's worried, confused eyes.

"I should have told him where I was going when I left," she said in a grudging voice.

Knowing she was acting like the kid she'd been when she'd first met Kemp, she forced herself to meet his eyes.

"Thanks for letting my dad know."

Kemp grunted in response, then pointed to his unmarked cruiser with one thick finger.

"You want a ride home?" he asked. "I'm heading that way."

Not wanting to spend any more time with the surly detective than was absolutely necessary, Bridget started to shake her head. But the image of her father returned.

She shouldn't keep him wondering and worrying.

Best to bite the bullet and get back to the house.

"Okay," she agreed, trying to keep the reluctance out of her voice. "I'd appreciate that."

As she climbed into the detective's car, she had to move a stack of file folders off the front seat in order to sit down.

She didn't see Kemp's phone resting on top of the stack.

Grabbing for it as it tumbled toward the floor, she picked it up and held it while he climbed into the driver's seat and clicked on his seatbelt.

Her eyes widened as she saw the missed text message from Angelo Molina on the display.

Wow, found alive, huh? Any blue duct tape on this one?

Bridget's eyes narrowed as Kemp plucked the phone from her cold, muddy fingers and dropped it into his pocket.

Before she could ask what the text was supposed to mean, Kemp started the engine and pulled the cruiser onto Landsend Road.

CHAPTER THIRTY-THREE

Vic Santino was in his Chevy pickup heading toward the interstate when he got the call that Althea Helmont was gone. Taking the next exit, he circled back to Arlington, cursing himself for telling Althea about Colby Crast, suspecting he knew where she must be headed.

Skidding to a stop outside the swanky safehouse, he jumped out of the Chevy and ran inside, not bothering to knock.

The house was exactly as he remembered, only everything Althea had brought with her was missing.

Even the toothbrush and toothpaste he'd picked up for her at the drugstore down the road were gone.

Dropping onto the plush sofa in front of the fireplace, he closed his eyes and tried to think.

She has no money and no way of knowing exactly where Colby is staying. She doesn't even know his new name.

Or did she?

He remembered telling Althea that Colby had been adopted by a family in Florida, but had he told her their last name? Would she know to look for Colby Darnell?

Pulling his phone out of his back pocket, he saw the

parking ticket fall again to the floor.

He grabbed it up and stared at it, then groaned.

The location of the parking violation was clearly written across the ticket, and Althea had seen it.

She knows where to go to find Colby. She's already on the way.

Jumping up from the sofa, he ran down to the Chevy and jumped in, not sure what she would do when she found Crast's son but knowing whatever she had planned, couldn't be good.

Santino made it back to Georgetown in record time, nosing the pickup into the same spot he'd parked in the previous time, not caring about the possibility of a second ticket.

Taking the stairs two at a time, he reached the second floor and ran down the corridor, skidding to a stop outside room 211.

He stuck his head inside, not sure who or what he was expecting to see but saw only a thin young man with curly black hair and wire-framed glasses.

"Where's Colby Crast?" he demanded.

"Crast?" the boy said with a frown. "I only know Colby Darnell. You sure you got the right dorm?"

Santino shook his head.

"No, you're right," He agreed. "I'm looking for Colby *Darnell*. Are you his roommate?"

"Yeah, I'm Luke Frazier. Who are you?"

Santino produced his badge.

"I'm Deputy Marshal Vic Santino," he said, not liking Luke's tone. "You know where Colby is now?"

The young man's eyes widened behind his glasses.

"No, but he ran out of here like a bat out of hell when I told him that lady had come here looking for him."

"That lady?" Santino asked. "What did the lady want?"

Shrugging his shoulders, Luke shifted on the bed as if he was tired of the conversation.

"I guess she wanted to see Colby," he said dismissively. "She was pretty worked up, so I told her that he'd gone over to the cafeteria. I wasn't sure he had, but that got rid of her."

"And then Colby came back?"

Luke nodded.

"When I told him some lady was looking for him, and that she'd used the wrong last name, he went batshit."

"But he didn't say where he was going?" Santino prodded, wishing he could shake the information out of the insolent young man. "You have no idea where he could be?"

Luke flashed a look at Santino's badge, then hesitated.

"He asked me not to say anything..."

Santino leaned forward to stick his face directly in front of Luke. They were so close they were almost touching.

"Where did Colby go?" he asked slowly. "Tell me now, or I'll drag you in for obstruction of justice."

"He said he was...going home," Luke stammered. "He said he wanted to put things right."

The words momentarily silenced Santino.

"Home, as in, home to Orlando?"

"That's what I asked," Luke admitted. "I told him he wasn't likely to find a flight to Orlando at this time of night, but he said he wasn't going back to Florida. He said his real home was in Wisteria Falls."

Santino nodded grimly.

"What else did he say, Luke?"

"I don't remember."

His voice had faded into a whine.

"Colby was upset. He wasn't making a lot of sense. But he did say something about a *disciple*. I never knew he was religious or anything but..."

Unable to stop himself, Santino banged a hand down hard on the small desk beside the bed, sending the desk lamp tottering toward the edge.

"What did Colby say about the disciple?" he demanded.

Leaning back in his chair as far as he could go, Luke tried to distance himself from Santino.

"He said the disciple knew where the truth was buried, or something like that. I wasn't really listening."

A stone settled into Santino's chest as he turned away.

"I told you it didn't make sense," Luke called after him in a sullen tone.

But Santino was already walking toward the door.

Colby Crast knew about the disciple. Maybe he even *was* the disciple. Maybe he was willing to act out his father's threat to finish what he'd started with Althea Helmont.

Crast's son most likely knew a great deal more than he'd admitted during their brief conversation that afternoon.

Santino's stomach turned. He'd been taken in by Colby's innocent routine. The young man had lied to give himself time to slip away, and now he and Althea Helmont were looking for each other.

They were heading for a collision that would surely prove

deadly for one of them.

Santino needed to get back to Wisteria Falls right away.

Thinking of the town instantly brought thoughts of Bridget.

If Colby is headed to Wisteria Falls, she could be in danger, too.

Digging in his pocket, Santino tapped on Bridget's number.

He listened to the phone ring with growing concern.

When the phone rolled to voicemail, he forced his voice to remain calm and collected.

"Please call me back, Bridget. It's urgent. Colby Crast was in D.C. and now he's most likely heading for Wisteria Falls."

Not sure how to end the message, he exhaled.

"Just please be careful, Bridget. I'm on my way."

CHAPTER THIRTY-FOUR

Terrance Gage sank into the chair behind his desk and turned to his computer. He'd been so focused on the Second Strangler task force, and so preoccupied with his imploding relationship with Vivian Burke, that he hadn't had a chance to check his emails or voicemails for several days.

He winced as he opened his overflowing inbox, then decided he'd rather start with voicemail.

Picking up his phone, he started going through the messages with brutal efficiency, deleting non-urgent or unwanted voicemails with a firm tap of one long finger.

When he heard Anne's voice in his ear, he hesitated, his finger hovering over the delete option.

"Hey big brother, I know you've been avoiding me, but I wanted to remind you about Sarge's appointment. Don't you dare forget again or there will be-"

Tapping on the display, he deleted the message, then moved on to the next. Several messages later, he heard Anne's voice again. This time she sounded distinctly unhappy.

"I can't believe you missed the vet appointment after I called and

reminded you twice. I've never met a more inconsiderate, selfish-"

Again, he deleted the message, his blood beginning to boil at his sister's single-minded focus and unfair accusations.

"I've spent the last twenty years trying to keep the public safe," he muttered into the empty room. "How the hell do you figure that's inconsiderate and selfish?"

"You talking to yourself again?" Vivian asked, suddenly standing at the open door. "I know your eyes have been going, but perhaps your mental faculties are on the decline as well."

She didn't soften the words with a smile as she dropped a brown paper bag on his desk.

"That's the tie you forgot at my house last week."

He opened the bag and peered inside.

"I didn't *forget* this," he protested. "I couldn't find it when I was rushing out after you said your husband was on the way."

Acting as if he hadn't spoken, Vivian crossed her arms over her chest and cocked her head.

"The lab found fingerprint evidence on several of the letters Deputy Santino submitted for testing," she said without enthusiasm. "It looks like they were handled by someone whose prints were in IAFIS."

"You mean the letters Deputy Santino got from the WPP archives? Including the letter Ernest Crast intended to send to Althea Helmont before his execution?"

Vivian nodded.

"Okay, you now have my full attention," Gage said, leaning forward in his chair. "Whose prints are on the letters?"

"Fingerprints on the envelope belong to an employee of the state prison system," she said, pausing for effect. "A psychologist over at the prison in Waverly. A man named George Sommerville."

She slapped a folder on the desk in front of him.

"I took the liberty of reading through his file," she said. "It looks like he started working at the prison back when Crast was on death row, and he still works there now."

"I know Dr. Sommerville."

Gage pictured the prison psychologist's blonde hair and cold blue eyes. The man was in his mid-thirties now, maybe older.

"Could Sommerville have written the letters?" Gage wondered aloud. "Or was he just a courier?"

Then another possibility slammed into him.

Or could he be the disciple? The one who's supposed to be delivering Crast's message to the world.

It didn't seem possible. But whoever had killed Brooke Nelson and Libby Palmer knew Crast's M.O. in detail and had gained access to his supplies.

Could Sommerville have gained Crast's trust?

Could he have used Crast's psychosis against him to plant the delusion of the disciple in his mind?

Was Sommerville some sort of sick psychopath who was getting his kicks by reenacting Crast's crimes?

Flipping through the file Vivian had prepared, Gage saw that Sommerville had worked at the prison during the same time frame Bridget had conducted her research on Crast.

"I've got to call Bridget and see if she thinks Dr. Somerville could be the Second Strangler," he said, picking up his phone.

Ignoring Vivian's annoyed huff, he waited for Bridget to pick up, then ended the call when it rolled to voicemail.

"I need to talk to my SAC," he said, looking pointedly at the door. "I need to see if I can bring this Sommerville guy in for questioning without tipping off someone at the prison first."

Shaking her head in disgust, Vivian watched him head for the door. She held out a hand, barring him from passing.

"That's all the thanks I get?" she said. "I work all weekend to get your task force the evidence you need and all you can do is call Bridget Bishop to ask for advice?"

"Move out my way, Vivian."

Once again, she pretended not to hear him.

"What is it about Bridget that gets you so hot and bothered, Gage? She quit the BAU and left your ass behind, but you still can't get over her, can you?"

"It isn't like that, and you know it, Vivian," he snapped. "Unlike you and I, Bridget actually has a moral compass. She's out there at a crime scene trying to save lives while you're standing here trying to malign her due to petty jealousy."

She narrowed her green eyes in outrage, but he spoke again before she could reply.

"Here's what's going to happen," Gage said quietly. "I'm going to go see my SAC, and you're going to leave my office. And we will pretend our misguided relationship, and this conversation never happened."

Ducking under Vivian's arm, Gage walked down the hall and turned the corner without looking back.

* * *

Gage was relieved to see that Vivian was gone by the time he returned from the SAC's office. Taking a seat behind his desk, he reached for his phone, checking to see if Bridget had called him back.

No new messages. No missed calls.

He was tempted to try her number again when his desk phone rang.

"I've got Warden Pickering on the phone for you," a nasal voice said. "I'll put him through."

Gage held the phone to his ear.

"I was just walking out to my car to go home, Agent Gage," the warden said. "I'm assuming this is an emergency?"

"It might be," Gage said. "It's about an employee of yours. George Sommerville. It seems his fingerprints were on a letter Ernest Crast wrote to a victim. We need to know how they got there."

A door slammed shut on the other end of the call and Gage heard the sound of a seatbelt clicking into place.

"You really think Sommerville could have something to do with the Second Strangler murders?" Pickering asked. "I just saw the news. Another woman dead and a third on her way to the hospital. It sounds like a real bloodbath out there."

"Which is why we need to bring Sommerville in for questioning tonight," Gage said. "My SAC wanted me to give you the courtesy of a call before we picked him up."

Pickering grunted.

"Sommerville's a cold fish but he's no serial killer," he said. "But it's no skin off my back if you want to talk to him. I certainly won't stand in your way."

"Good," Gage said, glad Pickering hadn't thrown a wrench in his plans. "I'll update you if anything comes of it."

Ending the call, he again picked up his cell phone and stared at the little display. Something was bothering him.

Suddenly he realized what it was.

The message icon no longer showed that he had waiting messages, just as the phone icon showed no voicemails.

Scrolling to the missed calls list, he frowned.

The list was gone, as was his list of text messages.

His phone had been cleared.

Gage pictured Vivian's angry green eyes and sighed.

Petty jealousy, and now petty revenge.

Reaching for his laptop bag, Gage pulled out his iPad and navigated to the messages list, which mirrored his phone.

He frowned as he saw a missed text message from Vic Santino. It looked like the message had come in around the same time Vivian had been in his office.

Once he'd read it, Gage had no doubt she'd seen the message and had deleted it out of spite.

Althea Helmont is missing. Colby Crast is heading for Wisteria Falls. Find Bridget and warn her while I track down Colby. Must assume he's armed and dangerous.

Gage stared at the phone, trying to process the information, then jumped to his feet and headed toward his car.

It would take an hour or more to get to Wisteria Falls.

He just hoped he'd make it in time.

CHAPTER THIRTY-FIVE

Bridget eyed Harry Kemp from the passenger's seat as he drove the unmarked cruiser toward Maplewood Drive. She was suddenly glad she'd accepted the detective's offer of a ride back to her father's house since now she knew the true source behind Angelo's in-depth articles on the Second Strangler investigation.

"Was he paying you?" she asked, although she doubted a struggling reporter could pull together enough cash to offer a bribe to the police. "Or is there some kind of bartering going on? What's Angelo supplying you with? Is he an informant?"

Kemp barked out an ugly laugh, causing Hank to jump nervously in the back seat.

"This is Wisteria Falls, not D.C.," he said. "We don't need informants. Anything I told Angelo Molina was in the best interest of the public, who had a right to know what's going on around here."

"That really isn't your decision to make though, is it?" Bridget asked. "Sneaking around behind the back of Chief Fitzgerald and the FBI task force isn't the way to do it. You could risk lives by giving out too much information."

Aiming a disdainful glare at Bridget, Kemp shook his head.

"You're going to sit there and judge *me* after the way you've treated your own father?"

The animosity she heard in his voice shocked Bridget.

"Why did you think he had his stroke in the first place?" he asked. "You have no idea how stressed out he was over your antics with Ernst Crast. I mean, you really had to go witness that scumbag's execution? After everything your father and I went through to get him off the streets?"

Kemp was practically spitting with rage.

"And then getting hooked up with the FBI and the BAU on the Backwoods Butcher case? Your father couldn't sleep for weeks worrying about you."

Steering the car around a sharp curve, Kemp momentarily lost control of the wheel. For a second Bridget thought they were going to careen into oncoming traffic.

Then he wrenched the car back into its lane. Looking in his rearview mirror, he slowed and pulled the cruiser onto the shoulder of the road.

"What do you think you're doing?" Bridget asked, still reeling from the accusations he'd hurled at her.

"I'm doing what I should have done a long time ago," he said. "I'm giving you a piece of my mind."

Bridget glanced back to check on Hank, then raised her eyes defiantly to Kemp.

"Okay, I get it," she said. "You blame me for Dad's stroke. You think I've been a terrible daughter. Now take me home."

"Oh, it's not just your father you've hurt," Kemp said. "You brought Ernest Crast's evil back here to Wisteria Falls."

He reached for the pack of cigarettes on the dashboard.

"Your little research project put a big fat target on this town," he continued, tapping out a cigarette and sticking it between his yellow teeth. "The wacko who's killing women around here likely decided to follow in the Shenandoah Valley Strangler's footsteps because you made Crast's crimes front-page news for years after he'd been caught."

Lighting the cigarette, Kemp took a long drag, then blew a puff of smoke toward the open window.

"You turned a serial killer into a fucking celebrity."

Bridget reached for the handle, tired of listening to Kemp's tirade, ready to walk the rest of the way to her father's place.

Then she looked back at Hank.

Could she get out of the car and open the back door to get the dog before Kemp could react? What if he tried to drive off? Would the detective do something foolish in his rage?

"And then your interference in the Felix Arnett case…"

Kemp shook his big head in disgust.

"You couldn't just leave well enough alone, could you?" he demanded. "You had to ask Cecil to call in the FBI, for fuck's sake. I mean, why would we need the feds poking around on a local homicide which was no more than a domestic dispute?"

"I didn't interfere in the Felix Arnett case," Bridget said, trying hard not to match his angry tone with her own. "Liz Reardon hired me to evaluate the defendant. She knew there was something off with the case."

Kemp banged his hands down hard on the steering wheel.

"There's nothing wrong with the case," he insisted. "Other than the fact that Liz Reardon and that sorry excuse for a judge let Arnett walk on bail. He could have killed a cop.

And here you are trying to get him off."

"I'm not trying to get anything but the truth," Bridget protested, not sure where all Kemp's fury was coming from.

How long had he felt this way about her? Was he really just worried about her father and feeling overly protective? Or was there something more behind it?

"What about the other gunshot?"

The question came out before she could stop it.

"Two different witnesses confirmed there were two gunshots before the police even showed up."

She stared over at Kemp, watching his reaction.

"I'm convinced there were two gunshots fired that night, but we only recovered one bullet."

When he still didn't respond, she leaned toward him.

"Where is that other bullet, Detective Kemp?"

Averting his eyes, Kemp leaned back in his seat and ran a big hand through his sparse gray hair.

"Witnesses can be mistaken," he muttered.

Bridget was about to protest when she noted the sheen of sweat on his wide forehead and the way he had started fidgeting with the cuff of his shirt.

He's lying. He knows where the bullet is.

Suddenly certain that Kemp knew more than what he was saying, she tried to meet his eyes, but he started the engine and looked over his shoulder before pulling back onto the road.

"What is it you're not telling me?" she demanded. "You know where that bullet is don't you?"

Kemp didn't answer as the cruiser approached Maplewood

Drive. When he pulled onto the driveway, Bridget turned to him with a look of incredulity.

"You took that bullet, didn't you?" she said slowly. "You knew it would raise questions about what had happened, and you took it."

"I don't know what you're talking about," Kemp said, pushing open the door and climbing out. "As usual, you're sticking your nose in where it doesn't belong."

Climbing out after Kemp, Bridget looked up toward her father's house, disappointed to see the little truck Angelo used for paper deliveries still parked outside.

She opened the back door and released Hank, allowing the Irish setter to run toward the backyard, knowing she needed to rinse off his muddy paws before letting him inside and onto Paloma's impractical white carpet.

"You stay back there, Hank," she said, latching the gate behind the dog. "I'll come wash you up after I check on Dad."

As Kemp walked up the driveway to the front porch, Bridget decided she'd go around to the side door.

Stepping inside the kitchen with a tired yawn, she froze.

A man in a black ski mask stood in the middle of the room pointing a gun in her direction.

Bridget cried out as she saw the figure sprawled on the floor at the masked man's feet.

A red puddle of blood had spread over the white travertine marble under Angelo Molina's body.

"Shut up or I'll shoot."

The man began to advance toward Bridget, then jerked around in surprise as the kitchen door swung open.

Harry Kemp stopped to gape at the gun, then turned to flee.

The shot echoed in the little room, reverberating through Bridget's ears as she lunged toward the side door.

"Stop now or I'll kill you, too," the man warned as her hand fell on the doorknob. "Although that's not what my mentor had planned for you, Bridget. At least not yet."

Recoiling at the sound of her name on the man's lips, Bridget let her hand fall back to her side.

"Good girl," he said softly. "My mentor told me you were a good girl. That's why he honored you above all women. Why he allowed you to witness his death. And why he wants you to bear witness to the second coming."

Hearing the madness in his voice, Bridget knew better than to challenge the man's delusion.

She would end up floating in the Shenandoah River like Libby Palmer if she said the wrong thing or made the wrong move.

"My father," she said, trying to keep the terror out of her voice. "Where is my father?"

The man hesitated, as if surprised by the quiet question, then jerked his head toward the ceiling.

"He's upstairs," he said, stepping closer. "I haven't killed him if that's what you're wondering."

"I...I know," Bridget said, swallowing back a sob of relief. "Your mentor wouldn't want that, would he?"

She watched as her words worked their way through the man's feverish mind.

"No, he wouldn't want that," he finally agreed. "He wants

me to kill the evil women. The instruments of the devil. That was his mission. And now as his disciple, it's mine."

His eyes fell to Angelo's motionless body.

"I didn't want to kill the reporter. He wasn't supposed to be here," he said, then shrugged. "But he got in my way."

Jerking his head up, as if listening to a sound in the distance, the man nodded.

"Yes, I know," he said, lifting the gun so that it hovered only inches from Bridget's forehead. "I'll take her now."

He nodded toward the side door.

"They'll be coming for us," he said. "We've got to go."

Desperate to stall for time, Bridget inched backward.

"Yes, but shouldn't we–"

"Go!" he screamed, shoving the gun toward her, and grabbing her by the arm.

Bridget could feel the cold metal of the barrel under her chin as he hustled her out the door to the back of the house. A black sedan waited with its trunk open.

"Please, I don't want to–"

Her voice faltered as she saw the thick roll of bright blue duct tape resting on the bottom of the trunk.

And then she was screaming in terror, unable to stop as the man lifted the gun and brought it down hard on her head.

Stunned into silence, she felt him lifting her into the trunk, unable to resist as he wrapped the sticky blue duct tape around her wrists, then moved down to her ankles.

"I'm sorry it has to be like this, Bridget," he said. "But it's your fate, just as it was foretold in the handbook."

Hearing Hank's frantic barks, Bridget forced her eyes open

just as the man pulled off his mask and stared down at her. Suddenly, she understood, and everything fell into place.

CHAPTER THIRTY-SIX

The disciple drove down Landsend Road in the black sedan, speeding past the Gas & Go before reaching the old truss bridge spanning the Shenandoah River. Soon enough he was making his usual turn onto Old Mill Highway which, despite its name, was no more than a poorly paved country lane with few cars and frequent potholes.

Ignoring Crast Farm on his right, he continued another mile, then slowed as he neared the nearly hidden dirt road leading out to Old Mill Pond.

He checked his rearview mirror to make sure he wasn't being followed, then turned onto the road, bumping and bouncing along, surrounded by a dark, unruly forest of pine trees and overgrown shrubs.

Finally, he reached the grassy clearing by the small, murky pond, lit only by the waning crescent moon above.

At first glance, it appeared that the old mill, for which the pond and the highway had been named, had been dismantled and taken away.

But on closer inspection, it was possible to see that, although the wheel had been removed long ago, the wooden structure still stood behind a stooping swamp willow tree and a profusion of dense foliage which had grown up over the years to hug the water's edge.

Parking the sedan under an overhanging branch to shield it from view, the disciple climbed out and pushed his way through a narrow opening in the greenery, using a small flashlight to guide the way.

Soon he was standing in front of the mill's narrow wooden door. Taking the metal key out of his pocket, he turned it in the lock and pushed the door open, then returned to the sedan.

The disciple leaned forward to rest his ear on the lid of the trunk and listened. Hearing nothing, he popped the lid open.

Shining the light into the trunk, he tensed, waiting for Bridget to lash out at him, but she didn't move.

Her motionless body was curled into a fetal position with her bound arms and legs pulled closely against her chest.

Bending over to lift her out of the trunk, the disciple heard a voice speak behind him.

You've brought the chosen one home. Your work is almost done.

He smiled down at Bridget's slack face and closed eyes, glad she wasn't resisting her fate as the others had done.

Take her inside to the altar.

Following the voice's instructions, the disciple carried Bridget's limp body through the branches and vegetation to the open door.

He laid her on the cracked wooden floor in front of the small table where the bones had been arranged, then took a book of matches out of his pocket and lit several candles, smiling again as light filled the dark cabin.

Gazing down at the tableau in front of him, the disciple felt a warm surge of pride work its way through him.

"I did this for you," he said, lifting his eyes to the wall, where he'd taped a picture of Ernest Crast, along with various photos of each of his victims. "I've brought her for you."

He leaned forward and ran his fingers through Bridget's thick, chestnut brown hair, reveling in the silky feel of it against his calloused hands.

It felt good to be safe and relaxed beside the altar after the jarring events of the evening.

He had gone to the house on Maplewood Drive after the voice had reminded him that children always run home when they're in trouble.

But he hadn't expected Angelo Molina to be there, and he hadn't planned on killing the reporter.

In fact, he'd been enjoying reading the reporter's stories about him in the local paper. It had been Angelo Molina who'd first started calling him the Second Strangler.

The reporter had acted as a herald, spreading the news that his mentor wasn't truly gone and that the second coming was close at hand. But then he'd had to get in the way.

It was unfortunate, but anyone who tried to stop the second coming must be sacrificed, just as his mentor had instructed.

And then he'd been forced to shoot Detective Kemp, who had suddenly appeared without warning, although the man's death had been inevitable.

The mentor had hated the detective, who had taken such

delight in his capture. His desire for revenge had been recorded in the handbook, and the disciple knew the voice would eventually have led him in Kamp's direction.

But regardless of the unexpected interruptions he'd encountered, the mission he'd set out to accomplish had been completed.

Bridget Bishop was now on the altar as planned, and his mentor would surely be pleased.

As the candlelight flickered around him, the disciple wondered if he should take the chosen one down to the lower level for safe keeping.

The room his mentor had instructed him to fortify was now empty. The room where the other women had been held was ready for its next occupant. But something stopped him from carrying Bridget below.

He wanted to keep the chosen one with him until the end. He wanted her beside him for as long as possible.

Bending over to inhale the scent of her skin, the disciple sighed with pleasure. He was living the dream.

It was the very dream that his mentor had raved about for hours while he'd stewed in his cell on death row.

He had been obsessed with Bridget Bishop but had never gotten the chance to lay so much as a finger on the pretty young psychologist.

But now the disciple was getting the chance to live out his mentor's dream, although, when it was over, he'd have to send Bridget to be with his mentor on the other side.

Tracing the line of Bridget's face with a trembling finger, the disciple tried not to think of the sacrifice he would have to make when it was time to let her go.

She was so very good. His mentor had told him so.

Not like the evil women on the wall.

Not like the women who had tried to snare him and trap him, or the women who had tried to trick him with their lies.

Bridget wasn't like the mentor's wife, Norma, who had run off and left her own child behind. Or like the disciple's wife, Eileen, who had deserted him when all was lost.

The thought of Eileen caused the disciple's hands to clench into fists. She had been so angry when he'd lost his job. Calling him useless. Telling him he had no purpose.

But as he'd packed his bags, he'd found the handbook again. After all those years, his mentor had placed it right in front of him. And when he'd opened it and read the words written on the front page, the voice had finally spoken to him.

The voice had revealed his true purpose was to fulfill the instructions written in the handbook.

And the handbook made it clear that only the chosen one would be allowed to die on the altar. Only she would be reunited with the mentor.

Soon the voice would speak again, and once it did, the chosen one would have to die.

CHAPTER THIRTY-SEVEN

V ic Santino's red Chevy sped into the Gas & Go parking lot and skidded to a stop in the fire lane. Jumping out of the pickup, Santino ran to the door and flung it open, bypassing the short line of customers standing in front of the counter waiting to pay for their purchases.

"I'm looking for the Crast Farm," he said to the clerk, who didn't look up but instead continued to count out change to the customer at the counter in front of him. "You know where that is? Can you give me directions?"

"I know where the Crast place is."

Santino turned to a small woman standing in line. She was holding a six-pack of beer and a bag of chips.

"Although if you knew Odell Crast like I do, you may not want to go out there," she added.

"I'll take my chances," Santino said with a grin that earned him appreciative glances from several of the women in line.

The woman hooked a thumb over her shoulder.

"Head west on Landsend Road. Go over the old truss bridge and watch out for the sharp turn just past Beaufort Hollow. Keep on going until you get to Old Mill Highway. Turn right and the Crast place will be a few miles up on your right. I believe there's a sign outside. Can't miss it."

Santino was running back toward the Chevy as soon as the words were out of her mouth, gunning the engine out of the parking lot and careening down Landsend Road, hoping Althea Helmont wouldn't get there before he did.

The lights were on inside the old farmhouse, which sat off Old Mill Highway just where the woman said it would be.

Two vehicles were parked outside, including one with D.C. tags and a *Georgetown University Mom* bumper sticker.

Cursing himself for not confiscating Althea's keys, Santino flipped off the Chevy's headlights, then winced as the truck's tires began to crunch over the gravel on the drive leading up to the farmhouse.

He had hoped to arrive unannounced. Maybe even get a look inside before anyone knew he was there.

But there was no cover around the house. Anyone looking out the window was bound to see him approaching.

A gunshot rang out as Santino opened the Chevy's door. Pulling his Glock out of his holster with one hand, he tapped 911 into his phone with the other.

"Shots fired at the Crast Farm on Old Mill Highway two miles west of Landsend Road," he told the operator. "Get ahold of Chief Fitzgerald and tell him Deputy Marshal Santino is at the scene and needs back-up."

Shoving his phone back in his pocket, Santino made his way toward the house, keeping his Glock out in front of him as he scurried across the patchy, uneven yard.

He headed toward the front porch, climbing the steps with

slow, stealthy steps, expecting someone to fling open the door and start shooting at any minute.

Raised voices drifted out from behind the front door.

Santino listened, trying to judge where the voices were coming from. Hoping to overhear what they were saying.

Resting his hand on the doorknob, he tried to turn it and was surprised to find it moved easily in his hand.

That's a small town for you.

He inched open the door, holding the Glock in front of him while trying to keep an eye out for someone sneaking up behind him.

"I'm not leaving here until you tell me where Colby is."

Santino recognized Althea Helmont's voice.

"I told you I don't know, lady. What are you, crazy?"

The old man on the floor stared up at Althea with wide, frightened eyes. Santino assumed he must be Odell Crast.

"Put the gun down, Althea," Santino said, careful to keep his voice smooth and calm. "We don't want anyone to get hurt. He's not worth spending the next ten years in jail for."

"His grandson's out there killing women," she said, keeping the gun aimed at Odell. "Just like his son did before the state put him down like the animal he was."

Santino took a step forward.

"We're looking for Colby now," Santino said. "And at this point, we can't be sure he has anything to do with the abductions and killings in Wisteria Falls."

Headlights flashed across the living room window as a car pulled up to the gravel drive, coming to a stop by the fence.

Hoping it was Cecil Fitzgerald or one of his officers,

Santino inched back slowly toward the window.

His heart dropped as he saw the small Uber sign lit behind the car's windshield and the tall, muscular figure climb out and begin trudging up the drive.

Colby Crast had hired a ride service to bring him to the farm.

Looking back at the wild gleam in Althea's eyes, Santino realized that she must have seen Colby, too.

She sprang toward the front door before he could stop her, wrenching it open and running down the front steps.

Santino shoved his Glock back in its holster and chased after her, his heart hammering in his chest as Althea headed toward the drive, her gun clutched tightly in her hand and her legs pumping.

Colby froze as he saw the figure hurtling toward him.

"Get down!" Santino yelled toward Colby, seeing only one chance to stop the disaster that was unfolding in front of him.

Summoning a sudden burst of speed, Santino executed a diving tackle he'd last used on the high school football field to bring Althea heavily to the ground.

The gun in her hand went flying, disappearing into the overgrown weeds beyond the gravel driveway.

"What the hell do you think you're doing?" Althea wheezed once she'd rolled over and caught her breath.

"Stopping you from going to jail," he said, sucking in air and pushing himself back to his feet.

He looked toward Colby, who was still standing frozen near the end of the drive.

"What are you doing here, Colby?" he called, moving forward. "You lied to me."

Colby shook his head.

"I didn't lie. Well, I didn't mean to," he said.

Wrapping his arms around his body in a defensive gesture, he walked forward to meet Santino.

"What do you know about the disciple?" Santino asked. "Luke told me you said the disciple knew where the truth was buried. What did you mean by that? And don't lie to me."

"That boy's been a liar from day one," Odell called out from the porch. "Don't you trust a word he says."

Colby turned hate-filled eyes to the porch.

"You're the liar!" he cried out, pointing a big finger at Odell. "You're the one who caused those women to die. The way you treated my father...the things you did. To him and to me."

He wiped at his eyes, unable to hold back the tears.

"You're a monster, just like he was," Colby cried.

"I don't know anything about those women," Odell said, turning around to go back inside. "Now get off my property, the lot of you, before I call the police."

As if summoned by his words, a cruiser turned onto the gravel drive, the bar of lights flashing, lighting up the dark.

Santino watched as the car jerked to a stop and Cecil Fitzgerald climbed out of the passenger's side door, his hand hovering over the gun in his holster.

"Now, what exactly is going on out here?" the chief of police asked, looking at the disheveled state of Santino and Althea with a dubious expression.

He looked over at Colby and did a doubletake.

"Are you..."

"He's Ernest Crast's son," Santino confirmed. "I guess he came out here to talk to his grandfather-"

Colby snorted.

"He's no grandfather of mine," he said, sniffing hard. "I didn't come out to see him. I came out here to find the disciple. I wanted to stop him. I think he might be the Second Strangler."

A jolt of adrenaline shot through Santino at the statement.

"Are you saying you know who the disciple is and that he's out here at the farm?"

Colby shook his head.

"I don't know who he really is. I came out here a few months ago to see the place where I grew up," Colby said, wiping at his eyes again. "I figured all the ghosts would be gone by now. I mean it's been over ten years..."

His voice trailed off and his eyes glazed over.

"Colby!" Santino snapped, stepping forward. "You saw a man here? What did he say? Think...we need to know *who* the disciple is and *where* he is."

Clearing his throat, Colby nodded.

"Well, I came by here, and then I went out to the old pond. The place I used to play when I was little," he said. "It was the only place around here I ever remember being happy."

A small smile lifted the corners of his mouth.

"My mother used to bring me there before she...left."

Santino inhaled slowly, forcing himself to be patient, to let the traumatized young man tell the story at his own pace.

"I decided to look around for the old mill. My father...my biological father...used it as a fort when he'd been little. Well, as I was looking around, a man showed up."

A pained look settled over Colby's face.

"The man said he'd known my father in prison. That he'd been his mentor, and that he'd made him his disciple."

Coby shrugged.

"I figured the man must be a little crazy, you know? I was kind of scared, so I just went along."

Swallowing hard, Colby dropped his eyes.

"When he showed me the old mill...how he'd laid out all these old bones and stuff...I had to get away. I told him I needed to leave, but he made me promise to come back. He said the second coming was at hand. That I was destined to take over my father's legacy."

"And what did you say, Colby?"

Santino knew his question sounded like an accusation, but he couldn't help it.

The young man had been given the chance to stop the Second Strangler months ago, back before either Brooke Nelson or Libby Palmer had died.

"I told him I didn't want anything to do with my father. I told him I was a different person now. But he told me blood didn't lie. He told me eventually I'd follow in my father's footsteps."

He turned pleading eyes to Santino.

"I know I should have told someone, but I didn't want anyone to know who I really was, and I didn't know he was going to hurt anyone," he insisted. "I thought he was just another crazy guy who was obsessed with serial killers. There are plenty of them out here, believe me. "

He looked toward the farmhouse as if looking into the past.

"That's why I had to go into protection in the first place. People would come to the farm and try to talk to me. Reporters and writers. People who said they were fans. They'd want autographs. Want to take pictures."

His voice turned hard.

"But I guess it was lucky for me they did. At least their harassment got me taken away from my grandfather. And that was the best thing that ever happened to me."

"Who was the disciple?" Santino asked when he realized Colby was done with his story. "Did he tell you his name? Can you give me a description? Where's the mill?"

Before Colby could respond to the barrage of questions, Cecil's radio erupted.

"Chief, we've got reports of a man down over at 5322 Maplewood," a woman's voice crackled over the airwaves. "And it looks like a woman's been abducted from the same address. Bob Bishop's daughter is missing."

Santino met Cecil's eyes.

"Bridget?" he said. "He's got Bridget?"

Turning back to Colby, Santino took hold of the young man's arms, tempted to shake him.

"Who's the disciple, Colby?" Santino demanded. "And where's this mill? Where has he taken Bridget?"

CHAPTER THIRTY-EIGHT

The splintered wooden floor scraped Bridget's cheek as she tried to move, and her eyes felt almost too heavy to open. But an urgent sense that she needed to wake up, that she was in danger, wouldn't let her drift back into the dark comfort of sleep.

She forced her eyes open just wide enough to make out the flickering shadows on the walls around her.

Where am I? What is this place?

The creak of a floorboard broke the silence, and she flinched as a man spoke beside her.

"You're awake."

Bridget froze as everything that had happened at her father's house came flooding back.

"I didn't think I'd hit you that hard," he said. "But you shouldn't have screamed. I told you not to."

Leaning forward, her abductor frowned down at her. The mask that he'd worn in her father's house was gone.

He stared at her with concern, just as he had the day she'd visited the state prison in Waverly. The same day Crast had broken Dr. Sommerville's nose.

"Officer Hoyt?" she asked.

"You can call me Wendall," he said. "I don't work at the prison anymore. Warden Pickering laid off the whole crew on death row once they repealed the death penalty. No need for us anymore, I guess."

Bridget tried to swallow, but her mouth was too dry.

"I'm...sorry," she managed to say. "About your job I mean."

She struggled to lift her hand, then looked down at the blue tape wrapped around her wrists. Flexing her numb feet, she felt the tape around her ankles, as well.

Panic began to seep in as she looked around the dark room, dispelling the sleepy shock of waking up in a serial killer's den.

Bringing her eyes back to Wendall Hoyt, she tried to remember everything she knew about the man who'd spent the last years of Crast's life guarding him on death row.

The man she'd met back then had always come across as quiet and efficient. He'd even expressed concern for her when Crast had attacked Sommerville.

He hadn't displayed the expected characteristics of a psychopath. He hadn't tried to charm her. He hadn't been boastful or made up any stories or lies.

Bridget could only assume that her theory had been correct.

The man Crast had called the disciple in his letter, the Second Strangler who'd been terrorizing Wisteria Falls, was suffering some type of psychotic break.

Her best option would be to stall for time until she could be rescued. Someone was bound to hear Hank barking in her father's backyard. Bound to discover the scene at her father's house soon and send help.

Fear rolled through her at the thought of her father. Had Hoyt hurt him? Maybe even killed him, like he'd killed Angelo?

She couldn't let herself think about it. Couldn't let herself lose control. She'd need to stay calm and keep her wits about her if she wanted to get out of this alive.

"Where are we?" she asked, letting her eyes move around the dark room, hoping to spot a way to escape.

Hoyt raised his eyebrows and produced an unsettling smile, his front teeth appearing too big for his mouth.

"Old Mill Pond," he said in a hushed tone as if telling her a secret. "My mentor grew up just down the road. Played on the pond as a child."

"Your mentor?" Bridget asked.

The unnerving smile widened.

"Ernest Crast," Hoyt said. "He's still here you know."

When Bridget didn't respond, Hoyt sighed and gestured around the room.

"A hundred years ago this used to be a grist mill, but the water wheel was taken away before I ever saw it."

Hoyt stared down at her, as if deep in thought, then reached toward the table behind her, seizing hold of a dagger with an eight-inch stainless steel blade.

Bridget screamed as he brought the knife down to her hands and sliced the tape from around her wrists.

"I brought you to my mentor's sanctuary," he said, gesturing to the table behind her. "And you're at his altar. I guess that makes you an offering. Or maybe a sacrifice."

Pushing herself into a sitting position, Bridget looked back at the table, her eyes widening as she took in the altar.

Candlelight lit up a grisly assortment of bones and illuminated the collection of photos taped to the wall.

A tattered notebook rested at the center of the altar.

Bridget reached out a tentative hand, but Hoyt grabbed her arm, crushing the tender skin around her wrist, which was pink and sore from the duct tape.

"The handbook is mine," he said, dropping the knife and snatching up the notebook. "My mentor gave it to me. He told me to give it to his son when the time came."

Sensing Hoyt's agitation, Bridget didn't reply as the ex-guard began to pace the floor holding the book, his eyes blazing in the flickering candlelight.

"I guarded Crast for years out in Waverly," he said indignantly as if Bridget had denied the fact. "I listened to him for hours at a time. He told me about the voices."

Hoyt flicked his eyes to Bridget, but she remained quiet.

"His mama talked to him all the time after she passed on to the other side, you know. She told him to seek out and kill the instruments of the devil."

He lifted a big hand to scratch absently at a patchy spot in his blonde crew cut.

"The handbook says his mama always hated the devil. She even tried to get the devil out of him before he died. But when that didn't work, she spoke to him from the other side."

A glassy sheen fell over his eyes as he spoke about Crast

and his mother, who had obviously contributed to her son's transformation into a serial killer.

Bridget was tempted to tell Hoyt that Crast had been psychotic. That he hadn't been hearing the voice of his mother or anyone else. That he'd been taking anti-psychotics for years before they suddenly stopped working.

But she knew it would be pointless. And likely dangerous.

She couldn't risk challenging Hoyt's delusions and throwing him into a rage. Not with the dagger near at hand.

"You spent a lot of time with Crast at the end, didn't you?" she asked. "Did you bring him his medications?"

Hoyt shook his head.

"Oh no, he stopped polluting himself with those pills long before his execution. Dr. Sommerville told him they weren't necessary since he wasn't psychotic or crazy."

A slow burn of rage mixed with Bridget's fear as she realized what must have happened.

Sommerville had never believed Crast suffered from a psychotic disorder. He'd always thought the serial killer had been faking it.

If the psychologist had somehow convinced Crast that his medicine was unnecessary, he may have stopped cold turkey.

That was probably enough to cause Crast to fall into full-blown psychosis near the end. And that had likely prompted the delusions of grandeur and the stories he'd filled Hoyt's susceptible brain with.

It was clear that now, all these years later, Hoyt had suffered his own psychotic breakdown and was acting under the delusion that he was Crast's disciple.

"How did you get the duct tape?" she asked, nodding toward the tape on her ankles. "Isn't it the same stuff Crast used?"

Hoyt narrowed his eyes as if he suspected she might be trying to trick him, then shrugged.

"I guess it can't hurt to tell you the truth now," he said. "You won't be around to tell anyone else."

The casual way he said the words made her heart pound.

So, he is meaning to kill me. Just like the others.

"My mentor left instructions in his handbook," Hoyt said, stroking the cover of the book. "Directions, too. The handbook led me to this old mill where he'd played as a boy. The place he'd first started hearing the voices."

Bridget looked at the altar, trying to hide her revulsion.

"These are the sacrificial bones of his victims," he said, running a finger over a small bone Bridget recognized from anatomy class as a distal phalanx. "They were evil women. Instruments of the devil. Like Eileen."

"Eileen?"

Bridget hadn't heard of any victims named Eileen.

"She's my ex-wife. Well, she's somebody else's wife now," he muttered. "Left me when I got laid off."

Suspecting Hoyt's wife had left him once he'd started having delusions and hearing voices, Bridget felt a twinge of empathy for the man.

Or perhaps his wife leaving him was what instigated his psychosis.

Either way, the man had begun to spiral, and many innocent people had ended up getting hurt or killed on his way down into madness.

"Once I'd read the handbook, I knew I was the disciple," Hoyt said, starting to pace again. "I had to find the mentor's son. I had to make sure he was ready for the second coming."

"The second coming?"

The question slipped out before Bridget could stop herself.

"That's what the handbook calls it when the mentor's son arrives to take over his work," Hoyt said, sounding belligerent now. "The second coming will be proclaimed by heralds on high throughout the world."

A sound in the distance caught Bridget's attention.

Is that a car outside? Is someone here?

Hoping to keep Hoyt talking, she tried to think of another question. Something that wouldn't upset him.

"Did you ever find his son? Did you find Colby Crast?"

"He found me," Hoyt said. "One day I was up here, and I saw a man who looked just like my mentor. I thought he'd come back. But it wasn't him, it was his son."

The words were thick with disappointment.

"I showed Colby the handbook. I begged him to understand what had to be done. But he wasn't ready. He needed more time. So, I acted on my own. I prepared the way."

"Is that when you went out and abducted Brooke Nelson?"

Hope stirred as Bridget heard faint shouts outside, but Hoyt didn't seem to hear anything. He just shook his head.

"Brooke Nelson wasn't the first."

Bridget saw a flicker of irritation cross his face.

"I made a few attempts before her. Almost got killed," he said, revealing his big front teeth in a terrible smile. "I'm just a disciple, you know. I'm still learning how to hunt and kill. But soon, I'll be as good at it as my mentor was."

"Ernest Crast wasn't perfect," Bridget said without thinking, listening for more shouts or signs of rescue. "He allowed Althea Helmont to escape."

Hoyt frowned.

"Don't you worry, I plan to get her, too," he promised. "Once I'm done with you."

A chill ran down Bridget's back at the eager look in his eye.

"My mentor has been guiding me. Telling me what to do."

"Are you hearing his voice right now, Hoyt?"

His eyes narrowed at the question. He hesitated as if unsure he should admit it, then nodded.

"Yes, I can hear him just as clear as I can hear you."

His voice deepened into a low growl.

"And he's telling me it's time."

Leaning forward, Hoyt picked up a strand of her hair and held it to his lips, inhaling deeply.

"He wants you with him. He's been waiting a long time for this, you know. *We've* been waiting a long time."

Bending over her, he snatched up the dagger, prompting a blood-curling scream from Bridget.

She scratched at Hoyt's face, but he grabbed her wrists and held them in an iron grip, lifting the dagger high in the air.

He froze as a loud bang sounded on the door, and then another. Someone was trying to get in. Someone was trying to rescue her. Hoyt released his grip on Bridget's hands and lowered the dagger.

Pulling a gun from his waistband, he pointed it at the

wooden door as Bridget felt for the dagger on the table.

Her hand settled on the handbook as the door burst open and Terrance Gage appeared, his eyes wide in the dim light of the candles, his gun drawn.

Bridget heaved the book at Hoyt as a shot rang out. Splinters of wood flew around the room as the gun went flying, slamming into the wall and sliding into the darkened corner.

Bringing her knees up to her chest, Bridget thrust her bound feet into Hoyt's groin with savage force, eliciting a loud grunt as she rolled out from underneath him.

The shine of the knife's blade slashed past her face as Bridget pushed herself to her knees.

"Get down, Bridget!" Gage yelled as another shot echoed through the little room.

As she threw herself to the floor, a door slammed somewhere behind her. Spinning around, Bridget realized Hoyt had disappeared through a narrow door in the back wall.

She also saw that the handbook had landed on one of the candles and had flamed to life.

A line of fire was working its way up the soft wood walls, illuminating the room as Gage ran in and scooped Bridget up in his arms.

Carrying her out into the night air, Gage lowered Bridget onto the damp grass, her ankles still bound with duct tape.

He held his Glock toward the mill door, ready to shoot if Hoyt reappeared as two figures ran toward the mill carrying flashlights. As the figures got closer, Bridget saw that Charlie Day and Tristan Hale had arrived.

"Wendell Hoyt is in there," Bridget said, pointing to the old wooden structure, which was now sending billows of gray smoke into the dark sky above. "We can't just leave him in there to burn, can we?"

"I'll go after him," a deep voice said.

Bridget spun around to see that a third figure had jogged up behind Charlie and Hale.

Vic Santino stood in the light of the now raging fire, his dark eyes already focused on the door leading into the flames.

"No!" Bridget cried out, suddenly sure if he went into the shaky wooden structure he'd never come out. "It's too late."

But Santino was already heading to the door, holding his jacket up over his face as he disappeared inside.

Bridget tried to struggle to her feet, but Gage stopped her as Hale ran after Santino, following him into the burning building despite Bridget's cries for them to come back.

As she stared in shock toward the door, Charlie knelt beside her and pulled out a pocketknife.

"Let's get this tape off you," she said, her voice strained as she glanced toward the door.

As soon as Bridget's ankles were free, she forced herself to her feet, holding on to Charlie for support.

Sirens sounded in the distance as the mill door slammed open and Hale burst through. Soot-covered and coughing, he sucked in a lungful of fresh air.

Bridget's heart leapt as he turned back to the door, holding it open as Santino appeared with Wendall Hoyt draped over his shoulders in a fireman's carry.

Dropping Hoyt onto the ground, Santino bent over and

coughed out a lungful of smoke, before pulling out a pair of zip ties from his pocket.

"These are a lot easier than that damn duct tape," he said as he grabbed Hoyt's arms and secured them behind his back.

He looked up at Bridget and attempted a smile, but only managed to set off another round of coughing.

By the time he'd regained his composure, an ambulance had pulled into the clearing.

Two paramedics jumped out and ran to Hoyt, who lay on the ground, still unconscious but visibly breathing.

"We found him on the stairs trying to get out," Hale said as they checked his vitals. "The fire never reached him, so I'd say it's smoke inhalation. And I'll have to ride along. Your patient is under arrest."

"It's been a busy night for law enforcement," the paramedic said as they hoisted Hoyt onto the gurney. "I just took a detective with a gunshot wound to Wisteria Falls General."

"My father," Bridget exclaimed, looking up at Charlie. "Hoyt attacked my father and my stepmother. And he shot Angelo Molina and Harry Kemp."

"I know," Charlie said. "I called to let Chief Fitzgerald know we were heading over here, and he told us Detective Kemp had called in. Said there'd been a fatal shooting. According to the Chief, your father and his wife are safe."

Relief flooded through Bridget at the confirmation that her father was alive, but it was quickly followed by a pang of guilt over Angelo.

"You said you were already on the way to the mill?"

Bridget asked. "How'd you guys find out I was here?"

"Santino notified everyone on the task force that Hoyt was hiding out at this old mill, so we all hurried over here."

Bridget frowned.

"Santino? How did he know?"

"Colby Crast told me."

Spinning around, she came face to face with Santino, who was almost as filthy and disheveled as she was.

Seeing the questions in Bridget's eye, Santino sighed and ran a soft finger over a bruise on her cheek.

"It's a long story," he said in a tired voice as another ambulance pulled into the clearing. "And you need to get to the hospital and get checked out. For now, I think it's enough to say that it's been a very busy night in Wisteria Falls."

CHAPTER THIRTY-NINE

Terrance Gage waved to Warden Pickering, who stood waiting for him at the end of a long corridor. He'd been invited to the warden's retirement party the following week and would be sorry to see the old guy go, although he figured it was probably a good time to bring new leadership into the old prison.

I guess nothing and no one lasts forever. We all just have to accept that fact gracefully and know when it's our turn to leave.

Shaking the warden's hand, Gage followed him down another corridor toward the maximum-security ward.

"I appreciate you letting me interview Hoyt," he said, as they waited for a guard to unlock yet another door. "It's rare that the BAU gets to interview a serial killer so soon after he has committed his murders."

The door slid open to reveal another long corridor. Gage was dismayed to see Dr. George Sommerville walking toward them.

He wasn't sure what it was, but there was just something about the man that rubbed him the wrong way. He suspected Sommerville had been a tattletale in school, always running to the teacher hoping to get the other children in trouble.

The psychologist stopped to greet Gage, blocking his way.

"Congratulations on the Second Strangler case, Agent Gage," he said, producing a thin smile. "I look forward to studying Wendall Hoyt while he's here at Waverly."

Gage cocked his head and looked back at Pickering.

"For a while, I thought Dr. Sommerville might be the Second Strangler," Gage said, giving Pickering a sideways grin. "You remember when I called to ask permission to bring him in for questioning?"

Sommerville's face drained of color.

"Me? The Second Strangler?"

His face creased into an indignant frown.

"Why in the world would you suspect me?"

"Because your fingerprints were found on threatening letters to one of Ernest Crast's victims," Gage said, enjoying Sommerville's discomfort. "Why was that?"

Opening his mouth, and then closing it again several times, Sommerville finally came up with an answer.

"You must mean the letters that were discovered during Crast's last cell search," Sommerville said stiffly. "Based on the disturbing contents of the letters, they were rightly turned over to me for evaluation. I read them and decided to turn them into the proper authorities."

Gage raised his eyebrows as if he had doubts about the reason given, but he figured the prison psychologist had done the right thing, although Gage suspected Sommerville had enjoyed confiscating the letters and turning them into the WPP a little too much.

"I'm willing to sit in on your interview with Wendall Hoyt

if needed," Sommerville said as Gage started to walk away. "I understand there may be some question as to his mental fitness to support his own defense."

"It's my understanding that Mr. Hoyt's court-appointed lawyer has already retained a psychiatrist who will evaluate the defendant," Gage said coldly. "And nothing Hoyt tells me during our interview can be used against him in a court of law anyway, as you well know. So, your assistance won't be required, Dr. Sommerville."

Sommerville's nostrils flared at the dismissal.

"Next thing you know the federal prosecutor will hire Bridget Bishop to come in and evaluate Hoyt," Sommerville said with a sardonic smile. "I'm sure she'd have a unique perspective on his mental fitness."

"You know, you really can be an asshole sometimes, Sommerville," Pickering said, shaking his head.

He put a hand on Gage's arm to guide him around the psychologist, who was left standing in the hall with an open mouth.

"That man makes me glad I'm retiring," Pickering said as they approached the visitor's room door. "You've got thirty minutes with Hoyt and no more. I've got golf scheduled this afternoon."

Pickering motioned to a guard who pulled open the door.

Stepping into the room, Gage saw Wendell Hoyt sitting at the table. His blonde crew cut and prominent teeth made him look younger than his thirty-three years.

The ex-guard had started working at the prison when he'd barely been legal, and now it looked as if he'd be spending the rest of his natural life there.

"Thanks for agreeing to meet with me, Mr. Hoyt," Gage said, taking a seat across the table. "I know you must be feeling a bit overwhelmed. Now that you're facing federal charges that could get you the death penalty it looks like you might get to follow in Ernest Crast's footsteps after all."

Hoyt stared up at him with a bewildered frown.

"I don't really remember anything that happened during the last few months if I'm honest with you."

He raised a hand to stifle a yawn.

"The doctors have me on these meds that make me tired, and I just want to sleep all the time."

"Are you still hearing voices?" Gage asked.

He'd been told Hoyt had been prescribed antipsychotic medication but wasn't sure he'd been taking them.

"No," Hoyt said. "I feel like my old self again since I've been in here."

Gage nodded and jotted a note on the small pad he'd brought in with him.

"You say you don't remember what happened during the last few months, but what about your long-term memory?" Gage asked. "Do you remember when you were guarding Crast on death row?"

"Yeah, all that's pretty clear," he admitted. "I remember Crast saying his mother talked to him in his cell and stuff like that. Once he'd stopped taking his meds, he started keeping this handbook and writing letters."

Gage frowned.

"Did you know what was written in the letters, or in the

handbook?" he asked. "Did he show them to you?"

"He'd read stuff to me," Hoyt said. "When I'd get bored, I'd go listen to him. He said some crazy things, but it started to make sense after a while."

A furtive look passed over his face and he narrowed his eyes.

"You know what happened to that handbook?" he asked. "Crast gave that book to me, and I'd like it back."

Gage struggled to maintain a neutral expression.

"The handbook burned in the fire," he said, watching Hoyt's expression. "It was completely destroyed."

Something that looked like rage rolled over Hoyt's face and then was gone.

"It meant a lot to you, didn't it," Gage asked.

Hoyt crossed his arms and leaned back in his chair.

"At first, I just stuck it on a shelf," Hoyt admitted. "Crast told me to give it to his son when the time was right. But then I found it when I was packing up my stuff to move out. I ended up reading it from cover to cover."

He dropped his eyes.

"That's when I started hearing Crast talking to me," he said. "I don't remember a whole lot after that."

"You ever think about that first time you heard Crast's voice in your head and wish you'd ignored it?" Gage asked.

Hoyt thought about the question, then shook his head.

"That'd be pointless," he replied. "As the handbook said, you can try to ignore your destiny, but it'll just come and find you anyway."

* * *

Gage made it back to Quantico with only minutes to spare before the final Second Strangler task force meeting.

Vivian Burke was waiting outside his office when he arrived. Her flame-red hair was in its usual tight knot on the top of her head, but Gage had a disconcerting image of it spread out in silky waves on his pillow.

They hadn't been on speaking terms since their abrupt break-up, but he figured it was about time they started acting like adults and made amends.

"Look, I'm sorry for-"

"Don't," she snapped, her green eyes flashing. "I don't have time for your too-little, too-late apologies right now. The lab has completed processing the evidence your friend Bridget Bishop turned in and there's something she's going to want to see. I figured you'd like to be the one to let her know."

Shoving a file folder at him, Vivian turned on her heel and strode away.

Gage opened the folder and studied the contents with growing excitement, then tucked it under his arm and headed toward BAU Conference Room 3.

The folder and its contents would have to wait.

First, he was scheduled to attend the final task force meeting. The case had been officially turned over to the federal prosecutors and the resources on the task force would be reassigned to new cases.

Charlie Day stood in front of the room as he entered,

already giving the team her update. He saw Hale, Bridget, Santino, and Tony Yen among the faces around the table.

"Federal prosecutors are preparing the case against Wendall Hoyt for the deaths of Brooke Nelson, Libby Palmer, and Angelo Molina, as well as the attempted murder of Jacey Wallace, Harry Kemp, and Bridget Bishop."

She motioned to an empty seat up front next to Vic Santino.

"I think our case against Hoyt is solid, so long as he doesn't get off on an insanity plea."

Gage saw her throw a warning look at Bridget, who sat near the back of the room.

"Don't worry, Charlie. As I've already told you, I have no intention of evaluating Wendall Hoyt or testifying in his defense," Bridget said with a sigh.

"Good," Charlie said. "And I'm pleased to say that Althea Helmont's protection services have been discontinued and she's now back at home."

Santino cleared his throat.

"What about Colby Crast?" he asked.

"The prosecutors have decided not to file any charges against Colby for his failure to report Hoyt. They said it would be too hard to prove what he knew," Charlie said. "Although they are considering filing charges against Odell Crast for child abuse if Colby will testify."

Murmurs of approval sounded as Charlie wrapped up the meeting and Gage waited by the door, hoping to intercept Bridget before she left the room.

She smiled as she saw him waiting for her.

"I have thanked you for coming to my rescue already, haven't I?" she asked. "I'm happy to say it again."

"It's always good to hear," Gage teased. "Although you could show me true gratitude by agreeing to come back to the BAU full time."

Bridget rolled her eyes and sighed.

"I have a full-time job already," she said. "Which I'm sure you remember. Now that the Second Strangler case has been resolved, I can concentrate on my evaluation of Felix."

"Actually, that was why I was waiting for you," he said, handing her the folder. Vivian Burke found some evidence that I wasn't expecting. I think you're in for a surprise."

* * *

Gage decided to stop by his house and change clothes before his next appointment. He ran inside, exchanged his suit for jeans and a polo shirt, and poured fresh food into Sarge's bowl.

The cat purred and rubbed against Gage's legs before digging into his dinner, prompting Gage to stop and scratch the tomcat between the ears, suddenly glad he hadn't given into Anne's demands.

There may be a day that Sarge would go under the knife, but Gage wasn't ready for that yet. And when the time was right, he would make that decision for himself.

Anne would just have to live with it, like it or not.

Jumping back into his Navigator, Gage headed out on the increasingly familiar route to Wisteria Falls.

Of course, seeing a therapist so far away had its drawbacks, but the ninety-minute drive gave him time to think, and the distance from his home and office gave him the privacy he needed. He didn't want any of his friends or coworkers to know he was in therapy, although of course there was one person who knew. One person who'd made the recommendation.

Knocking on the side door of the bungalow, Gage waited patiently for Faye Thackery to appear.

He was soon rewarded by the appearance of Faye's silvery hair and cheerful smile in the doorway. Following the tiny woman into the cozy room where she held her sessions, Gage took a seat on the plush sofa.

"I do have to wonder why you're coming all the way out here for your appointments," Faye said as she set a cup of steaming Chamomile tea in front of him. "I do offer virtual, online appointments you know."

Looking around at the peaceful room Gage shrugged.

"I like it here," he said, leaning back on the sofa. "And I like to talk to people in person, even if that makes me seem old-fashioned."

"Does that worry you?" Faye asked, cocking her head. "That you may seem old or outdated?"

Gage automatically shook his head, then shrugged his broad shoulders, and produced a sheepish smile.

"Yeah, it kind of does," he admitted. "In fact, I think I've been worrying about a lot of things lately. Things I have no control of. Like getting old. And being alone."

He exhaled, feeling lighter somehow as if the words and

the worries that had been weighing on his chest for months had lost some of their power.

"Well, verbalizing your worries is a positive start," Faye said. "And seeking out help is a good first step."

He nodded, ready to take the next step. Suddenly ready to let the future unfold.

CHAPTER FORTY

Bridget leaned over to survey the near-empty parking lot again, letting her eyes linger on the redbud tree outside her office window, admiring the changing colors of the leaves as spring began to make way for the coming heat of the summer months.

"Bridget, I've been meaning to stop by to congratulate you."

Jumping at Gary Zepler's sudden appearance at her door, Bridget turned to her boss, seeing that Zepler had woken Hank from his afternoon nap.

"Dr. Zepler, that's very kind of you."

When the psychologist continued to stand in the doorway, Bridget motioned toward the chair across from her desk.

"Is there something you wanted to talk about?" she asked. "Would you like to sit down?"

"Oh no, I just wanted to say good job for your work on the Second Strangler case. I'm glad you're back safe and sound."

He started to turn away, then hesitated, clearing his throat.

"I do hope you'll think twice before you take on another case for the BAU," he added. "We'd hate to lose you."

Bridget stared after him as Zepler inclined his head and withdrew from the room. She was still looking toward the door when Aubrey March knocked on the frame.

"Felix Arnett is here for your appointment," she said.

"Oh good, show him in."

A twinge of anxiety settled in her midsection as Aubrey led Felix into the room. The young man was tall and thin, his dark, shaggy hair unbrushed, and his complexion pallid.

As disheveled as he looked, he did appear to be more alert than the last time she'd seen him. And his eyes had lost the blurry, unfocused look that had worried her.

"Sit down, Felix. I've got something quite important to discuss with you," she said. "You see, new evidence has come to light in the investigation. Has your lawyer talked to you about it?"

Felix nodded.

"He told me the police found a second bullet."

"That's right," Bridget said. "Which means it's likely someone else was outside your house the night Whitney died."

A pained look twisted Felix's pale face at the mention of his wife. Bridget wondered again if he was mentally and emotionally ready to remember what had really happened that night. His physical brain injuries had healed nicely according to the neurologist.

His psychological injuries had been harder to treat.

"Felix. I think you're ready to try to remember what happened to Whitney," she said. "Your statement will be important in determining what happens with the case, and if justice is done for your wife."

Felix swallowed hard and nodded.

"Are you willing to undergo hypnosis?"

He nodded again.

"Great, then let's go ahead and get started."

As Bridget walked Felix through the initial stages of hypnosis, she was surprised at how quickly he sank into a deep, trance-like state.

"Now Felix, I want you to think back to that night. You said you remember getting home from work early. You were in the house. Tell me what you were doing."

Felix spoke in a hesitant voice, his face passive.

"I was making dinner for Whitney. I'd gotten off work early and wanted to surprise her. I was making fettuccine alfredo. It was her favorite. But then I heard something outside."

Felix tensed and began shifting in his seat.

"Remember you're safe here, Felix. Nothing here can hurt you. It's okay for you to remember what happened next."

When Felix didn't speak, Bridget gently prodded.

"So, you're cooking fettuccine alfredo for Whitney, and you hear something outside. What did you do then?"

Felix's forehead furrowed and his voice deepened.

"I ran to the door and opened it. I saw Whitney and...there was a man. He was behind her. He had his arm around her throat. And he had a gun."

Felix's eyes remained closed, but Bridget saw movement underneath his lids as if he were watching someone.

"I grabbed the gun by the door. I was scared. The man was

dragging her to the car. She pulled away and I took my chance. I aimed the gun and I...I shot him. Only he shot at the same time and I...missed. *I missed...*"

The words were a strangled cry.

"You aimed the gun at the man attacking Whitney?"

Felix didn't seem to hear Bridget.

"I missed and Whitney fell."

Panic filled his voice.

"There was blood. So much blood. And the man...he ran."

"What did you see next, Felix?"

"Whitney's on the ground and then, the police were there. They're yelling at me. Telling me to put down my gun, but I didn't want to."

His voice cracked with emotion.

"I didn't want to put it down!"

Bridget leaned forward, wanting to put out a hand, wanting to comfort him, but knowing it might pull him out of his trance-like state.

"Why didn't you put down your gun, Felix?"

"Because Whitney was dead!" he yelled. "She was dead, and I wanted to die, too!"

Flinching at the anguished shout, Bridget noted Felix's rapid breathing and the sheen of sweat on his forehead.

She spoke softly, careful to keep her voice calm.

"Felix, listen to my voice. You're safe in my office. You're safe here. Everything is alright. You need to come back now."

Felix's eyes snapped open.

"That's good, Felix. Now, inhale slowly, and exhale."

As he continued to breathe slowly in and out, Bridget

spoke in a soft, soothing voice. Comforting him. Explaining that his head injury and the emotional trauma had likely prevented him from remembering the events once he'd woken in the hospital.

But now that his brain had healed, he'd done it. He'd remembered.

Opening a folder on her desk, Bridget pulled out a photo.

She stood and crossed to Felix, putting a soft hand on his shoulder as she held it out to him.

"That's...*him*," Felix said in a hoarse whisper. "That's the man who attacked Whitney."

Bridget released the breath she'd been holding in.

After months of wondering, she finally understood what had happened, and who was ultimately responsible for Whitney Arnett's death.

"This man is Wendell Hoyt. You might have even seen him in the paper. He's the Second Strangler."

She knelt in front of Felix as tears streamed down his face.

"I know you must feel guilty. But this wasn't your fault," she said gently. "You were trying to save Whitney. If you hadn't been there, she would have been his first victim."

* * *

Bridget parked outside the Wisteria Falls Police Department and strode inside, making a beeline for the conference room.

Liz Reardon stood by the window, her sleek bob aglow in the late afternoon light flooding in.

"Finally," she snapped. "I thought you'd never get here."

Holding out a thick folder to the anxious prosecutor, Bridget glanced over at Cecil and Opal, who were both seated around the conference room table, and shrugged.

"Some things take time to get right," she said. "And we definitely had this one all wrong. But I think now we know what really happened."

Liz dropped the folder on the conference room table and began scanning through the pages.

When she got to Bridget's final report, her eyes lit up.

"He remembered?" she said in a triumphant voice. "He'll make a statement? He'll testify?"

"You'll have to talk to Felix and his lawyer about that," Bridget said. "But yes, he's starting to recall the night of his wife's death. And I believe he'll be able to identify Wendall Hoyt as the man who attacked her and shot at him."

She nodded toward the file.

"My report and his statement match up with the FBI investigator's findings that there had been a second gunshot," she said. "They found the bullet discarded in the bushes further down the driveway."

Looking at Cecil, she raised her eyebrows.

"The FBI ballistics lab was able to match the bullet to a gun found in Wendell Hoyt's possession."

"So, Whitney Arnett was another victim of the Second Strangler?" Opal asked, looking stunned.

She glared over at her husband.

"How did you not know about this, Cecil?"

But Bridget wasn't done.

"Fingerprints on the bullet matched a detective at the scene," she said. "Detective Harry Kemp. The FBI agents who questioned Kemp about the bullet said Kemp admitted to picking up the second bullet and throwing it in the bushes."

"But why?" Opal asked as Cecil stared in silent shock.

Bridget sighed.

"He said he wanted to prevent Felix from getting away with murder. Despite evidence to the contrary, he felt sure Felix had killed his wife and didn't want any unexplained evidence to muddle up his case."

A hush filled the room as Bridget closed the file folder.

"How is Kemp recuperating, by the way?" she asked.

"He was doing pretty good, up until today," Cecil said, jumping to his feet. "But now? Now I'm going to kill him."

* * *

Bridget came out of the police station and walked toward the Wisteria Falls Ice Creamery.

She'd agreed to meet Daphne and Ginny for an afternoon treat before heading back to the office to pick up Hank.

Then it would be another Friday night spent on her own.

"Bridget! Over here!"

Ginny ran toward her, her ponytail bouncy along behind her with every step. "Mommy says I can get a puppy!"

"I did not!" Daphne cried out as she tried to keep up with her daughter, despite the three-inch heels she was wearing. "I said we could go *look* at them after our ice cream."

Giving Bridget a wink, Ginny smiled.

305

"With Mommy, looking always means buying."

Daphne rolled her eyes as they walked toward the corner.

"She's been talking about nothing but puppies ever since we took Pixie back home. How is Jacey, by the way?"

"She's doing as well as can be expected," Bridget said. "It helps that she's seeing a new man. A doctor who took care of her at Wisteria Falls General. She's smitten. Says he's very handsome."

"Speaking of handsome."

Daphne looked past Bridget's shoulder.

Bridget spun around and saw Vic Santino striding out of the courthouse toward a red pickup.

"Isn't that your man over there?" Daphne asked.

"He's not *my man*. He's just a colleague."

Raising both of her perfectly arched eyebrows, Daphne looked unconvinced. She put a hand on Bridget's shoulder and nudged her in Santino's direction.

"Hurry up and go get him," she said. "He's getting away."

"I thought we were meeting for ice cream," Bridget protested, even as her eyes followed Santino to his truck.

Daphne waved away her objection.

"I'll take Ginny to look at the puppies and we'll get ice cream afterward. If you're not too busy. Now go!"

With a gentle shove from Daphne, Bridget headed toward the courthouse, her feet moving faster as she saw Santino opening the Chevy's door.

"Santino!" she called out, feeling foolish.

He stopped and turned around, giving her a wide smile that caused her heart to swell in her chest.

"You're becoming a regular around here," Bridget said as she hurried up to him. "I'd have thought with everything you've seen lately we'd have scared you off by now."

"Oh, I've seen some pretty bad stuff in my line of work," Santino said. "It'd take more than a psychotic serial killer to keep me away."

Bridget grinned.

"I was just going to come look for you," he said. "I had to drop off some paperwork first. Looks like charges will be filed against Odell Crast after all this time."

"That's great. It's about time someone holds that man accountable for all the pain he's caused."

She stared up at him, not sure what to say, only knowing she wasn't ready for him to leave yet.

"You said you were going to come check on me?"

He nodded, his clear, hazel eyes filled with concern.

"I saw you at the task force meeting but didn't get a chance to ask how you're doing. I've been worried about you."

The softness in his voice stirred the hairs on the back of Bridget's neck. She swallowed hard and shrugged.

"I'm good, I guess. Keeping busy."

"Gage tells me he's determined to get you back at the BAU. Are you thinking to return to the Bureau?"

It was a question Bridget had asked herself over and over again in the last year. She still hadn't found the answer.

"I'm not sure what will happen," she admitted. "But I have a feeling the Bureau and BAU aren't through with me yet."

Checking his watch, Santino pointed to his truck.

"I was just heading back to D.C., but I have time for dinner."

Her heart flip-flopped in her chest, but she shook her head.

"I'd love to, but Hank's waiting at the office for me."

Bridget saw a flash of disappointment in Santino's eyes.

You've got to take a chance someday, Bridget. Why not today?

The little voice sounded annoyed. But it was also right.

"Isn't there someone waiting at home for you, Santino?" she asked softly, her eyes dropping to the silver band on his finger. "Did someone special give you that ring?"

Santino followed her gaze. He studied the ring.

"Yes, Maribel was very special," he said, lifting his eyes to hers. "But she's not waiting at home. Not for many years."

He cleared his throat and looked toward his truck as if suddenly thinking of escape.

"I'm sorry, I didn't mean to pry," Bridget said. "I just...wanted to know more about you."

A blush filled her face.

"It's been hard for me to talk about Maribel," he admitted. "Telling people that she died makes it seem so real. So final."

His voice was raw.

"Talking about someone you've lost can help keep them close," she said. "It keeps them alive in your memory."

Santino nodded, seeming to like the idea.

"Although, in my case, the person I lost is the one who does the talking," Bridget said. "I always imagine I hear my mother's voice in my head. Giving me advice and trying to stop me from making silly mistakes. You know, the kind of things she'd say if she were still around."

"So, you're telling me you hear voices?" Santino teased, cocking an eyebrow.

"Does that sound crazy?"

"No, it sounds wonderful," he said. "It sounds like you're very lucky to have your mother with you."

Bridget nodded, knowing he was right.

"And I'd feel lucky if you'd agree to have dinner with me tonight," he said. "We can pick Hank up on the way."

"Sounds good to me," Bridget said, moving toward the truck before he changed his mind. "I'm ready if you are."

THE END

Ready for the next Bridget Bishop thriller?
Read on for an excerpt of:
Taken by Evil: A Bridget Bishop FBI Mystery Thriller, Book Two

TAKEN BY EVIL

A Bridget Bishop FBI Mystery Thriller,
Book Two

Chapter One

Adrenaline coursed through Bonnie Lambert's body as the lights in the cavernous room dimmed and an electronic dance version of Beethoven's Fifth Symphony rose into a thudding, pulsating rhythm. A collective gasp rose from the sold-out crowd as a dazzling spotlight suddenly illuminated the solitary figure on stage.

Tate Everest's long, lean body remained perfectly still as his ice-blue eyes scanned the room, taking in the sea of spellbound faces before him.

Bonnie's breath caught in her throat as he stalked to the edge of the stage with panther-like grace.

Lifting a leanly muscled arm, he curled his hand into a fist and thrust it into the air, shouting toward the audience.

"This is your night, Sable Beach! This is your time!"

His deep, raspy voice sent a shiver of pleasure down Bonnie's spine as she cheered along with the rest of the crowd.

"Time to find your strength!" he growled. "Strength over weakness! Strength over self-pity! Strength over suffering!"

Voices all around Bonnie responded in unison.

"Strength over suffering!"

As the music faded and the lights brightened, a high-pitched voice echoed through the packed room.

"We love you, Tate!"

The audience erupted into spontaneous applause as a smile spread across Tate Everest's handsome face.

"I love you, too!" he replied. "All of you! Which is why I'm standing here...why I'm willing to share my secret with you."

His voice suddenly lowered into a more intimate tone, and a somber expression replaced the smile on his face.

"I know each and every one of you out there have suffered," he said quietly. "I know that's why you came here tonight."

Bonnie blinked back tears as she gazed up at the man who'd changed her life. The only man who seemed to understand what she'd been through. What she was still going through.

"You've had enough pain to last a lifetime," he continued as his perfect features creased into a pained scowl. "And you can't go on like this anymore. I know...I've been there, too."

Swallowing hard, he shook his head.

"I was ready to give up...ready to give in," he said in a raw voice. "And then *something* happened that changed my life. That *something* transformed me from a victim into a victor!"

Pointing toward a man in the front row, he cocked his

head.

"Are you ready to be transformed?" he asked, then swung his hand toward a woman to his left. "How about you? Are you ready to leave all your pain behind?"

Suddenly Tate Everest was pointing at Bonnie, who stared up in rapture, captivated by the intense blue eyes above her.

"What about you?" he asked, his voice softening into a caress. "Are you ready for your whole world to change?"

Bonnie nodded numbly as Tate moved away, her legs shaking and her eyes wet with emotion.

She followed his sinewy figure around the stage, absorbing every word he uttered with growing resolve.

No more fear for me. No more suffering and stressing over the past. I'm going to be strong from now on, just like Tate Everest.

He had the answers she'd been looking for all this time. The secret to overcoming her PTSD once and for all so that she could live a normal life.

That was all she wanted. The reason she'd taken time off work to travel to the luxury Sable Beach Resort on Virginia's coast in the first place. The reason she'd dipped into her savings account for the event ticket, which had cost close to a month's rent.

Tate Everest had saved her life when she'd been ready to give up. His online videos had kept her focused on the present instead of the past. He'd motivated her to keep putting one foot in front of the other until she'd been walking and then running toward a new future.

With his help, she was starting to believe she could become the strong, confident woman she'd once been.

Of course, that had been before everything had unraveled.

Shaking the unwanted memories from her head, Bonnie lifted a hand to tuck a strand of reddish-blonde hair under her headband. She winced as the long sleeve of her wrap-around dress fell back to reveal a thick white scar on the inside of her wrist.

She tugged the sleeve down, covering the scar along with the bad memories it summoned. Returning her eyes to the stage, she gasped to see Tate standing in front of her again.

He seemed to be staring directly at her.

"Don't give into fear or shame," he commanded in a deep voice. "Don't let the past rule your future..."

A tear slipped down Bonnie's cheek as she pushed back her sleeves and then lifted both hands toward the ceiling, baring her scars and her pain for all to see.

Electricity rolled through her as Tate reached out and squeezed her hand before moving on, leaving her staring after him with wide green eyes.

She'd been empty of hope or happiness for so long. She'd almost forgotten what it felt like to feel whole and full of life.

If she could feel like this, maybe it wasn't too late for her after all. Maybe she was going to make it back to normal.

But too soon, Tate was waving to the crowd, wrapping up his speech with a final message of encouragement.

"What do you say when the past comes for you?" he shouted toward the crowd.

"SOS!" the crowd roared back.

"What do you say when fear tries to take over your life?"

The response thundered through the room.

"SOS!"

"That's right, Sable Beach! You know the secret. You've got the power. You're stronger than your suffering. You're more than your pain. Now, go and spread the word!"

As Tate left the stage, the crowd began to chant.

"SOS...SOS...SOS!"

Bonnie chanted along, but her heart dropped as she watched Tate retreat. She kept her eyes on him as a burly man with a walkie-talkie guided him toward the back.

She recognized the man as Barney Cash, Tate's manager, as his eyes scanned the crowd, clearly ready to combat any over-enthusiastic spectator who may try to rush the stage.

Then Tate was gone and the house lights brightened, earning an audible groan of disappointment from the audience.

A deep voice sounded from the loudspeaker.

"Thank you all for joining us on the SOS Everest Tour! If you enjoyed meeting Tate tonight, be sure to subscribe to the Everest SOS YouTube channel for new videos each week."

Bonnie turned to leave, feeling strangely let down. Like most of the people in the room, she was already a dedicated subscriber to Tate's popular YouTube channel, but now that she'd seen Tate in real life, had even touched his hand, she wasn't sure watching him online would ever be the same.

She'd been an avid fan of his *Strength Over Suffering* self-help program since its inception, but as she followed a jostling throng of fans toward the exit, Bonnie was still amazed to see how many people had turned up to hear Tate speak in person.

His promotional summer tour, which included show dates in cities all along the East Coast, was obviously a hit.

"Excuse me! Can I get through?"

A bearded man in a red beanie held a small handheld recorder above his head as he pushed his way toward the stage, fighting against the flow of bodies moving toward the exit.

Feeling the heel of the man's boot crunch down on her toes as he moved past, Bonnie winced in pain.

She looked back to see him shove his recorder at Barney Cash, who was blocking the access to the backstage area while arguing with a middle-aged man in an expensive-looking suit.

Tate's manager batted away the recorder with one big hand as the man in the suit pled his case.

"I need to speak to Tate," he insisted as he adjusted his tie. "I'm sure he'll see me if you tell him I'm here."

"I told you he's busy, Doc," Barney said, jerking a big thumb toward the door. "Now we gotta clear this room."

The man in the suit spun around with a scowl. His eyes narrowed as he caught Bonnie's curious stare.

Quickly looking away, Bonnie once again joined the exodus toward the lobby, relieved that she'd decided to splurge on an overnight stay at the hotel.

Picturing the small, empty apartment waiting for her back in Richmond, Bonnie felt a familiar stab of loneliness as she rode the elevator up to the sixth floor.

The hotel room was dark and quiet as she let herself in and crossed straight to the minibar. She removed a miniature, screw-top bottle of sparkling wine and then dug in her purse for her pill bottle.

The plastic bottle was light in her hand as she shook out two pills and popped them in her mouth, grimacing at the bitter taste on her tongue.

I've gone through these way too fast. I'll need more soon.

Ignoring the nagging voice in her head, Bonnie twisted the lid off the wine and washed down the pills, then stood in the quiet room, listening to the waves crashing below her window.

Lulled by the soothing sound, she opened the sliding glass door and stepped out onto the balcony.

A gust of wind picked up her long hair and whipped it around her face as the ocean churned in the darkness beyond.

Looking up at the full moon, she allowed the warmth of the wine and the pills to settle over her.

I'm safe. He can't get me here. I'm finally free.

An unwelcome image of her ex-husband's angry face flashed through Bonnie's mind. She tried to make it go away by quoting one of Tate Everest's favorite sayings.

"The past is dead and gone. Bury it, so it can rest in peace."

The whispered words were followed by a wave of dizziness. Bonnie swayed and grabbed for the railing. She looked down at the beach below, suddenly remembering that she hated heights.

Draining the remaining wine in the bottle, she turned and stumbled back into the room, pausing only long enough to grab her room key before heading out the door.

* * *

Stepping out of the elevator onto the marble floor, Bonnie walked briskly, as if she knew exactly where she was going.

Her head was still a little fuzzy, but the bright lights and the noise in the lobby were starting to clear away some of the fog.

Following the signs to the beach, Bonnie paused to admire a colorful promotional poster displaying the Everest SOS Tour dates, including the previous stops in Savannah and Charleston, as well as the next stop in Washington, D.C. the following Friday.

As she approached the exit to the beach, she hesitated.

The bearded man who'd stepped on her toe earlier now stood in the lobby talking to a slender woman with waist-length blonde hair. Neither of them seemed to be aware that they were blocking the door.

"So, you follow Tate Everest around to each new show?" the man asked. "Don't they have one like...*every week?*"

The woman nodded.

"I haven't missed a city yet," she said, lifting her chin in a defiant gesture. "And I've got tickets for next Friday in D.C."

"Some people would consider you a groupie...or a stalker."

The man's mocking tone set Bonnie's nerves on edge. She took a small step forward, indicating she needed to get around them, but they continued to ignore her.

"But I'm guessing you're more of a follower," he added. "Like those creepy girls who followed Charles Manson."

"I don't expect you to understand," the woman said stiffly.

317

"Tate's the only one who understands what it's like to truly suffer. People like *you* never will."

With a flick of her long hair, the woman pushed past him and strode down the hall, almost colliding with Bonnie in her haste to get away.

As the smirking man turned to follow the woman's retreating figure, he nodded at Bonnie.

She tried to look away, but it was too late, he was already honing in on her.

"What about you?" he asked, taking a step closer. "Is this your first time seeing Tate Everest, or are you a *follower*, too?"

Bonnie grimaced at the term.

"I'm Chase Grafton, by the way," he said, brandishing a small voice recorder. "You may have heard my *Chasing Killers* podcast? It's top of the true-crime charts right now."

She hesitated, studying the man's bearded face.

Come to think of it, he does look kind of familiar.

"Did you know women have been getting abducted and killed after going to these Tate Everest events?" the podcaster asked. "Two women are dead...and those are just the ones we know about."

Bonnie frowned and shook her head, then looked back the way she'd come, suddenly wishing she'd stayed in her room.

"I've heard of your podcast," she admitted, forcing herself to meet his intense gaze. "But I'm not a fan of true crime. That stuff creeps me out."

She cleared her throat, prepared to tell Chase Grafton his podcasts on violence and death hit way too close to home for her to ever consider them entertainment, but he held up a hand to stop her.

"I understand. You don't want to hear about real criminals being held to account," Chase said with a shrug. "You'd rather listen to the fake self-help bullshit Tate Everest is shoveling. And most of the people in here would agree with you, I imagine. It's actually kind of sad."

Before Bonnie could reply, Chase's phone buzzed in his pocket. He dug it out and stared down at the display, then began frantically tapping out a message.

Taking advantage of the distraction, Bonnie hurried to the exit, shoved the heavy door open, and stepped through.

As the door clicked shut behind her, she surveyed the terrace, hoping the podcaster wouldn't follow her outside.

The crashing of the waves mixed with the echoes of Chase Grafton's words as Bonnie headed toward the beach.

Two women are dead...and those are just the ones we know about.

She wondered what he'd been talking about. She hadn't heard of anyone getting killed.

Admiring the strings of twinkling lights draped along the railing between the resort and the dark beach beyond, she stood at the head of the stairs, her hair whipping around her face as it danced in the gusty wind off the ocean.

Smoothing the silky material of her dress over her slim hips, she sucked in a deep breath and squinted against the sand that stung her eyes and skin.

She scanned the deserted shoreline, tempted to turn around and go back inside, then squared her shoulders.

"What do you say when fear tries to take over?" she whispered into the wind, imagining she heard Tate Everest's voice joining hers in the dark. "SOS..."

Suddenly feeling foolish, Bonnie descended the stairs and slipped off her heels. Her feet sank into soft, cool sand as she made her way toward the edge of the water.

She'd had a fear of dark water ever since she'd seen the movie *Jaws*, where a beautiful young woman had run into the ocean at night only to be attacked by a monstrous shark.

I could never do that. I could never...

But suddenly she was walking toward the water, feeling the sand becoming wetter and harder under her feet, wincing as she stepped on a scattering of broken shells.

Heart pounding, Bonnie froze as the first wave splashed over her feet. But the water was warmer than she'd expected, and she smiled as she moved forward, inching further and further into the ocean, the hem of her dress now wet and clinging to her legs.

I'm doing it. I'm standing in the ocean at night.

Tempted to let herself sink down into the water, to allow herself to just float away, she looked up at the callous face of the moon.

Isn't that what I wanted? To drift away and never return? Isn't that why I have these?

She lifted her arms up in the moonlight, studying the scars left behind by her grief and her weakness.

No, that was before. It's different now.

Now that she'd found Tate Everest and his SOS videos, everything was different. She was different. She was stronger, and she knew better.

She knew she wanted to live.

And she knew that no matter how painful life could be, she was strong enough to get through it.

Backing away from the endless pull of the ocean, Bonnie turned toward the shore, suddenly tired and wanting to go back to her room, ready for a good night's sleep.

She saw the man's dark figure coming toward her just as her feet found dry sand.

He appeared to be alone, and he was moving fast, his body a long, ominous shadow against the pale glow of the sand.

Heart pounding, Bonnie tried to think. Should she stand her ground and fight or run like hell in the opposite direction?

By the time she'd made up her mind to run, it was too late. The man was already standing in front of her, his face clearly visible in the soft light of the moon.

"You?" she gasped, trying to wipe the salty water out of her eyes as he stepped forward. "What are you-"

A powerful hand shot forward to grab Bonnie's throat, abruptly choking off her words.

Seizing a fistful of her hair with his other hand, he jerked her head back, forcing her to her knees.

"He told you to be *strong*, didn't he?"

The words erupted in a guttural growl, penetrating Bonnie's panicked mind, alerting her that she was in terrible trouble.

"But he didn't tell you he's a *weakling*...and a *coward*."

He spat the words at her as he dragged her backward, his

feet splashing into the surf as waves crashed in a shimmering spray all around them.

Feeling the world start to spin around her, Bonnie clawed futilely at the man's hands, but he forced her head down into the rough, salty water, again and again, her fingernails no match for the thick leather gloves he was wearing.

As she tried to scream, salt water rushed in to fill Bonnie's nose and mouth, turning her shriek into a weak, watery gurgle.

She struggled against the man and the churning ocean until her lungs burned and her arms grew too heavy to lift.

Just as she'd given up all hope, a powerful wave crashed over them, wrenching Bonnie out of the man's grip and depositing her on the shore.

Staggering to her feet, Bonnie looked back to see the man splashing through the water toward her, his eyes wild and his mouth twisted into an evil smile.

He let me get away. It's all part of his game, and he's enjoying it.

She turned to run, already knowing it was no use even as she dared to hope that maybe she'd get lucky and reach the sand dunes ahead.

Maybe he'll let me go. Maybe I'll get to...

The crack of the gun was drowned out by the crashing of the waves. Bonnie didn't realize she'd been shot until her legs gave out and she saw blood staining the sand beneath her.

Writhing in pain, she flinched as a flash illuminated the sky and a shadow fell over her. The man was there, taking pictures.

"Come on, smile for me," he said as another flash of the camera lit up his face. "You owe me that much."

Shoving his phone into his pocket, he lifted the gun.

"You'll need to be strong now."

He spoke between clenched teeth as he pointed the gun down at her, his finger tightening on the trigger.

"Cause this is gonna hurt."

Vist Amazon.com to purchase a copy and continue reading *Taken by Evil: A Bridget Bishop FBI Mystery Thriller, Book Two.*

And don't forget to sign up for the Melinda Woodhall Newsletter to receive bonus scenes and insider details at www.melindawoodhall.com/newsletter

ACKNOWLEDGEMENTS

STARTING A NEW SERIES IS BOTH DAUNTING and thrilling. I loved the idea of starting a new year with a new series and was eager to introduce Bridget Bishop to my readers early in the year. Luckily, I had wonderful people in my life to help me meet my short deadline.

As always, my amazing husband, Giles, helped me find the time and space to write, while my five talented children, Michael, Joey, Linda, Owen, and Juliet provided the inspiration to keep me typing along on even the most difficult of days.

I'm also truly grateful for the unending support of my extended family, including Melissa Romero, Leopoldo Romero, Melanie Arvin, David Woodhall, and Tessa Woodhall.

The kind feedback and interest of readers always seem to make the long days (and some nights) of writing a little easier.

And finally, I always give thanks to my mother, who inspired my love of books and continues to live on in my writing.

ABOUT THE AUTHOR

Melinda Woodhall is the author of heart-pounding, emotional thrillers with a twist, including the *Mercy Harbor Thriller Series*, the *Veronica Lee Thriller Series*, and the new *Bridget Bishop FBI Mystery Thriller Series*. In addition to writing romantic thrillers and police procedurals, Melinda also writes women's contemporary fiction as M.M. Arvin.

When she's not writing, Melinda can be found reading, gardening, chauffeuring her children around town, and updating her vegetarian lifestyle website. Melinda is a native Floridian and the proud mother of five children. She lives with her family in Orlando. Visit Melinda's website at www.melindawoodhall.com

Other Books by Melinda Woodhall

Her Last Summer	*The River Girls*
Her Final Fall	*Girl Eight*
Her Winter of Darkness	*Catch the Girl*
Her Silent Spring	*Girls Who Lie*
Her Day to Die	*Steal Her Breath*
Her Darkest Night	*Take Her Life*
Her Fatal Hour	*Make Her Pay*
Her Bitter End	*Break Her Heart*

Made in the USA
Middletown, DE
08 May 2024